HIGHLANDER'S DAWN

SWEPT INTO THE HIGHLAND PAST
BOOK I

Thank you • Happy Reading!

MICHELLE
DEERWESTER-DALRYMPLE

ISBN: 978-1-959225-12-6 (E-book)

ISBN: 978-1-959225-13-3 (Paperback)

ISBN: 978-1-959225-14-0 (Hardcover)

Cover designed by MiblArt.

Spiteful Books LLC
PO Box 1991
Woodbridge, VA 22195

www.spitefulbooks.com

Content Warnings

Content warnings
(and potential spoilers)
can be found at the end of this book.

To learn more, go to
www.spitefulbooks.com/content-warnings

This book is dedicated to my husband, without whom the book would not have been written, for showing me that love will indeed return in a different way.

Acknowledgements

I would like to thank a few people for their encouragement and assistance in writing this book.

First, thank you Michael Roberts for helping me conceive the idea and helping me write the most unbelievable fight scenes. You have a singular talent for fight scenes. And thank you for showing me that listening when someone talks about grandma is important.

Second, thank you to Dawn Fraser, my beautiful, eternal cheerleader and conjurer of brilliant ideas for how to share the reach of my books. And for my beautiful Highlander's Dawn mug.

Finally, thank you to my family - close and extended - because you all have been the most staunch supporters, reading my books and sharing them with your friends. A writer could not ask for a better support system.

Everything you love is very likely to be lost, but in the end, love will return in a different way.

–Franz Kafka

Chapter One

Eastern Scotland, 900 CE

Gray early morning mist unfurled like a banner across the Highland moors.

Alpin Grant sat on his tall black horse, adjusting his sword belt as he looked around the open field, occupied by both his clansmen and the MacIntosh clan. His reins jingled in the eerie quiet as the horse pawed at the ground. Even the steed could feel the tension in the air. He gave his mount a pat on the neck as he whispered a soothing word into the beast's ear. He was a spirited animal and wanted to bite anyone and everyone who got close to his mouth.

Only thirty men from each clan were in attendance at this meeting. Most of the men were from the outskirts of his chieftain's stronghold. None known to be extremely close to his chieftain, with Alpin being the only strong tie to the Grant clan as the chieftain's tanist, second in command. That was part of the deniability built into this plan. Thirty had been the agreed number and both clans had abided by it. No banners were carried identifying their clan or crest.

From the Grant clan, none but Alpin knew the true reason why they were here or what was to be discussed.

It felt unnatural riding in the countryside without banners. Alpin always found the sound of the cloth flapping in the wind to be soothing, a display of the pride that always surged through him as he rode at the head of the column, a banner on each side of him, declaring him a Grant man.

His liege and chieftain, James Grant, had sent him here to this neutral ground, halfway between the MacIntosh clan and the Grant clan's homes. They were here to talk with the MacIntosh clan about a common threat. James Grant and Lucas MacIntosh could not risk being at this meeting themselves, needing some deniability if the king ever learned of it. If they were discovered consorting with one another in this manner, the savage, bloodthirsty king would not hesitate to wipe out the whole clan, from every last old woman down to the newborn babes still sucking at their mother's breasts. This was the safest way to do what needed to be done as well as protect the innocent.

Thirty men was a decent number to have. More than enough to defend themselves from outlaws and with a total of sixty men they could defend themselves from most other clans, none of which would have this many out on guard.

This meeting concerned their *Ri Alban*, King Donald II, the son of Caustantin I and current king of Scotland. A man known for his temper and ability to use violence in a brutal but effective manner. A man who was quicker to kill any clan leader who questioned him rather than reason with them. A man who was supposed to continue the legacy of a unified kingdom of Alba but instead sowed division among the old clans. This was why the words that would be spoken today and promises made could not be written down. Letters risked being intercepted and falling into the wrong hands, and thus today's discussion required to be said aloud in person.

An oath to be made in blood, but if God was with them, only two men would spill their blood today. All of Scotland knew that Alpin Grant spoke for his clan chieftain just as Ian MacIntosh spoke for Lucas MacIntosh.

Words spoken today would bind the two clans together in an alliance to defend each other against the king if he ever chose to move against either of them. If the king did decide to move against the MacIntoshes, this oath taken by Alpin would drag the Grants into a bloody war with the king. Alpin did not know if the Grants could survive a bloody war against such a violent king and the army he commanded. The risk was worth the promise that if the king moved against the Grants, James Grant could call upon the MacIntosh clan to ride to his aid.

The hope was not only for these two clans but for other clans to make similar alliances and bring the king to his senses so he might hear the voices of the Highland clans. Alpin had to hope that if they were successful, the nearby Gordons, MacDougals, and eventually the Keiths, and with the grace of the gods, even the power-hungry Morays, might join them.

Alpin scoffed to himself. *Morays and Keiths. 'Twould take a miracle.*

Yet if enough clans united and spoke these words, it would go far in preventing the king for mistreating, molesting or attacking any of them. If he attacked one, he would attack all, including those who supported him.

Horses from both clans were tied to picket lines while men milled around grasping arms, slapping backs, and speaking with kin and friends not seen in months. Some of these men, from different clans, were related by marriage. The two clans were friendly together and it was a fortunate sign that no fights had broken out. His men had been given orders that the whole MacIntosh clan was to be treated with due respect. Too much depended on this meeting to have it go awry just because some prideful young man wanted to show off his love for his clan.

Ian MacIntosh sat on his own horse that trotted towards Alpin. Ian was a tall, hard man, known for his loyalty as his chieftain's tanist and second in command and for his fighting skills with his war hammer. He wore an unnatural and unsettling smile on his lean, leathery face, thus Alpin knew that the MacIntosh clan had been given the same orders as he about making every effort to ensure this alliance went smoothly and without any snags.

Ian MacIntosh stuck out his arm and Alpin clasped it. Alpin opened his mouth to speak but a sound like thunder rolled across and over the hills stopped him. Mungo Grant, who stood at Alpin's right, dropped to one knee and pressed the flat of his palm to the damp ground. He felt the vibration, trying to identify the rumbling's source. The two warriors glanced at each other with knowing in their eyes, then looked to the north.

Young Rudy Grant rode over the hill on his brown steed like the devil himself was chasing him. He rode high on the saddle, leaning forward over his horse's neck to squeeze every ounce of speed from the beast. He wasn't yelling but he didn't need to; there was only one reason for him to be riding hard and fast back to camp.

Alpin had ordered men out to all four directions as lookouts to ensure no one rode up on them without warning. Rudy, as the youngest and fastest rider in the clan, had been sent north. Due to the hills and wooded valleys, they would have the least amount of warning afforded to them if an attack came from that direction. The hills were low but long and a sizable force could snake their way close without giving warning if precautions had not been made.

Alpin and Ian immediately reined their horses around and shouted orders for their men to mount up and ready themselves. Men drew their weapons to prepare for the oncoming danger, and spotting Rudy answered their unasked questions.

"Run or fight?" Ian asked Alpin.

"Run if we can," Alpin answered in a tight voice. "Fight if we must."

Men from both clans rushed to their mounts, climbed up, and whipped them around, looking to Alpin and Ian to command their next actions.

A throng of armored horses crested the hill in a fury of clanging and hoof beats. Not in columns of twos but like an arrow, extending in a line at the top of the hill. Men and horses crested the hill, spreading out to the left and right. First two then four, then six and in the span of seconds there were a hundred strong. An army. The king's army.

They were discovered.

"Ten for every six of us," Alpin observed.

"All on horseback so at least we dinna have to worry about the bastard bringing any of his blasted bowmen," Ian replied sourly.

The king favored his bowmen and their ability to decimate an attack from a distance. It was rumored that he'd paid a Welshman to come to him and make their famous longbow for him. The only thing worse than being attacked by a Welsh bowman was not having the opportunity to fight back.

"If we fight, we die, but at least we might take half of them with us," Alpin added, looking around at his men. "If we run, they'll ride us down, but a few may get away."

"We stick to the agreed plan," Ian growled. "We knew 'twas a possibility. Half of each clan runs in different directions while half of each clan stands and fights to buy the runners time."

"What do your men ken about the meeting?" Alpin asked with concern.

"Same as yours. That is to say naught. If any of them are taken alive, they cannae talk or give witness against either clan."

"Then ye and I are the only hazards to our people," Alpin stated as fact. "And I willna be taken alive."

"Nor I, Alpin," Ian said, puffing his chest out.

Fighting was preferred, running was acceptable, but if neither was possible, a last resort plan had been agreed upon. Each of the leaders had already designated a group of men to ride if the order had to be given. And the order was now being given. Men drew swords, axes, and war hammers while others protested about having to ride away like cowards, even as men formed up to repel the onslaught to come.

Alpin did not know who he felt worse for, the men staying to die or the men ordered to ride away, living at the cost of those who stayed. Rudy tried to argue that he should stay, but Alpin slapped the haunches of his horse so it took off under him.

The mad king himself crested the hill in the center of the line, flanked by two of his own banner men. Alpin watched the king remove his helmet and survey the field. Alpin imagined he could see the vile man smirk as he looked down on them and knew the numbers were on his side.

The king drew his sword, holding it high for all the men to see. Even from this distance Alpin squinted at the dull, mist-covered sunlight reflecting off the king's blade.

"Sheath your sword and ride, damn ye!" Alpin hollered to his next in command, waking the man from his battle-ready mindset.

With a loud curse, the man kicked his horse as if he blamed the animal for what he'd been ordered by his commander to do. The horse protested, rearing up on its hind legs with a harsh whinny, then bolting forward, south bound, followed by fourteen other clansmen who felt the same as he did.

Ian's second was no happier than Alpin's second, as he and fourteen of the MacIntosh's men rode hard eastbound to the river they'd have to cross, then broke up into smaller groups going in three different directions.

As the two groups rode hard, kicking up mud and grass, it looked as if all of Clan MacIntosh and Clan Grant were running in a panic. The king screamed and sliced his sword down through the air in a quick, violent act as if he was cutting off the head of an enemy. His one hundred warriors spurred their horses as one and charged down the hill with their battle cry, believing they gave chase to a fleeing foe.

Alpin waved his sword in the air to rally his men, as Ian drew his sword and war hammer from his belt. With a yell of anger, they charged ahead hoping to meet their combatants at the bottom of the hill.

Both men knew that if they waited for the king's men to come to them, they would be surrounded and dispatched with little effort and no losses on the king's part. By meeting the charge, they would fight man for man in the middle while those on the king's ends would have no one to fight. If the clans clashed against the king's men and broke through the line, they could avoid the circle of death and survive to turn and clash again. They'd no chance of victory unless they reached and killed the king himself.

Horses screamed as they careened against each other in a brutal clash of horse flesh and muscles. Riders from both sides were thrown to the ground, rolling to their feet as others managed to stay in the saddle. The clans did well against the king's men but didn't break through the line as hoped.

Alpin swung his sword, taking the man on a grey horse in the neck. Holding onto his sword with experience and knowledge as much as muscle, the blade ripped free of bone and muscle as the dead rider fell from the saddle.

Ian's horse collided with another, and Ian was the victor having veered at the last second and collided with the other horse's leg and not straight on. The king's soldier's horse crashed down, landing on its rider, breaking the man's leg under its weight. Horse and rider screamed together as one. Ian threw his war hammer at the next man, his spike ripping through the man's helmet and taking him in the face, and tearing him out of the saddle. Ian's sword came up just in time to stop the blade of the man on his left. As the man raised his blade to strike again, Alpin blocked a spear thrust cutting the shaft in half, then spun his horse and stabbed the man attacking Ian in the side.

Pulling his blade free with a twist and jerk, Alpin spun his horse again, to see that their thirty men had been whittled down to twelve in a matter of seconds. Four of their men were on their feet on the ground, twice that for the king's men.

Riderless horses panicked and fled the field at a full sprint. One of the king's riders rode down one of Alpin's men. His man had swung his sword at the rider, but the horse had reached his man first and after being slammed into by an eight-hundred-pound horse he tumbled to the ground rolling and was then trampled by the beast, with no chance of getting back up.

Men from both sides littered the ground, face down or in impossible positions, arms, and legs bent in ways they were not meant to go.

Another of his men on the ground sidestepped a charging horse and managed to remove the rider's left arm with a strong swing of his sword. Blood sprayed from the rider's open elbow. Alpin watched in horror as the lad, Rudy, who should have had the best chance to ride away, took a spear in the back right before he collapsed against his horse's neck before slipping into a dead heap in the mud.

The lad!

But Alpin had to let the lad's death go to face the king and his army.

The two ends of the king's line had circled around and in, and the clans ended up right where they'd tried to avoid being, in the center of the circle of death. There were more of the king's men dead on the ground than clansmen. But there were also more of the king's men still alive than the clansmen. Sixty plus king's men against a total of now ten men from the two clans was not worth celebration. The king's men pushing ever forward and the circle around them kept shrinking.

The ground that had been wet to begin with was now soaked in blood, the grass having been churned up by a hundred and thirty horses stomping across it.

Two of the king's men that had been knocked off their horses and had lost their swords in the fall, were on the ground, grabbing onto Alpin's right leg. They were trying to pull him out of the saddle where he, too, could be trampled to death. Alpin's sword came down hard, caving in one of the men's helmets, and the man collapsed to the ground as his eyes rolled back into his head. Instead of swinging his sword again, Alpin spurred his horse pulling away from the other man's grip, to help Ian who was fending off three attackers.

Alpin ducked under a random sword as he rode past the attacker without stopping, just to again collide with a king's man's horse, knocking that man to the ground and under his own horse's hooves, as Alpin drove his broadsword into the second attacker, dispatching two of Ian's attackers. Ian deflected the sword of the third, then opened the man's throat with a spray of blood, as the man had raised his arm and dropped his guard. The man's horse bolted and the rider tumbled backwards off his mount.

One of the MacIntosh men took a sword in his side under his ribs, and fell out of the saddle after a second sword ripped through his stomach.

MacIntosh and Grant clansmen fell even as the king's men fell. They would not give up their lives cheaply. The king may not pay the price but his men by God would.

Ian was now the only MacIntosh left alive and only two Grants along with Alpin remained on their horses. The two remaining Grants pushed hard to come up behind Alpin trying to protect him from behind.

Alpin and Ian moved as one, spurring their horses for one last attempt to break the line and reach the king. Ian was trapped between two horses. He managed to slice down and through the chest of the rider on his right, separating tunic, skin, and muscle, exposing the man's rib cage as he fell. The king's man on his left swung wide and hard, taking Ian in the back of the neck and removing his head from his shoulders.

Ian's body sagged to the ground, as Alpin's horse pushed through the line, as he killed one man and was stabbed in the side by another. His horse regained its footing and pushed uphill. Alpin was but thirty feet from the king when a spear lodged itself a foot deep into his horse's flank. The beast was loyal but that did not stop him from tumbling headfirst into the ground, throwing Alpin ten feet into the air.

Alpin landed hard on his back, breathless, wounded, and bleeding. Ignoring the pain, he rolled onto his stomach and pushed himself off the ground, stumbling to his feet, sword lost, facing downhill just as the last of his men were killed. Turning to face the king with fifty of the king's men behind him, Alpin pulled his knife with one hand while holding his injured side with the left. He took a step forward to finish the job one way or another.

On his second step another spear took him in the back as a horse rode past him. A good eight inches of black steel came out his stomach, just left of his navel. His knife dropped from his hand as he fell to his knees and gripped the spear at his belly and coughed up a splatter of blood.

Looking down at the spear tip in shock, Alpin knew he lacked the strength to stand back up. Blood poured out the gash to his side as well as the spear that was impaled in him.

Alpin had served his chieftain well today and would die a good death. He had to hope that at least one rider made it out to tell the tale of what happened here today.

The king's horse galloped down the hill to stop in front of him.

King Donald the Second himself slid off his horse with grace and hung his helmet on the pommel of his saddle. He clutched his long, black-hilted sword in his black-gloved hand. The giant silver signet ring he always wore, a Celtic cross with a dark red ruby at the center, glinted against the black. His black leather tunic flapped in the wind where it hung below his long chain mail cover. He pushed his black leather hood off his head as he turned toward Alpin. He didn't hurry but ambled slowly with deliberation to loom over Alpin.

"If you're going to torture me, ye better be about it. I've only a moment left," Alpin panted with a grim smile, spraying blood from his lips with each word.

"I don't need answers from ye," King Donald spat out, raising his sword high. "My men will capture at least one of your clansmen. I'll torture them in your stead. I just need ye to deliver a message for me. Fortunately, ye dinna need to be alive to deliver it."

The king's strike was the final blow of the battle.

Chapter Two

Modern-day Scotland

Emilie jumped off the bus less than a quarter mile from her father's farm. Otherwise, she'd have a long walk back to the Gordon farm from Stonehaven.

The town was north of her family farm and historical touring company that was her father's pride and joy. Though he fancied himself a historian, he was a pragmatic man as well, and made sure his only daughter had the skills and strength to kick ass when needed. She might be home from college for the summer, but her martial-arts training did not take a summer break. Her father, Jack Gordon, made sure of that.

Turning her face to the setting sun, a thankfully dry setting sun, Emilie hitched her satchel higher on her shoulder and made sure her bo-staff, her preferred weapon and one that she excelled in, was tight and not falling out of her pack. The velcro was secure, so she started down the main road to her farm.

More of a hobby farm, and she loved it. Most of her father's, and therefore her, efforts went into the tours. Gordon farm, one of the last of the Gordon properties near Stonehaven or even Aberdeen, housed small animals – goats and chickens mostly. However, its location just northwest of the infamous Dunnottar Castle and other Scottish historical markers was what made it special. Her grandfather had created the Dunnottar Tours company when he was a young man, helping to establish the Dunnottar Cliffs Trail, and her father and now Emilie were the purveyors. And fanatics.

Such fanatics that her dual study of history and business at Ashbond College in America was intended to help her run the business once her father could no longer do it.

But that was far in the future. Jack Gordon was a youthful, hale man. He'd run the farm and tour company for a long time yet, of that Emilie was certain.

As she made her way down the road, the silhouette of the man himself appeared, and Emilie smiled to herself. His shoulder, still broad for an older man, curled around the rake he used to collect fallen oat stalks in the field. Coming up next to him, she stood on her tippy-toes and kissed his sun-weathered cheek.

"Hello, Da! Making progress on the field are ye?"

Jack smiled at Emilie as he raked. He joked that during the year while in America, her Scottish lilt lessened, at least to his ear. Coming home to Scotland brought it back in full force and did his heart good.

"Och, lass. A never-ending chore."

"Any tours of Dunnottar castle or the local sights today?" she asked.

Emilie had realized early on that she might be studying history, but she'd be an old woman with one foot in the grave before she had a smidge of the knowledge her father had. Some of her favorite stories were those of the castle ruins and the history surrounding it. Such a long history, and tourists came from all over the world to visit and hear those stories. Emilie adored visiting the old castle as much as any tourist. There was something almost other-worldly about it.

"Nah. Today is for cleaning up the barns. Get ye changed and help with chores. I'll be here in field. Ye can care for the sheep before joining me."

Emilie gave her father a mock salute at his command, then ducked hard as he threw a fluff of oat chaff from his rake at her. She giggled and ran toward the modest farmhouse where she had lived her whole life until she left for college.

Slipping out of her t-shirt, she threw an old, long-sleeved shirt over her jeans and changed her sneakers out for her boots. It might be summer, but summer in the Highlands was not summer in even the northern parts of America, and with the sun tucking itself to bed soon, the Highland air held a chill. With a hard stomp on each foot to adjust her boots, Emilie raced from the house to the sheep pens adjacent to the run shed. She made sure the water trough was full and fluffed the hay and peat and raked up any refuse before putting the tools away and heading toward the field where her father toiled.

She had just joined him and was reaching for a rake when the sound of an engine on the road grabbed their attention.

They stood side by side and watched as a worn-down car, gray with rust damage around the chassis, wound its way down the road. The car stopped and a handsome, dark-haired young man wearing a dark blue, short-collared coat over black pants and boots emerged from the driver's seat. He stood at his door, staring at them for a moment before slamming the door shut and making his way around the front of the car to the rear passenger door.

Like a chauffeur, he opened the rusted door and reached his hand in to assist whoever was in that seat. After several seconds, a scarf-covered head appeared. The scarf was sheer and dark purple, edged in golden rounds and gems and draped over a face that was a patchwork of wrinkles. The woman wasn't just old, she was ancient. Yet she stood straight, her brown broom skirt reaching nearly to the dirt as she strode purposefully toward them. The young man scrambled to follow.

Emilie stiffened at their arrival. "Travelers?" she asked.

"No Irish travelers that I have seen. But Gypsies from the continent are encamped near Stonehaven."

"Romani, Dad," Emilie commented off-handedly.

Jack whipped his head around. "What?"

"*Romani* is the correct term, if they aren't travelers, then they're Romani. *Gypsy* is an insulting term loaded with stereotypes, Da."

"Och, look who's got fancy American college learning," he teased.

Emilie rolled her eyes exaggeratedly then returned her attention to the old woman. She stopped several feet in front of them, and her eyes sharper than Emilie expected roved over her father, then herself. Emilie's breath caught in her chest.

"Are ye the Gordons of Glenbervie?" the woman asked in a voice as strong as her walk. She sure didn't behave like an elderly woman.

Jack coughed into his fist then smiled weakly at the woman. "Aye. Jack Gordon. How can I help ye? Tours are closed for the day."

The Romani woman's eyes remained level as she studied Jack. "Have they been here yet? The scientist people. Have they spoken to ye?"

Emilie shared a confused glance with her father. Scientists? What was she talking about?

"I can see from your faces, nay. Not yet. They will come though, and ask about a cure for the sickness."

Jack's body stiffened. "What concern is it to ye?"

Emilie, on the other hand, felt her heart go out to the woman. She must be suffering from dementia. But why would the young man bring her here if her mind was suffering?

The woman's eyes narrowed to slits. "'Tis of significant concern to me, Gordon. This sickness, many of my people are ill and dying. 'Tis no' a concern for scientists until wealthy people start dying. But my people, and many others in communities like mine are suffering."

"Other Romani?" Jack asked. Emilie gave him a sideways glance. Was he humoring the woman?

"And travelers, and homeless, and the elderly," she finished for him. "And the very young."

She said the last few words with emphasis, and Emilie understood her meaning.

"Is someone ye know dying? A child?" A lump formed in Emilie's throat as she asked the question. If it was true, how unfortunate that was.

Her father coughed again, and the Romani woman's gaze cut hard to him before returning to Emilie.

"Aye. My young grandson. He will perish if there is no cure." The woman paused, and for the first time, her tough visage faltered. "The scientists will come and ask ye about a plant. 'Tis a way for a cure, and I know a way to retrieve the plant you seek, but it is unconventional and dangerous."

"Ye are wrong" her father answered. "There is no cure. No plant will cure it."

The woman nodded. "Aye, no plant today. In this time, the mushroom the scientists seek is gone. 'Tis the plant that they believe cure. Extinct today, but it was here centuries ago, aye?"

"That's an odd bit of information to have, an odd thing to say," Emilie commented.

Her father had stiffened again under the woman's odd appearance and questions, and Emilie had slowly shifted to stand in front of him, protecting him.

The woman's hard face softened as she nodded. The gold coins on her scarf jingled. "'Tis my job to have information. 'Tis a gift from my grandmother and from her grandmother before her. And 'tis their knowledge that I now share with ye. 'Tis unconventional as I said, but I ask that ye listen and no' judge."

Emilie's attention was on the woman, ready to listen as she bid.

"Many secrets, stories, and old knowledge have I, the gift from my ancestors. I have other gifts as well. One is I can take ye back to that time. there ye can protect the mushrooms so they dinna go extinct, and the scientists can use them today."

"Ye cannae change history," Jack commented flatly, as if what the woman claimed could actually happen. "And your story is beyond unbelievable."

The logical side of Emilie wanted to agree with her father, but something else inside her, in her chest as well as her mind, told her to listen to everything the woman had to say.

"I can take ye back, Jack Gordon, but ye can never return. I've seen it in my dreams, this mushroom and this time in history. No' ancient, but close. Ye are the last of the male bloodline of the Glenbervie Gordons, Jack." The woman's gaze riveted on Emilie's father. "I have a way to send ye back to the time of grandfather's grandfather before the land was razed.""

"What?" Jack's voice cracked. "Ye are crazy, lady. It's time for ye to go."

She stepped closer to Emilie, her eyes pleading. "I'm no' crazy. With the right words and herbs, I can send ye back into the body of your ancestor Seocan Gordon. There ye can protect the fungus from the ill-tempered king and save everyone today."

Emilie was immobilized by the woman's words that sounded absolutely preposterous, but why would she come to them unless she could do something? Maybe not travel through time, but something.

The woman's face grew impossibly paler, and her voice rose as she continued to speak. "It's the only way! We have to save them! My grandson!" Then she pointed her knobby, arthritic finger at Jack. "Ye and my grandson!"

Emilie's gaze followed from the woman's fingertip to her father. He had coughed this afternoon. Did the Romani woman know he was sick?

The dark-haired young man (*a son? A nephew? An older grandson?*) pulled on her upper arm to calm her and drag her backward.

"Nonni, come on. I told ye they would no' listen."

The woman's eyes grew hard again, more stone-like than when she had exited the car. "Ye shall regret this," she told Jack, then spat on the ground by his feet. She spun in a flash of purple and another jingle of charms and stormed away.

Instead of following her right away, the younger man remained. Unlike the fiery older woman, his lowered gaze appeared sheepish and apologetic.

"When the scientists come, listen to them. Pay attention. We are at the Stone Haven cleaning if ye care to discuss it more. Ask for Eladon. Or the witch. She's known by that as well," he said with a curt bow, then followed the older woman back across the sunset field.

Emilie waited until the woman was in the car with the young man and driving away before she spoke.

"What was that?" Emilie asked her father. "Did that just happen?"

The encounter with the woman resembled a fairy tale more than reality. Emilie honestly expected to awake from this strange dream. Her father's comment, however, assured her that she was indeed awake.

"I dinna ken. 'Tis like a bad joke. Forget she was here." He broke off into a fit of coughing. Emilie's insides turned to ice.

"Are ye okay, Da?"

He waved his hand at her. "I'm fine. So much dust with the stalks and the car kicking up dirt. Go on and head to the barns. I'll join ye straight away."

Chapter Three

Emilie made her way to the barns but stopped short when she noticed a car off to the side of the access road, unnoticed after the interaction with the old woman. Three people emerged, heading right toward her father. She froze where she stood near the barn because one of the men wore a white lab coat.

What was a doctor doing out here? Wasn't he busy? Or was he . . . was he a scientist?

Oh my, had the old woman spoken the truth?

The sickness, these scientists visiting her family, it was suddenly too real. Her mind flitted back to her martial arts class today, and of how many people were absent. The world had dealt with a pandemic a few years ago, and now it seemed something else was making people sick. The news hadn't been sharing much–and she hated how governments kept things like this secret–but her friends at Ashbond had researched it. Some odd disease wasn't just making people sick; people were dying in large numbers, and doctors and scientists were worried and confused. And with the peculiar visit from the Romani, this mysterious illness was all she was thinking about.

The amount of contradictory information was shocking, and like everyone else, Emilie didn't know what to believe. Her friends from college had said they heard that the school might be closing again, but Emilie hadn't been able to confirm that. All she knew was she was glad she hadn't heard any grumblings about it at Stonehaven, and that they lived in a relatively remote area. And that her father was healthy. Or so she thought. The woman, Eladon, hadn't believed her father to be as hale as Emilie believed.

That lab coat guy, though, *he* worried her. Why was a doctor or scientist here? It was out of place, even if the woman had said scientists would come. Emilie certainly hadn't believed that Eladon woman.

She scrambled up the side of the hill toward the field where her father was collecting his tools. Focusing her attention on the lab coats and keeping her distance once she reached them, eavesdropping on the conversation. She only heard bits and pieces, but what she heard was more than enough, and she was too stunned to move any closer.

Impossible. The old woman must have seen the scientists' car or something.

The field was wide open, so Emilie lingered by the split rail fence to see her father and the visitors' profile and read their faces. Drifts of their conversation reached her ears, and studying their faces filled in the rest. The person leading the trio, a sharp-dressed woman in a pantsuit and sensible shoes held her hand out to Jack.

"Hello, Mr. Gordon. My name is Willa Anderson, and I'm with the World Health Organization. My associates and I would like to ask you a few questions if we may?"

Jack rested his elbow on the pit of his rake and swept his hand toward them. He stared at them as though Eladon hadn't just predicted their arrival. Her father had an unrivaled poker face. "Ask away, but I dinna know what a historian farmer can do to help the likes of ye."

"We are looking for a rare plant believed to have once grown in this area. The fungi *amanitagorenlandica arctic* species is a rare parasitic fungus, a strangler for its ability to take over other fungi. Since you are the owner of this property and your family has lived here for centuries, we hoped you might be able to help us."

Jack rubbed at the stubble on his chin as he regarded the woman. Emilie could see he was weighing her words against the strange Romani visit.

A rare plant? Emilie thought. The plant Eladon spoke of. A fungi – a mushroom, just as she had said? *No, it isn't possible . . .*

"I'm no' a student of flowers, nay a botanist," Jack drawled in his rolling Highland burr. "I dinna ken one flower much from the next."

"But you're a farmer and a historian. And you know the area. Please." The woman's voice bordered on begging. Emilie raised an eyebrow. This plant, the one they were searching for, must be a final straw. And the Romani woman had said it was extinct.

The man in the lab coat stepped closer to her father and held out a piece of paper. "Gordons of Glenbervie. You're the last, are you not?"

Lab coat's words echoed the Eladon's, and Emilie shuddered. Jack nodded, but remained silent, his golden green eyes studying the paper.

"We can't find many Gordons left in this area. We were told of your farm and the study of history near where a fossilized piece of the fungi was found. Can you help us?"

Emilie's eyes narrowed as she watched her father hand the paper back. What was on that paper?

"I'll do my best, but as I said, I'm no botanist."

The lab coat man dipped his head. "Yes. Understood. You've heard of the most recent illness sweeping the globe?"

Jack rolled his eyes and Emilie inched closer, her curiosity peaked even more. Was there truth to the rumors? To Eladon's worries about the illness?

"Another supposed sickness. If it's not the flu, it's something else . . ." Jack's words trailed off as the trio shared a peculiar glance.

The woman cleared her throat. "There is a bit more to this illness than the WHO and other health organizations have let on. We are trying to avoid some of the panics of the past."

Jack straightened and sniffed hard. "What are ye hiding?"

"I can't share everything, of course," the woman answered through tight lips. "But unlike other illnesses, we can't seem to find an antibody or a vaccine for it. We are at a loss. This disease has markings of something seen in the ancient world and early medieval times. Our scientists were stumped until one of them came upon this." She pointed to the picture.

"I dinna understand. What does any of this have to do with me? 'Tis no' of my concern if ye cannae find a vaccine for a flu."

The taller man in the fitted suit finally spoke up. "It's not a flu. It's more like a plague."

Emilie's brow furrowed. A plague? *Come on*. Even she wasn't buying this, no matter what the Romani woman had predicted. But then, why send out three people, including one scientist, to interview her father if it wasn't serious? And how could her father help? It seemed so far-fetched, almost as far-fetched as changing the past. She took a few steps closer to hear better.

"We found small, fossilized fragments in a museum, of all places," the scientist explained. "From historical and scientific records, we've learned that this plant, this fungus blights other mushrooms, and today, it appears mushrooms are causing this global illness."

Jack crossed his arms across his chest. "Mushrooms?" he asked, disbelieving. To be honest, Emilie didn't blame him.

"Through airborne spores," the scientist continued. "This is not a viral thing, and we've tried to destroy the mushrooms but there are so many, and the spores have traveled in the air and once in the lungs, one person can pass the infection to the next just through breathing." She lowered her voice. "And it's killing people. Millions. The death rate is nearly 50%."

Emilie stood as stock-still as her father. *What?* This illness was so much more than she'd heard on the news. Eladon had not mentioned that. Her roommate Angelina didn't know the half of it, even with all the news in her America!

Yet, after living through the foolish chaos that came with previous global infections, from a flu to Ebola, she understood why the health organizations might want to keep this information under wraps.

But, if it was as bad as all that, wouldn't deaths or illnesses be leaking or reported? How had they kept it on the down low?

The scientist pointed to the paper as well. "We have learned this one fungus can be converted into a vaccine to cure it. It strangles the spores just as it does as a plant, and can strangle the infection in someone who's sick. We need a fungus to kill a fungus, if you will."

Jack rubbed his chin again. "But you dinna have this fungus. You only have this fossil. And you need the plant."

Just as Eladon had said.

Willa nodded.

"And ye cannae find it anywhere?"

Willa fidgeted, her sensible shoes sinking into the muddy ground. "We've been informed that it's extinct. But we held out hope that maybe that information wasn't 100% correct. We've heard the last known location of the plant was near here. We hope maybe a small patch or a single stool grew in this area still."

Jack opened his mouth to ask another question, the lab coat man must have anticipated it because he picked up where Willa left off. "The flowers only grew on the field behind castle Dunnottar." He reached into his pocket and pulled out a map, pointing. "The castle was situated on this headland here, smart for defenses –"

"Aye," Jack agreed. He brightened even as his brow furrowed. This was his field of expertise now. Emilie took another step closer. "With three sides surrounded by sheer cliffs and the volatile sea and this narrow strip land leading to it, 'twas a brilliant choice for occupancy by King Donald the Second. Then again, Donald was known as a skilled warrior and tactician."

"Yes, and here," the scientist brushed his finger over the northern face of the strip of land. "This is where those fungi grew, in the shadows of the castle. Might there be more growing there that we don't know about?"

Jack snorted. "Ye have a problem then."

"A problem?" Willa asked.

"Aye, a problem. Ye'll need a new solution to your vaccine. There's nary a flower from that time growing there."

Willa's face tightened. "What? How do you know? Have you checked every underbelly of rock?"

Her voice rose with each question. Emilie could feel the woman's panic waft off her, and with good reason. Eladon had spoken the truth. Those mushrooms were gone today.

"Nay. I dinna have to. In 900 CE, Donald battled the Norse and his own men who tried to invade Dunnottar. He defeated the Norse, and to send a message to those who might try again, he took their boats, weapons, and bodies, and lit it all on fire. Myth said it was big enough for all the northern nations to see. As a result, the fire raged out of control and scorched the entire eastern seaboard, from the headland inward, destroying all the landscape and flora in the surrounding countryside, including this flower. If it grew on that headland or miles inland, it was gone. Donald took the scorched earth approach to the invaders, and only in the past centuries or so has anything grown back.

Thin grasses and moss that blew from Scotland proper to the sea. Your information about the extinction of the fungi was accurate."

Emilie's hand flew to her mouth. Eladon's information was accurate! Emilie was intimately familiar with that history – most in the Highlands were. King Donald was renowned as a warrior king, but also as a violent and temperamental one. That scorched earth effort had included burning the houses, villages, and farms of the surrounding clans, and killing anyone who might have had a hand in aiding the Norse, who only wanted to settle, not necessarily invade, according to several different historical documents. The King had turned that desire to settle into a power move, and many Highland clans suffered for it.

King Donald and his allies – the Morays and the Keiths – were the reason her father was the last man of the Glenbervie Gordons, and she was the last of them all. He had killed as many of the Glenbervie Gordons as he could find, and their allies. 900 CE had been a bloodbath for the Highlands.

The trio hung their heads. "So there is nothing we can do?"

Jack shook his head sadly. "Nay. The plant is gone."

Emilie's chest clenched. It seemed that King Donald had managed to reach through time with his vengeance and would yet kill them all.

The scientist thanked Jack and returned, shoulders slumped and heads hung low, back to their car.

"Dad, what's up with the scientists? Why are they talking to ye?" Emilie asked as she raced up to her father. He rested his elbow atop his rake as he watched dust gather behind the departing car.

His gaze lingered, then he turned and coughed again into the dusty air.

"How much did ye hear?" he inquired.

Emilie had the good grace to blush heatedly at her father's question. "Most of it. What of this disease? This plant? Was that old woman right?"

Jack didn't answer right away. "What do ye know of this illness? Have ye heard anything at college?"

Emilie shook her head. "Nay. My friend Angelina said she had heard something of yet another flu or the like, but I passed it off as another health scare."

"Mmm," her father grumbled with a brief nod. He handed her the papers that the scientist had left with him. "I dinna ken what to believe, no' having heard anything. But if many are dying and they are desperate enough to come to me, then perhaps it's as bad as they said. The scientists found a fungus or something that they believe would cure the disease." He handed her the picture and botany drawing of the fungus.

Emilie had to admit it was a beautiful mushroom, red-pink gradient top with creamy white freckles. "It's like a fairy tale mushie," she commented.

Jack grunted again. "They wanted to find this, but it's gone."

Emilie nodded, recalling both her father's words to the scientists and her own knowledge of history.

"And ye dinna believe any to be left? At all?" She didn't have to say the rest of the sentence, *like the Romani woman claimed?*

Jack sniffed the air and rubbed his nose. "Nay. I've never seen this plant outside of your fairy tale books when ye were a wee lass. If that cliff was the only place it grew in the tenth century, it's gone now." Jack's face shifted and he cupped the back of Emilie's head, his rough hand light against her reddish-blonde bob. "Come. Since ye are here, grab a rake. Ye can help me bring the tools in. We're losing the sun and this dusty air is making me miserable. Let's head home for supper."

She fell into step next to her father, keeping a wary eye on him. After everything she'd heard today, dust allergies seemed like too pat of an answer. Was he sick? Her insides chilled more. If what those people had said was true, her father's cough was a death sentence. A 50% death rate, especially among seniors? Her father didn't seem old to her -- he had always appeared healthy and strong, but what if . . .

What if Eladon was right? Just as she had been correct about everything else this day?

If Da is sick, maybe I can do something. As they entered the house, Emilie made the firm decision to head out to Stonehaven, find out what Eladon woman meant by sending back.

Because if she could save her father, she would. No matter what it took or how crazy the idea was.

He didn't have her train to be a fighter just to sit back and do nothing.

Chapter Four

Eastern Scotland, 900 CE

When the rider appeared from the mist like a demon from the old god's Otherworld, Brian MacDougal held his hand up to his nephew William MacDougal, before he dropped his hayfork and approached the rider.

William's muscle-packed body tensed, and he narrowed his eyes as he watched his uncle approach the stranger. Men riding like the fires of hell lapped at their heels were never a good sign, that was something William understood well.

Brian reached the horse and the rider, covered in sweat and mud, all but fell into his arms. William rushed to assist his uncle. He didn't know the man, but the rider peered at him with a measure of gratitude. Brian shouted for a nearby lad to take the man's horse as Brian half-walked, half-carried the weary soul to the Drumoak castle, seat of Clan MacDougal.

"Cormag! Man! We have an urgent matter!"

William supported the young man's left side while Brian carried the man's right. The chieftain's wife, Caitir, swept in, wiping her hands on a cloth as she came up from the kitchens to the great hall. Brian's gaze shot to Caitir.

"Find Cormag! Something has happened!"

William was uncertain what might have caused this stranger to ride like a fury, but the man had nearly killed himself and his horse riding here, so *something* was amiss. Brian laid the man on a bench set against the stone wall near the hearth. Nearing midsummer but cool, and fires roared near day and night, much to the man's fortune.

William's uncle Cormag, chieftain of Clan MacDougal, stormed into the great hall with the same urgency Brian beset upon Caitir as she swept in behind him holding more cloths. She stepped to the man, wiping his face as Cormag approached them.

"Who rides here like this?" Cormag asked.

William hovered between the rider and his uncle as Brian detailed the man's arrival, listening intently. Cormag turned his gaze to the rider. Color returned to his pale skin as Caitir brushed his long, light brown hair out of his eyes. His face might have been clear, but the blood and muck upon his tunic was unmistakable. Cormag, Brian, and William shared a concerned look.

"Grant," the man croaked out as he opened his eyes. Wild, amber, and frightened. He had witnessed something dire.

"What's your name, lad?" Brian asked in a low tone.

"Hamish. Hamish Grant." The young man groaned and tried to sit up. Caitir and William assisted him until he was upright and using the wall for support.

"What has ye riding here as if the demons of hell were chasing ye?" Brian pressed.

"The king. The mad king has slaughtered half the Grant and MacIntosh clans."

William stiffened at the harrowing words. But he didn't believe them. He couldn't bring himself to believe them. What reason would King Donald, mad though he was, have to attack the Grants and MacIntoshes?

"They were trying to form an alliance," the young man continued, answering William's silent question. "The king is running wild, and to prevent any retribution against the chieftains, their most trusted seconds came together for conference with a small force of men at Tewel Glen. The king must have found out because he attacked. Men fell as I rode away as instructed by my tanist, Alpin."

"Alpin Grant is dead?" Cormag interrupted the man's horrific tale.

William pressed his palms against the back of his blond head. He had heard rumors of the clans uniting in a show of strength to temper the king's mad violence -- they were yet a loose collection of the clans of Alba, and if the king did not respect them, then the clans did not feel the need to obey him, especially since he'd been sowing discord among the frail clan unity.

The clans were what made the kingdom of the Scots, not a king.

And the clans knew it.

William knew it. And as a brave son of the MacDougal clan, he'd fight to keep it that way.

Cormag tilted his head toward Brian and William and spoke quietly. "Brian, send a message to the Gordons of what this lad has said, and have some men meet me in Tewel. Like us, they share kin with many a Grant, and they should be there to see if it is as Hamish has said." He flicked a hard look at the Grant rider. "I want to disbelieve him. No' even the most mad king would slaughter a gathering of men such as he has described, but the man has no reason to lie. Go now. William, find your father and a few other men to accompany us. We will see this villainy for ourselves."

Brian bowed curtly and rushed off, racing for the postern gate and stables beyond. William searched for his father, Bernard, his broad chest tight with unease. A shift was happening in the Highlands, and William feared this recent attack might mean a turn for the worse.

William followed his father and his chieftain Cormag MacDougal through the thicket of trees toward Tewel. He doubted what he had heard about this slaughter -- he saw the same on his father's face. Bernard was naught if not pragmatic. He and William were of one mind. What purpose did it serve to have a king attack his own people? And powerful Highland clans, at that?

The horses stopped short as they exited the trees, and as a tall man, William didn't have to move much to see beyond his father and uncle to the field.

An abattoir, more like it.

The carnage defied the imagination. William had been in many a scuffle, reiving, fights, even a few battles with invading Danes and Norse, and he prided himself a true Highland warrior, but nothing like this.

This was a nightmare.

Silence encompassed the entire field as homage to the fallen that littered the grass, staining it crimson with their own blood. A mural of death. William shuddered and pulled his checked cape around his shoulders.

"William, ye and Ailbert ride to the north of the field, see what bodies lay there, if we ken any of them. I'll search the south with Cormag." Bernard tipped his chin to his chieftain to see if he agreed, and Cormag nodded once.

Digging his heels into the horse's ribs, he spurred the steed around the corpses to the north. He studied the bodies as he picked through the field, marking those he knew in his mind.

The echo of horses approaching rolled through the field, and all the MacDougal men spun around, the ring of unsheathing swords combining with the beat of horseshoes.

Seocan Gordon, chieftain of the Glenbervie Gordons, burst through the northeast woods to the edge of his field, his men filing behind him. He pulled up short, reining his horse until it reared at the sight of this killing field. His gaze remained fixed even as his horse pawed and pranced under him.

He shot a look to William. "What is this? Where is your uncle?"

William pointed. "'Tis evidence of the king's vile nature. Cormag would welcome your conference here."

"Have ye seen any Gordon kin here?" Seocan asked as his eyes flitted from one dead body to the next.

"No' yet, but we've just started looking."

Seocan reined his horse to the left before pausing. His gaze softened at William. "I hope ye find none of your kin, lad. For your sake and your uncle's." Then he rode around the field to Cormag and Bernard.

William understood Seocan's comment. Like the Gordons, MacDougal would not let any slight go unrewarded, even if it meant defying a king.

And William's handfast to Seocan's sister, Ailith, meant any quarrel they had with the king became Gordon's quarrel as well. This wedding was more than a union of two souls, but a union of two powerful clans. There were many other clans, including those that supported the mad king, who did not want to see it to fruition.

William cared naught for what those clans wanted. William's sole desire in this world was Ailith, and had been since he met her when he was but ten summers. The clans joining was merely a secondary benefit.

Thinking of Ailith, her deep red hair that curled down to her waist and her flashing green eyes that teased him at every turn helped temper his disgust and sadness at the sights before him. How might he keep these horrors from her? Taking a deep breath, he turned his horse northward.

"Let us start at the northern tree line, and move south, meet Father in the middle."

"Aye," Ailbert agreed and followed William. Then he gasped and leaped from his steed before William could turn around.

"Ailbert! Wait!" Why was his brother such a rash fool? The young man lacked all sense.

William slid off his horse, sword in hand, and reached the spot where Ailbert stood. He stared at a bloodied body crumpled on the ground, partially hidden in the trees.

"Is that –?" Ailbert lost his words. William's blood pounded in his throat and temples as he crouched to the young man. He gave the body a light shove, and the head shifted upward, glazed eyes staring at the heavens where his soul now walked.

"God's blood," William cursed and tried to swallow the thick, hot lump in his throat. "Aye, 'tis Rudy," William spoke loud enough for Ailbert to hear.

Rudy, their close cousin, so skilled with horses he'd helped William and Ailbert learn to ride. Their dear cousin who'd recently spent a fortnight at Drumoak, drinking and betting on a game of hazard, which he was terrible at.

Had been terrible at. William's trembling breathing was mirrored by Ailbert. Their mothers were close cousins, as close as sisters, and the news of Rudy's death at the hand of the mad king would devastate them both, as much as it devastated William.

Rudy wasn't much older than William's younger brother Wee Brian. This could be his broken body here. The thought choked him.

"William?" Ailbert called, but William didn't hear him over the sounds of his despair in his mind.

"William?" he called again, and wiping his hand across his eyes, William turned on his heels.

"Father and Uncle Cormag will no' take to this," Ailbert said in a tremulous voice. He was trying not to cry. William wiped his own eyes again. "'Tis bad, brother. So verra bad."

William nodded. Rudy was beloved by both clans. And he yet did not know who else had found their end here. Aye, this was bad indeed.

No longer would the clans be complacent in trying to temper the king's violent nature. Nay, William had been present many times as Bernard, Brian, and Cormag spoke, and they had already decided they could no' suffer the king to live if he abused or slaughtered the clans further.

Something *this* dire was exactly the spark to ignite that fire.

The king was just one man, after all, and Alba was and always had been a land of the clans.

Chapter Five

Modern-day Scotland

Emilie shut off her laptop and leaned against her padded headboard. Angelina's words twisted around Emilie's mind and she couldn't shut it off.

They had a live chat online, she and Angelina, and her other two housemates, Julia and Ashland, both from Scotland as well. Julia was working an internship in California, and Ashland had a summer class. They had agreed before Emilie left for Scotland to have the video chats with all of them at least once a week, so they didn't feel quite as distanced over the summer. This chat was on top of daily texts, chats, and phone calls. Her friends were not going to let her forget them over the summer. They had become the best of friends in so short a time, and Angelina often called them the Four Musketeers.

Tonight, however, the chat did not resonate or make Emilie feel as elated as it typically did. Once Ashland had heard Jack coughing in the background, the entire tone of the conversation had changed.

"Em, is your dad sick?" she had asked in a wary voice. Her pale blue eyes were wide. Ashland was the type who only wanted the best for everyone, and things like illnesses worried her too much. Pretty, blonde Ashland was too good a person for this world. And after all that Emilie had learned about the illness and the conversation with the Romani, she was wary, too.

"No, just allergies from working in the yard," Emilie assured her, keeping up her father's fib. None of her friends appeared to believe her – which prompted Emilie to ask her next question. Even in this moment, she didn't know what had possessed her.

"Hey, guys, what would ye do if someone said they had a way to stop the spread and save all these lives, but ye had to do something strange? Would ye do it?"

Her friends had fallen silent, their eyes shifting.

"It'd depend on what it was, I guess." Julia had spoken first, she of the sage advice, of a still water that ran deep and only spoke when it meant something. She brushed a frizzy brown curl out of her face. "I mean, if it meant something that would kill me, probably not. But as long as I wasn't dead or injured in the end, I'd probably say yes."

Ashland had nodded her agreement, but Angelina's round face remained stoic, and she narrowed her deep-set black eyes through the camera.

"Why? Did someone ask you to do something? Did your dad ask you?"

Emilie shook her head, her strawberry blond bob brushing against her chin, but she knew Angelina could read her better than she read herself. Angelina had a way of knowing who people were and what they were thinking before they did, and she unleashed that uncanny ability on Em now.

"Nay, no' him. I'm just asking. Call it an intellectual exercise." She hated lying to her friends but how could she begin to explain what had happened that day when she still didn't fully understand?

Angelina, the only American of the housemates, kept her hard gaze at the screen. "I don't know what's going on with you, Em, but I do know this. You've always been a fighter. You took down that handsy guy at the party with one move. But some things you can't fight. Think hard about what you can do before you act. Please."

Emilie had nodded, as did Julia and Ashland, and when her father's coughing started up again, she had bid her friends good night (and good afternoon since there was a seven-hour time difference) and closed her laptop.

You've always been a fighter.

Leave it to her American housemate to state it so plainly. Now, when it mattered, when her father was probably sick with this illness, was she going to sit by and do nothing? She'd lost her mother in a car accident when she was four – she couldn't fight for her mother.

But she could fight for her father.

That made up her mind. Grabbing her jacket from her chair, she slipped into the hallway. Jack was already in bed. The blue cough medicine he'd taken sat open in the bathroom. Emilie stuck the lid on, peeked at her snoring father, then locked the front door after stepping into the cool evening air.

This was probably a wild goose chase, but she had to try at least. She jumped into her dad's truck, started the engine, and drove down the access road toward Stonehaven.

Stonehaven clearing, to be more precise.

The Romani campsite reached her ears, a carnival of sound, well before she saw it around the trees. Not far from the Tewel Glen, separated by a throng of trees that seemed to dance to the music in the moonlight.

Following the curve in the road around the bed, the sight of the camp rivaled the musical cacophony, with fairy lights, camper lights, campfires, and lamps illuminating flapping tarp canopies, tents, and RV-style campers. People milled about, adding to the din and the force of color that brightened as she drove closer. Women in jewel-tone jackets, skirts, or scarves, and gold rounds and gems embedded in their clothing. Men wearing fitted pants and brightly colored shirts and scarf-styled belts. Not everyone she noted, chastising herself for making assumptions, but many.

She parked just outside in a ring of cars that served as a buttress between Scotland and their world. Emilie felt like an interloper. But the young man had invited her – well, her father – to come.

With a hesitancy unfamiliar to her, Emilie left the safety of her truck and made her way through the maze of cars and tents to the main part of the campsite. Couples danced and ate, families gathered and laughed as they shared stories, and children ran about with their games. No computers or phones, no hiding in tents or campers. This was a community in every sense of the word, and Emilie could understand why the Romani woman had been so fervent in her request.

Eladon, Emilie reminded herself. *The witch. The young man had called her 'Nonni'. Grandmother?*

If nothing else, maybe Emilie could make better sense of what the woman had been speaking about. She didn't really mean going back in time–scientists hadn't quite figured that one out yet, but perhaps she meant something else, like hypnosis? To use old memories to find old seeds or spores in another plant or location? Using another, older plant the same way – a plant that Eladon knew of? Or maybe the woman knew of a place on the Glenbervie lands or near Dunnottar that hid the plant. That could be what her metaphor of going back in time meant.

At the edge of the lively camp, Emilie paused, uncertain of where to go or who to ask. She searched for either the old woman or the young man, but she didn't find either of them.

A small body slammed into her side, knocking her off balance. Not too badly – she spread her legs in a ready stance as she evaluated her attacker.

Or rather, the wee child who had run into her. A little girl with wide hazel eyes and black hair gazed up at her. Then smiled.

"Are you a visitor?" she asked as she fidgeted in her blue dress.

Emilie nodded. "Aye. I was invited here by Eladon."

The girl's eyes rounded like teacup saucers on her face, and her body stilled. Eladon was a name with power, evidently. The girl threaded her hand into Emilie's.

"I can take you," she said in a suddenly mature voice as she tugged Emilie into the middle of the camp.

She didn't miss the stares as people paused in their activities and watched Emilie and the girl weave their way through the camp to the more northern side. They reached an unassuming caravan, one that Emilie might see at any campsite or RV park.

The girl knocked at the narrow door, then called out. "Evan! I have a visitor for your Nonni!"

Within seconds, the door swung open and the handsome young man from earlier stood at the door. His eyes rested on Emilie for a moment, then flicked to the girl.

"Thank you, Cherise. I'll take her from here."

Ominous words, and Emilie's stomach trembled. She took a deep breath and again put herself in a prepared position for whatever was to come. If this had been a bad idea, one that could end badly for her, then she was going to be ready to fight her way out of it. Her eyes rested on a broom on the RV stoop, one she could use as a bo-staff if needed.

Evan opened the door wide and stood to the side. "Please, come in."

In a slow series of steps, her eyes scanning the interior of the RV for anything threatening, she entered the RV.

Evan led her down the narrowest hall Emilie had ever encountered. She considered herself lucky that she was not claustrophobic as he reached a closed door at the end of the hall. There he paused and turned to her.

"*Nonni*, Eladon, is a self-proclaimed witch, but none would disagree with that proclamation. She knows things, sees things, and can do things. Impossible things. It's believed it's her inheritance from her grandmother, and her grandmother before her, going back generations. And know this." His voice grew stern. "What she says she can do, she can do. Never doubt it, so make sure you are positive, with absolutely no doubts, before you agree to anything. Do you understand?"

What's behind that door? she wondered as her shaky mind slowly comprehended the man's words. His face had paled starkly against his dark hair. *What am I getting myself into?*

She took a deep breath and nodded.

Then he turned the knob and opened the door.

Whatever Emilie had built up in her head about Eladon and this room -- what she saw was not it.

Unlike the rest of the camp, full of vibrancy and color, this room was stark. Brown carpet and white walls, no designs or paint; a plain brown bed frame; a white comforter on the bed. No television, but a small chest of drawers in the corner and a brown paneled door hiding the closet.

That was it. Oh, except for Eladon herself, the lone multichromatic image of vibrancy in this drab room. She sat on a kitchen chair by the bed.

Eladon nodded to Evan, who gave Emilie one final look before closing the door. Eladon swept her hand over the bed, inviting Emilie to sit.

"Thank you for coming," she said as Emilie perched on the edge of the bed across from Eladon.

Emilie's lips thinned. "Truthfully, I dinna know why I'm here. Ye spoke in riddles earlier today."

Eladon's face was a mask, unmoving. No smile, no frown, no emotions whatsoever. It unnerved Emilie to see it. But Eladon's heavily wrinkled eyes – they held everything, like dark tunnels to an unknown world.

"I never speak in riddles, lassie," Eladon countered. "I speak the truth, always."

Emilie shook her head. "No, because you talked about going back in time to fix . . ." she waved her hand around, "what's going on."

"The sickness," Eladon answered for her. The woman leaned forward and sniffed Emilie.

What –?

"You are the last of your people. That is a mighty weight to bear." Eladon sat up tall, her hair scarf tinkling in the spartan quiet of the room. "But it also makes what must be done easier."

"What? What must be done? What are you talking about?"

"I call myself a witch because the universe and my foremothers speak to me in dreams. What else would we call it? Our dreams, they can tell us so much, if only we listen. Do you listen to your dreams, Emilie?"

Her chest suddenly seemed heavy, as if it was difficult to breathe. Maybe coming here had been a bad idea. Was this woman insane?

"You should. My dreams are different than most. I see the world, the future and the past, in my dreams. And with those dreams comes a wee bit of ability." Eladon rose and stepped to her chest of drawers. She opened the top drawer and withdrew a small pot, a cup, and a leather packet.

"You will not believe me, but one ability is to move people through time. Have you ever heard of someone called an old soul?" Eladon looked over her shoulder at Emilie, who nodded slightly.

She was surprised she could move at all. Shock at this conversation kept her all but frozen in place.

"They are those who have traveled the expanse of time. But it cannot be done idly. Those stories of people falling through time willy-nilly, those are fairy stories. People always travel for a reason."

"Like the Irish Travelers?" Emilie asked as she tried to make sense of Eladon's words. Nothing made sense.

"No, not like that. They travel in a different way. They travel like my people have traveled for centuries. We share a lifeblood that way, a shared livelihood of people unencumbered by the trials and responsibilities of land, not in DNA but spirit. But the word is used the same way. There are many different types of travelers after all. But there must be a reason."

"And this reason is this illness?"

Eladon fiddled with her pot and cup, mixing the contents of the packet into the cup. Satisfied, she had the mixture she desired, she returned to the chair and sat, cradling the cup in her wizened hands.

"I am old," Eladon interrupted herself. "Older than any woman should be. It is part of my legacy as well as the dreams and the abilities. My granddaughter, she will be like me one day, but I cannot pass until

I teach her. So, I have seen and done more than you can imagine. And I have done this many times. Every time with a need."

She handed the cup to Emilie who took it without thought.

"The reason is a connection. The illness is just something you can fix, but you can only do it because of your connection. You or your father," she intoned as she sat back in her chair, her dark eyes unwavering as they focused on Emilie.

"Your father is the last man of his bloodline, and you are the last woman. My own grandmother from the middle ages spoke to me in a dream of your connection to your many times removed grandmother, a woman who lived in the time bridging the tenth century. Your connection to her is so strong, this should be an easy journey for you."

"Do ye believe you can send me back in time to the middle ages?" The words sounded like lunacy as she spoke them aloud.

Finally, a shadow of a grin crossed Eladon's wrinkled face. "I don't think, I *know*. But there are some things you must know before ye go." She held up one finger ravaged by arthritis. "One, your mind, your consciousness will go and you will awaken in the body of your great-great-grandmother. Her mind will slip into your body in return. When she awakens here, I will care for her, but she will not look or sound like her old self, and neither will you. Ye will have her looks, her shape, her tone of voice. You will be yourself in your mind, yet those around you will know you as your grandmother, not as a strange new woman in their land."

Emilie's mouth opened and closed like a fish out of water. Swap places? Force her many-time grandmother to live as a young woman in her modern time? Though Eladon said she'd care for her, what did that mean? And how would Emilie know she kept that promise? Could she do that to another person? Emilie had so many questions, but what could she ask that might make any of this more understandable?

"Second." Another ancient finger rose. "Your connection to your grandmother is all you will have, that and your mind. No one else will know you as Emilie or know why you are there. While your task will be to save some of these red mushrooms, no one else will be there to help you or even understand what you are doing. You will be on your own in this task. It will be difficult."

Emilie swallowed hard. "And the third?"

"You will not return. This door is one way. My foremothers have sent people into the future, and I have sent people into the past, but they never come back. You will have to leave your father forever, but if you do, you have the chance to save his life. If you don't go, then he dies for certain in three days. This I have seen."

Emilie's breath caught in her chest. "Ye lie. Ye say that to get me to do your dirty work."

Eladon moved more quickly than Emilie believed possible for an old woman. She grasped Emilie's wrist and yanked their faces close.

"I told you, I speak only the truth," Eladon bit out. Even the difficult truths, the worst truths. I have seen my grandson's death, your father's death, the death of many of my people. And it is dirty work. Saving those we love is always dirty work, but we do it because we love them."

Eladon threw Emilie's wrist down and glanced at the cup.

"It is the moment of your choice. And you have to be certain, otherwise it will not work. If you are certain you want to save your father and others you care about, such as your friend Ashland, then drink, lay back on the bed, and when you wake, you will be your grandmother in centuries past."

Eladon's eyes fixed on Emilie, who stared into those depths. She knew of her friend Ashland? That Ashland would expire from this mysterious illness? How could she know that Emilie even had a friend named Ashland?

"How do you know about Ashland?" Emilie asked quietly, steeling her nerves along with her gaze.

Eladon's lips thinned as she lifted her bony chin. "I have seen her. I have dreamed of you both." Then she nudged her chin toward her. "Check your phone, if you yet doubt."

A light line of sweat broke out on Emilie's hairline as her chest dropped. She had to force herself to reach into her pack pocket where her phone had started to vibrate. With trembling fingers, Emilie poked the screen.

She had missed a phone message, but a blue text illuminated the dim room. It was from Julia.

That thing you said you could do? Can you still do it?

Then another text right after that one.

Ashland. She's sick.

Every drop of Emilie's blood turned to ice. Her father, now Ashland.

Her finger hovered over the text screen. Eladon waited patiently, her eyes lowered. She didn't have to read the texts on screen. She knew, and her sympathy softened the deep lines on her face.

Emilie didn't have the time or really the understanding to relay to Julia what she was doing, so she took a deep breath and typed quickly.

I'm doing it. Tell the Musketeers I love you all.

That was what convinced her. Not her father, not Eladon's explanations, but that she was able to refer to Ashland by name and knew she was ill. That everyone Emilie loved might fall victim to this illness decided for her. She switched off the phone and set it next to her on the bed.

Eladon's tone was paper-thin. "What did your friend tell you?"

Emilie didn't have to answer – she could tell Eladon knew the answer from the intense fire in the old woman's eyes – but speaking the words aloud made them real.

"Ashland is sick," Emilie answered in a hollow voice. Her chest was just as hollow, carved out from this news and the weight of her decision.

With a heavy nod, Eladon offered up the cup.

"What is my grandmother's name?" Emilie asked. She should probably know what her own name would be in the tenth century.

"Ailith," Eladon answered. "Ailith Maeve Gordon. Sister to the chieftain of the Glenbervie Gordons, Seocan Gordon. You will awake at Glenbervie tower on this day, July 9th, 900 CE."

Emilie's breathing turned shallow, panting, and her stomach churned. She looked at the drink, a greyish tea, and wondered if she could even keep it down.

Eladon sat patiently, watching her but not pressuring or urging. It was as Evan said, Emilie had to be sure, and Eladon was going to wait for her to make that choice.

The strange tea swirled in her cup as everything from this crazy day swirled in her mind like the drink. Never return to Da? Never see her friends again? Live in the middle ages, hell, the early middle ages, the dark ages, for the rest of her life?

Her father's face flashed before her eyes, then Ashland's, then everyone else she knew. Aye, doing this – whatever it was – with her grandmother was worth saving millions of lives.

For Da. For Ashland.

Emilie lifted the cup and drank. The sour liquid burned over her tongue and throat like bad whiskey.

Eladon rose and put her hand on Emilie's forehead, pushing her back onto the bed as she chanted under her breath. Emilie barely felt her touch as her mind and body felt lighter, like she was on a dropping roller coaster, and her chest was heavy. She panted as she breathed.

"Pay attention to your dreams, lass," Eladon told her as she swept her hand over Emilie's eyes, closing them. A kaleidoscope of color filled her vision. "Your dreams will speak to you, guide you, and lead you. Pay attention to them."

Then Eladon resumed her chanting, but it sounded farther away as Emilie floated higher. Her mind spun out of control and her body was no longer hers. A pressure built under her skin, not pain but odd and uncomfortable. She commanded her mouth to call out and her eyes to open -- nothing happened. Only that lightness and pressure and dizzying kaleidoscope. The uncomfortable pressure increased until the kaleidoscope exploded, and she screamed out in her mind.

Eladon touched her forehead with a finger.

Then only blackness.

Chapter Six

Eastern Scotland, 900 CE

Emilie woke with her head spinning and something tickling her nose, her skin drenched from sweat. Her eyes didn't want to open, but she managed to crack open one, then the other, letting the bright, blurry world slowly come into focus. She wiped her fevered brow.

The tickling came from something furry on her blanket.

What's furry on my bed?

Her thoughts spun out of control again as she tried to focus her gaze. What had happened the night before? She recalled only strange dreams of bad whiskey and conversations about history. Something about her grandmother? She had never met her grandmother. Why would she be talking about her?

A knocking sound came from her door. But it was on the wrong side of the room. Wasn't her bedroom door to her right? Why was the sound coming from her left? Emilie opened her eyes wider, letting them adjust to the sunlight filling the room. Had she forgotten to close her blinds the night before?

With a groan, she sat up in bed.

And her heart stopped in her chest.

This wasn't her room.

Where the hell am I?

Instead of her downy comforter, several tartan blankets topped with tickling fur covered her bed. No cream-colored walls – raw brown and gray stone surrounded her, punctuated by narrow shuttered windows and dark blue and brown tapestries. A small metal bowl on legs was tucked into the corner of the room, next to a hard-backed chair, and a trunk had been set under one of the windows with a reflective silver oval propped atop it.

The door, the origin of the knocking, was a wide, wooden plank door, arched at the top and fastened with large iron hinges and a long bar across the center.

"Milady? Are ye awake? I have parritch to break your fast."

Milady? WHAT THE HELL?

A pinprick of pain shot through Emilie's head as memories from the night before flooded her head. She sat forward, and a long lock of curly red hair fell across her lap.

Emilie froze, staring at that hair.

Had it worked? Had she traveled...?

Nay. Not possible.

She grabbed at her head, feeling that hair. That thick, curly hair. Definitely not her smooth bob.

Throwing the blankets off her legs, she raced from the bed, across the woven mat-like rug to the silver round. As big as a serving platter and so shiny, she could make out most of her own reflection. It must be a type of mirror. Emilie fell to her knees in front of it.

The image that stared back was like someone pretending to be her, but not doing a good job. Her nose and lips were the same, her long nose and her much fuller lower lip. Her three-finger forehead was the same, but everything else . . .

The hair – that was most noticeable. Gone was her sleek bob, replaced with a head full of wild, deep russet red hair. Like some sort of cartoon princess. It fell around her shoulders and down her back, with thinner wisps that brushed against her bright pink cheeks. Leaning in she noticed her eyes, no longer blue, as far as she could tell in this poor mirror. Green, a bright green like the Great Glen in late spring.

I am a cartoon character! Emilie thought.

Nay, no cartoons here, not if what the Romani witch had told her was true.

Which it seemed to be.

The knock came again, and Emilie rose and immediately stopped again. Her breasts were loose under the nightgown she wore (*nay a nightgown, What was it called? A léine, that was i t*), and full. Much larger than her own! And she seemed taller, though she had no point of reference to really compare.

"Milady Ailith?"

"Aye, I'm coming!" Emilie shouted. *No more Emilie,* she reminded herself. *Ailith. I'm Ailith now.*

She hoped she could remember that.

"Coming?" the timid voice behind the door called.

Emilie - now Ailith – swung open the door to a shorter, wide-hipped woman holding a tray with food and a cup.

"Ye did no' have to open the door, milady. I would have managed it fine."

The woman's voice was thick with brogue, thicker than even Emilie (*Ailith, I'm Ailith*) was accustomed to in the more remote part of the Highlands. She was fascinated by the difference in accent when untampered by time.

"I have your honeyed mead and parritch." The woman bustled to the trunk and set it in front of the mirror, then turned to her. "Shall I return to help ye dress, Lady Ailith?"

Och, recalling that name would be difficult! Emilie vowed silently to call herself only that from now on. Emilie was gone forever, after all.

"Aye. 'Twould suffice." She tried to adopt what she thought the speech patterns might be – thank God for her history studies! – but it must have fallen flat because the woman looked at her with a raised eyebrow.

"Do ye have a throat ache, Lady Ailith? Ye appear fevered." The woman's face crumpled with her concern as she reached for Emilie.

Emilie (*Ailith!*) licked her dry lips and shook her head. The woman smiled, smoothing her worry lines.

"Fine then." She bustled to the bed and peeked under the bedstead. "Have ye used the pot yet?" she asked as she pulled out the cloth-covered bowl.

Oh, feck. Chamber pots. Conveniently forgotten in the hubbub of the night before. So many things she hadn't considered.

"Nay. I'll retrieve that when I return." The stout woman shoved the bowl back under and smiled at Emilie (*Ailith*!). I'll return shortly, milady." She eyed Emilie once more. "Are ye sure ye are well?"

Emilie pressed her hand to her cooling forehead and nodded. The woman curtseyed, then left, shutting the heavy door behind her.

Her stomach growled, and she regarded the food. Lifting the marbled cup (horn maybe?) to her nose, she sniffed, noting berry and nutmeg mixed. She sipped. The drink reminded her of a thick juice, and she smiled to herself.

At least I won't starve if I can drink this.

The parritch was next. A gloppy gray porridge made of oats in a wooden bowl. She crossed her fingers and hoped it had been sweetened with honey or something. The thought of plain oats made her gag. She grasped the wooden spoon, held her breath, and ate it. Sweetness exploded on her taste buds, and she smiled again.

Her ancient grandmother must have had the same sweet tooth.

Now if she only knew the name of the servant who had brought it, so she could thank her properly. How was she going to figure that out?

She finished the parritch and mead and used the chamber pot (*what an ordeal! How am I going to do that? Mayhap go in the woods like I used to when I went camping with Da*), and shoved it back on the bed when she didn't know what to do with it. Then she turned her attention to the trunk.

Time to get dressed and figure out where she was and what to do next.

She had pulled a fine, indigo-blue dress from the trunk. A selection of dresses (or where they called gowns? Kirtles?) sat neatly folded and stacked in the trunk, along with more cream-colored léines, a wide leather belt, what she presumed were woolen stockings, and an interesting leather hood attached to a fringed cape. Some of the gowns had long sleeves. The rest, like the indigo were sleeveless, like a tank top. Did she wear it like that? Or, she glanced down at her léine, did it go over this?

Tucked by the side of the trunk was a leather packet, and when she opened it she found a collection of jewelry and accessories – an etched round brooch with an attached spear-like pin, a circlet, an emerald ring, long pieces of fabric like thick ribbon, pieces of bronze that might be hair combs or pins, another gold circle that might fit her wrist and a small paring knife, presumably for eating.

The full content of her grandmother's belongings. Emilie thought about her closet at home, her bathroom, and sighed. And this was for a woman who was sister to the Chieftain, a woman of wealth and privilege for this time. It made her clothing collection at home seem gratuitous.

A pair of woven leather shoes with laces across the top sat next to the trunk. Neat, as was the rest of the room. Her grandmother Ailith (or her servant) prided herself on tidiness.

The knock sounded again, and the servant peeked her face around the door.

"Did ye use the chamber pot?"

Emilie nodded. The servant took the pot from under the bed and departed the room.

Where did she go?

As she waited, she studied the rest of the room – the four posters of her bed, the details of the tapestry – before rising and opening the shutter. The window, empty of any glass, opened to a courtyard (a bailey?) several stories below. A warm breeze, as warm as Scotland got in the summer that was, caressed her cheek as she leaned past the window's edge. The bailey was mostly grass-patched mud, and from her vantage, she saw part of the palisade wall and the corner of an outbuilding. Stables? Or a barn?

"Och, Lady Ailith. Do ye want me to open the shutters?" the woman asked as she returned the pot to its place under the bed. Then she turned and noted that Emilie had been digging in the trunk. "Lose something, did ye? Or did ye want to wear the blue kirtle? 'Tis fair enough with your light léine. But I presumed ye'd want to wear it tomorrow eve when your MacDougal arrives."

Emilie had been shoving the gowns back in the trunk and stopped.

My MacDougal.

Oh feck. She hadn't considered that. Women in the middle ages married young, very young. How would the sister of a chieftain *not* have a beau? And she didn't even know his *name!* Emilie gulped.

Who was this man, her MacDougal? She hoped he was decent looking and guessed he was probably well-muscled if he was a Highland warrior. Being tied to the man, well, that wasn't a concern. She wasn't here to get married, after all.

"Whatever ye believe is best," she deferred to the woman.

She wracked her mind to come up with a way to ask her name without appearing like a mad woman. Then it came to her. As the sister of a chieftain, there was a slim chance Ailith knew how to read. And maybe this woman knew how to spell her own name. "Last night I was speaking with my brother's man, and he said ye dinna know how to spell your name. I called him a presumptuous fool. Can ye settle the wager for us?"

The woman grinned widely, showing off a slew of crooked teeth.

"Och, my mam did no' raise any fools. O' course I can spell my name. "L-E-I-T-I-S." She enunciated each letter carefully and smiled proudly when she was done.

Leitis, that was it. *Feck*, she might have to use the wager lie frequently. It had worked brilliantly.

Emilie smiled and clapped her hands. "Och! I knew I was in the right! I'll have to collect on my wager."

Leitis patted Emilie's shoulder. "Good for ye, Lady Ailith. Let's wear the brown today, aye?"

Emilie let the woman tug the kirtle on, adjust the sleeves, and tighten the belt around her waist. She gestured to the chair, and Emilie sat while Leitis's deft fingers braided part of her hair, leaving rich red curls to unfurl at the base of her neck. Finally, she bent and tied the laces on the woven leather shoes that Emilie had slipped onto her feet.

She was dressed. The wool kirtle was soft, as was her léine against her thighs and backside – the odd sensation of no undergarments was one she would have to get used to in the meantime.

With a satisfied look on her face, Leitis admired Emilie. "Och, ye look fine, Lady Ailith. And thank ye for being so agreeable to the brown. I ken ye prefer your colors."

That one statement told Emilie much about her grandmother. A bold and bossy one, likely. Emilie tipped her head at Leitis in acknowledgment of the compliment. Leitis swept past her, grabbed the remains of Emilie's breakfast, and strode purposefully to the door.

"Shall we go down, milady?"

Down? Downstairs? Meet others? And do what? What did a medieval Scottish lady do all day? For all her historical studies of kings and dates and deaths, very little covered what a Highland lady did during the course of her day.

Emilie licked her lips and nodded. Leitis bowed her head and waited by the door. Emilie got it – she was waiting for Emilie to exit first.

And go where?

This was it, the moment of truth. And in that moment, Emilie made a decision. Once she walked past that door, any remnant of Emilie was gone. After that threshold, she was Ailith, completely.

The narrow, curved stone stairwell was the first moment of something familiar for Ailith, reminding her of the stairs in the Dunnottar tower. That tower overlooked the churning sea, a sheer drop down the tower and the cliffs on to the rocks and crashing surf below. At times, the view had been almost dizzying.

Here, the view was much more domestic. Yet, defensive curved stairwells were consistent across the board.

Ailith had urged Leitis to take the lead and did her best to ply the woman with questions to help her blend in.

"What are my duties for this day, Leitis?" she probed. She dragged her hand on the cool stone with one hand and held her skirts up with the other. Wearing a long skirt while managing the stairs was not a skill that Ailith excelled at. Give her a bo staff, however. . .

Ailith didn't think she'd be handling one of those ever again.

"Oatcakes and oat bread in the kitchens, milady. Ye must tell the cooks which ye want served for the meals, and if ye prefer the cock-a-leekie soup today or on the morrow. And we must prepare for the visit from the MacDougals the eve of the morrow. Your brother wishes to speak to ye first. He's had a messenger."

Keeping her mouth shut, Ailith's insides quivered at the prospect of meeting this man, her supposed lover. Were they engaged? Not married yet, not with his visit. Betrothed? Hand fast?

And how might she put that off or avoid it altogether? She couldn't marry some man she didn't know!

Well, she could, and given the time period, there was an excellent chance she might have to, or be forced to.

Why hadn't the Romani woman mentioned that?

And meeting the man who was Ailith's brother? The chieftain of the Glenbervie Gordons. How could she ever convince him that she was indeed his sister? She had a sinking sensation that she might end up chained in the dungeon before long.

"Aye. May I call on ye to assist me with that? I've no' felt myself as of late."

They had reached the base of the stairs that opened up to a main hall. Leitis twisted to face her as she moved to the next set of stairs.

"Och. 'Tis certain. I've noticed ye've seemed feverish myself, and I will do all to help ye, milady. Now your brother is in his antechamber."

Leitis must have noticed something in Ailith's expression because she shifted the tray to one hand and pointed. "The door on the left, just through there," she said in a kind tone.

Whether Leitis believed her ill or going soft in the head, it didn't matter to Ailith, as long as Leitis helped her as needed. Right now, the stout, kind servant was the only person Ailith had met that she might count on.

As Ailith strode through the main hall, past the few tables to the door Leitis pointed out, she practiced steady breathing and hoped that this man, her brother, might be a second person.

Chapter Seven

Ailith kept her eyes on the door – stopping to admire the castle as it was, not as a mysterious ruin with moss-covered crumbling hallways and secret passages, would only bring her more unneeded attention. She reached the door and waited, inhaling through her nose several times, gathering her courage before entering.

Ye can do this, she told herself.

How she was going to pull it off was the real question. This was more than a servant; this was a person who had known her for her entire life.

With a final deep breath, Ailith pushed the door open to the antechamber. She forced herself to leave off admiring the room and focus on the man who sat behind a sturdy, table-like desk extending from the stone wall and near the long dormered window opened to permit pale sunlight to filter onto the desk during the day. A simple candle stick rested near his elbow for when it did not. Overall, a rather spartan antechamber.

The man himself (she searched her memories for his name. *(Seocan. He's Seocan Gordon*) curved over the desk, squinting at a parchment. His baggy tunic hung well on his frame, but what caught her attention was his hair, the same bright, brilliant hair that she could see on her own head. Wavy and long, it brushed against his shoulders and hung in his face as he bent over his reading and marked her as Ailith's brother. Her brother.

Uncertainty overwhelmed her. Clasping her hands together, she stood in front of the desk and cleared her throat.

Seocan lifted his head and his eyes sparkled at her. Not quite as green as hers – his eyes held touches of amber, and when he smiled at her, they transformed into joyful triangles. His hair was braided near his temples, a series of small braids, most likely queued to keep his unruly waves out of his eyes.

He leaned back in his chair and set his mangy quill to the side. "Ailith, it pleases the heart to see ye. Ye look well, no' at all overly feverish."

His words expressed one emotion, but the tone of his voice spoke another, of a man who had something weighty to discuss. Ailith pressed her hand to her forehead in an almost automatic gesture.

"A bit feverish, yet, but hale enough. Ye look well, brother," she said, keeping her sentences clipped.

"We've had a recent incident, one tha' might affect ye a wee bit. Once I tell ye, I'm sure ye will understand the plight."

An incident? Nay! I'm no' ready to deal with anything like this! I cannae –

She shoved the grim through away and dipped her head to him. "Aye, brother. I am at your disposal."

Seocan smiled again, a weak smile that did not reach his eyes. He rose from his seat and approached her, embracing her in his thick arms. When he stood, she was able to get a better measure of him. Not overly tall, but thick, *built like a tank,* as her father would say. His clean dark brown tunic gathered at the waist in a braided belt, from which hung a fur pouch and a sword in his scabbard – wide with a curved pommel. The man was a Highland warrior chieftain in full.

He ran his hands down her arms to hold her hands. "Our entertainment tomorrow eve, with the MacDougals, must become something more. The king has set upon the Grants and MacIntoshes, for what reason I dinna ken. We have reached out to James Grant and Lucas MacIntosh for information on the matter, and they will arrive on the morrow, along with the MacDougals. A celebration for your upcoming nuptials, aye, but a conference regarding the king as well. My apologies for souring your celebration with such dire necessities."

A well-spoken man, one who seemed to understand the intricacies of the Highlands. She considered that he may well be another person she might trust. She dipped her chin again.

This was more than she had anticipated, more than her overwrought mind could deal with this morning. The MacDougal man wasn't merely a love interest, but a betrothed? She was getting married?

Oh, no . . .

Ailith took a deep breath. Maybe she could end that betrothal – say he was no right for her, or abused her, or . . . *something*. She'd cross that bridge when she got to it–another fun quote from her father. She swallowed the lump that had formed in her throat.

"I understand what must be done," Ailith said in the most timid voice she could muster.

Was Ailith a timid person? Would she be timid around her brother, or her potential fiance? Oh, but this was so much more difficult than she anticipated when going back in time was first propositioned a mere day ago!

Seocan leaned forward and kissed her forehead. "Ye are the dearest of sisters. Mairi was certain ye wouldna take the news lightly. It pleases me to see ye agreeable."

Well, that told her quite a bit about Ailith. And who was Mairi? His wife, most likely, to have such an intimate conversation about the chieftain's sister.

"There is much turmoil in the Highlands," she replied. "'Tis long past time since I recognize that."

His sad smile widened at her, seemingly pleased at his own news. "Och, it does my heart good to hear that. And I have a wee bit of good news to temper the bad."

Ailith lifted her eyebrows. "Oh?"

"Aye. As a result of this, I have spoken with both Cormag and Bernard. They are in agreement, as is William."

Ailith worked to keep her face still and interested while her mind rioted. *Who are these people?*

"In agreement with what?"

"That ye and William wed as soon as possible," Seocan answered. Ailith's chest dropped to her feet. Marriage? Oh no . . .

His name is William, another voice spoke up, her more rational voice. Your beau's name is William MacDougal.

"I offered a handfast, but William was no' in agreement. He prefers to wed ye in a kirk to ensure no one, no' even a king, can put your marriage aside. Which is a good thing, to be sure." Seocan added, dropping her hands and moving back to his desk. He gave Ailith a slight grin. "And I believe the man wants the formal wedding for ye, with all the Highlands in attendance, if he could. The MacDougal man is far too soft when he comes to ye, lass."

She tried to ignore his last comment. "A good thing?" she asked.

Did her voice waver aloud as much as it felt in her throat? She swallowed hard.

"Aye," Seocan said as he turned to her. "Ye know the Highlands are the clans. This king seeks to make Alba, the land of the Scots, his own.

But such will never be. Scotland is ruled by the clans, and the more aligned and more allied we can make them, the better. This wedding will go far into showing the King, and the leeching clans that support him, the power that the clans yet yield."

Her stomach sank impossibly farther. If she had hoped to weasel out of a marriage to a man she didn't know, that hope was all but extinguished. Ailith's brother sat in his chair and moved one parchment over another.

"And I cannot stress how pleased I am with this union as well. Uniting with the MacDougals will benefit us all."

Then he fell silent, his attention moving to the papers on his desk. Ailith recognized what his actions meant.

She was dismissed.

Without another glance, Ailith backed away to the door and exited the antechamber. She closed the door and leaned against it, exhaling a wavering breath. Getting out of marrying the man might be more of a problem than she initially thought. What if she did have to marry the stranger?

She hoped she convinced her brother that there was nothing wrong with her–nothing more than a slight fever. If he thought anything was wrong with her, Seocan didn't show it. Then again, he did have other, more pressing issues clouding his mind. Her lips pursed in a tight smile–she might have pulled it off.

Now that her main duty to the day was complete, Ailith took a moment to rest against the door and survey the main hall. Ruins she was familiar with, but to see a medieval Scots tower as it was supposed to be left her in awe.

Heavy, wooden double doors were at the farthest side of the hall, sealed with gigantic iron hinges and a wide iron bar. In the center of the hall and directly before her were several long tables, surrounded by a mix of benches and high-backed chairs. Candelabras stood in the middle of each table. One table appeared offset from the rest, edged in only high-backed chairs. The chieftain's seat, perhaps?

The opening to the staircase that led up to the second floor was visible at the other, darkened edge of the main hall, under an arched doorway flanked by ornate, Celtic knot torch sconces. Her eyes rose to the high wooden ceiling, noting the broad support beams seated in the stone walls and the two plain iron candle chandeliers hanging unlit from thick metal chains. More windows, partially shuttered, permitted a bit of light and the fair air to warm the still, cool air of the chamber. Narrower windows, not dormer windows, most likely as a means of defense for . . .

For what reason? The Romani witch had told her she was a Gordon at Glenbervie tower, but if this tower yet remained in the Highlands, it was nothing more than a pile of decrepit stone in a random field, nothing that she'd been able to tour in her lifetime. A tower, not a castle, which likely meant a smaller group of Gordons in this area – *a smaller group easily slaughtered by other clans and a treasonous king,* she thought sourly.

A decent enough tower, though. Another struck her on the heels of that one. The man everyone kept mentioning. Her betrothed. What would the MacDougal tower or castle look like? Was it as tidy? As welcoming? Would she live there with this strange William fellow, or somewhere else?

Before coming to this time, she had a set path in life–college, a job, an apartment. Now, nothing in her life was on a set path, and it made every step she took and every thought she had felt like the earth was shifting under her feet.

Pushing herself off the door, she made her way to the darkened edge of the hall and stairwell. Leitis had continued down the curving stairs, to the kitchens if Ailith guessed correctly. Given the duties Leitis had listed earlier, that seemed like the best place to go.

What else was she going to do? Search for the vital fungus? She had to gain her bearings first, figure out exactly how far she was from Dunnottar castle on the eastern shore, and then figure out how to get there.

So many steps in this plan, so many places, and things could go horribly wrong.

Dinna focus on what ye cannae do, focus on what ye can, then do what ye must, the voice of her father echoed in her head.

The dark stairs brightened as she descended into the bowels of the tower under the main hall. Dank scents of yeast, burning, and spices greeted her as she stepped through the low archway.

Three women busied themselves in the low-ceilinged kitchen, which was well-lit by high, narrow window slits and a raging fire in a huge hearth.

Two younger women worked near the hearth, one at a cauldron, her brown hair sticking to her face, the other next to her at the open-mouthed oven cut into the stone. It was heated by the hearth, and the buxom lass was pulling a platter-sized spatula from its mouth. In a skilled move, she spun around to the table behind her and slid the baked oatcakes off the platter to the table to cool.

At the table, Leitis labored on a round of dough, flipping it and punching it to make the bread it would become as light as possible.

The girl with the hot platter gave Ailith a quick curtsey and reached for a set of dough rounds ready for baking. Leitis glanced her way.

"Lady Ailith! What are ye doing here?"

Oh no, did preparing for the celebration tomorrow night mean something else?

"My brother, he has informed me that our guests tomorrow will increase in number. He must have conference with some of the clans, and they will be in attendance as well."

Leitis's eyes widened comically above her flour-stained nose. "More! With so short a notice? Och! Gwen, Isa! Fetch another sack of oat flour from the pantry, barley, pickled herring, bramble berry preserves, and curds. If the chieftain longs for a feast, then a feast he shall have!"

Ailith grinned at the woman's infectious cheer in the face of an overwhelming task. Then Leitis eyed Ailith.

"If ye come to help, then help. Here." She tossed the lump of dough down the table toward Ailith. "Put your hands to use."

Chapter Eight

The day passed in a rush–there was so much to learn, and so much to hide. Ailith had kept to herself the rest of the day, hiding in the kitchens with Leitis and her lassies, or in her chambers. Leitis had said the eve tide meal would be an informal affair.

What does that mean? "Och, an informal affair?" Ailith repeated, hoping to prompt Leitis into explanation.

It worked. "Aye. If ye are weary from today, rest in your chambers. I shall bring ye a platter and tell the chieftain and Mairi ye are resting for tomorrow."

Perfect. A grateful smile crossed Ailith's lips, then with a slight bow to all three women, she made her way up the winding stairs to her own chambers.

Once there, Ailith unbelted the flour-covered kirtle and tossed it over the ornate high-backed chair. She unlaced the shoes and returned them to their spot by the trunk but left her hair alone. If anything, the braids might keep some of her wild hair under control while she slept.

While she waited for Leitis to bring her supper, she opened the window shutter wide and peered at the activity below. Not much, most people were finishing their chores and returning home or the keep for their evening meals. Finally, a moment alone with her thoughts.

Ailith realized that she hadn't stepped outside the entire day – how was that going to help her find that fungus?

A breeze kicked up, blowing across her cheek and neck, refreshing her after a day in the stuffy kitchen.

Maybe not the best start, she told herself, but a good start. She had learned a lot and her mind was tired, if not her body. Truly, she was more than ready for bed.

After Leitis delivered the tray, Ailith asked Leitis to bid her brother good eve, ate what she could, and dropped into bed.

Time travel is tiring work, she thought right before she fell asleep.

***

Ailith almost believed the day before had been nothing more than a fevered dream as she came to consciousness the next morning. Yet when she opened her eyes to the four-poster bed and beams in the high-ceilinged chamber, she sighed.

It hadn't been a dream, and here was another day of pretending to be someone else, trying to be the person she was in 900 CE.

"Ailith," she mumbled as she rose from her bed. "My name is Ailith."

A shaft of sunlight, more brilliant than the day before, peeked through the slats of the shutter. A rare, sunny day in the eastern Highlands, and Ailith made herself ready for it.

The night before, Leitis had also brought up a small bowl of water and a clean linen cloth. "To wash in the morn, milady," she had said before departing.

As she washed her face in the tepid water, wiping grime and sleep from her skin and eyes, she was grateful Leitis had thought ahead to provide it.

Ailith's hands froze as she wiped her face and she stood up tall, flashing a frantic glance at the door. Was the original Ailith this forgetful? Everyone thus far had taken her questions and seemingly obvious lack of understanding in stride, blaming any differences on a wee fever.

Ailith twined the cloth between her hands. Maybe that was why she had been able to blend in rather seamlessly. The original Ailith appeared to be a wild child who did her own thing and had little care for what was going on around her, and that had been how Emilie had appeared since she'd woken up in her medieval bed.

If that was the case, perhaps being Ailith was going to be a wee bit easier than she had presumed. She could only hope that the real Ailith was finding it as easy to be Emilie in the twenty-first century.

Eladon knew what she was doing, Ailith mused. The Romani woman was too clever by far.

The knock at her door. "Leitis, enter!" she called out as she tossed her cloth into the bowl. Leitis's apple-cheeked face peeked in.

"I've your platter. Honeyed mead and parritch," she said as she pushed her way past the door. She set the platter on the trunk. "Used the chamber pot yet?"

Ailith lost her fight with her smile. She was starting to adore Leitis. "Nay, can ye –"

"Come back soon? Aye. Eat and I'll return to help ye dress."

The morning was a repeat of the day before, only with Leitis crinkling her nose at Ailith's kirtle.

"Och, but ye were a mess yesterday. Are ye feeling improved this morn?"

Ailith nodded as she slipped the kirtle over her head and tightened the belt. "A wee bit."

"'Tis fine. And ye can wash again this eve when ye dress for your mannie. Meanwhile, ye will suffice. Mairi will put ye to work to prepare for the celebrations tonight for certain. Nay rest of the weary, aye?"

"Aye," Ailith answered, following Leitis into the hall.

The day was warmer than the previous one had been, and sweat dripped down her back as she pointed to where the outside tables needed to be placed by the tower doors as Mairi had instructed.

Meeting the chieftain's wife had been a harrowing event, especially compared to her encounter with Ailith's brother, Leitis, and the kitchen lasses the day before. Mairi had eyes like a hawk and a sharp mind – a blend that meant the woman missed nothing.

One raven's wing eyebrow was high on her head the entire time she spoke with Ailith.

Or rather, spoke at her. Mairi, as her friend Julia once said, did not come to play.

Ailith understood why Seocan married her. The woman could carry an empire on her back – carrying a Highland clan was little effort for her.

When Ailith had come down the stairs that morning, Leitis had led her into the main hall where Mairi sat next to Seocan, her hand atop his.

Yep, wife.

She had the coloring of what her father called Black Irish – deep emerald green eyes and lustrous black hair that was pulled back from her round cheeks into loose waves that cascaded down her back. Those eyes. Ailith would have to be careful around her.

"Leitis says ye were feeling a wee bit feverish yesterday? I trust ye are recovered today?"

The bite in Mairi's tone had caught Ailith unaware, and she had to force herself to smile at the woman. And it *was* forced because Ailith had felt more like a mouse under the shadow of a falcon.

When Mairi had asked her to direct setting up the tables outside, Ailith had jumped at the opportunity. Anything to get out from under that predatory gaze.

Shading her eyes from the sun, a rare behavior in Scotland, even in the summer, Ailith directed several sturdy and bearded men in tight tunics and baggy pants (*braies? Trews? No, braies. Trews were tighte*r) to move the tables on either side of the door, so there was a path to the main tower doors.

The sounds in the inner bailey were so different from the noises from her time. No roaring cars or overhead airplanes. No hum of electricity or bells or phones ringing. Grunting men and animals, bleeting sheep, the laughter of young children chasing chickens or each other. Even the smells were different, grass and beasts and sweat, not gas or pollution. When she inhaled, she almost felt high from the purity of it all.

The men were both gruff and polite, as one would expect behavior to be around the lady of the clan. Most were crofters or husbandmen, accustomed to working with the animals at the keep, yet a few were younger men with scruffy patches of hair where one day beards would grow, and they seemed overly eager to assist Lady Ailith. She grinned. Och, there was something to be said for these larger breasts, and a lack of modern-day Internet which meant the only boobs these lads saw had to be on actual women, and any breasts were well appreciated.

One man stepped outside after the two sets of tables had been put in place, carrying a bench, followed by an eager-looking, younger red-haired man – with the same color hair as she and Seocan. Another brother? A close cousin? Why hadn't Eladon mentioned him? Then again, he was a younger brother, and rarely did younger brothers make history.

The man carrying the bench set it down by a table, then strode toward her. He was a decent-sized man, about the same height as Seocan, and nearly as burly, with a thick neck only partially hidden by a tawny brown beard that matched the hair on his head, and deep-set hazel brown eyes.

Who is this guy?

He looked her up and down before speaking. "Good day to ye, Ailith. How many more benches do ye need for the tables? Seven?"

From the corner of her eye, she noticed a pair of men carrying a bench from the thatch-roofed barn.

"Ask them? I dinna ken how many benches they have in the barn."

The man's brow creased, and Ailith clenched her jaw. Did she say something wrong? Why was he looking at her like that?

"Barn benches? Ugh. We might as well invite the Moray barbarians. They practically sleep in their barns."

Morays? Ailith wracked her brain, trying to recall what history she had learned about Clan Moray.

"Daniel!" the younger man piped up. *Thank God for him,* Ailith thought. "Da says he did extend an invitation to the Morays. He said he wants to feel out their loyalty to the King and see if their warriors had anything to do with the slaughter."

The thick man, Daniel, cut a deathly glare at the lad. "Dinna speak of such foul deeds in a lady's presence. Has Seocan no' taught ye anything?"

The red-headed young man blushed as deep red as his hair and Daniel turned back to Ailith with a quick bow.

"My apologies for Simon's loose tongue. He has much to learn about manners."

Simon, she thought, committing the name to memory. *Daniel and Simon.*

Who they were yet remained a mystery.

"'Tis of no concern," she assured Daniel. "Though my brother didna provide details, he did mention that the Grant and MacIntosh clans had been set up. 'Tis easy to presume what he meant."

Only she hadn't. Slaughtered? The king against his own people? Clan against clan? History had told how violent the Scottish middle ages might have been, but to hear about it, maybe see it firsthand, to live with those affected and even risk her own life was something altogether different. The drops of sweat on her backside increased.

Daniel threw another glare at the lad, Simon. "Aye, but your wee brother here must learn propriety. Isn't that right, laddie?" Daniel asked as he playfully slapped the back of the young man's head.

Ailith desperately longed to ask Daniel for more information regarding this slaughter and why invite the Morays who were in league with the king but bit her tongue. He had just chastised Simon for referring to the bloody deed, and the clan probably didn't yet know the level of betrayal the Morays were guilty of in their grim alliance with the king. Willing to slaughter a clan? That wording didn't mean one or two people–*slaughter* meant more. A lot more.

Ailith tilted her head to the men who brought the bench. "Do ye want them to bring more benches from the barn or the stables? Or would ye rather they retrieve them from inside?"

A vague question, but since she didn't know how many benches were anywhere on the premises, better to keep it vague. At least Daniel wasn't looking at her cross-wise this time.

The thick-necked man scratched at his beard. "Simon, come with me. We'll grab the benches from inside. Jamie! Farlan! Only bring out one more bench from the barns, then assist me inside." He turned to face Ailith again, and if she didn't know any better, she'd think his eyes were dancing with mirth, and then he winked at her. "We'll seat the Morays on the barn benches."

Chapter Nine

Leitis brought up a larger bowl of water, scented with lavender and heather petals. She carried a stack of clothes and bumped the door closed with her hip.

"Come, lass. Time to dress ye. 'Tis a celebration for ye, by the now."

Ailith nodded her head at Leitis in thanks, then a thought came to her.

"Do ye need to assist Mairi? Surely she must need your help. As chieftain's wife, all eyes will be on her."

Leitis clicked her tongue and patted Ailith's shoulder. "Och, lassie. Nay, all eyes will be on ye as William's betrothed. And Mairi has Elsbet to help with her and the bairn."

And the bairn? Mairi had a baby? Ailith was an aunt? Her mind spun again. If this kept up, she was going to have quite the headache by the end of the night.

"Rise, Ailith. Time to make ye the center of attention."

Leitis opened the trunk and drew out the blue kirtle from the day before. She flapped it to air it out, and it was then that Ailith got a good look at the gown. It was far more refined than the brown kirtle, with a much fuller rich, indigo skirt and darker blue floral embroidery around the bodice, enhancing her breasts and narrowing her waist. The fitted bodice boasted a square neckline and short sleeves that ended right at the edge of her shoulder.

"Do I wear this léine under the kirtle?" Ailith asked, wondering if she had a nicer one she might change into, when Leitis's eyes twinkled at her.

"Och, lass. Ye have more to that kirtle. Do ye no' remember the sleeves?"

God save Leitis for thinking Ailith was just forgetful. Maybe the original Ailith had been forgetful as well.

"Aye, the sleeves," Ailith agreed, her eyes fixed on Leitis as she reached into the trunk. What were these sleeves?

Leitis withdrew a fabric that Ailith had mistakenly believed to be stockings, a delicate, sheer material so thin, it looked like nothing at all. Then she dug into the trunk and with a victorious uplifting of her hand, she pulled out blue and silver ribbon-like laces.

Ailith returned her focus to the kirtle. The sleeves had narrow slits sewn into them, and the sleeves were attached with the laces.

No wonder Leitis told her to reserve the dress for tonight. It was truly a divine gown. Ailith recalled medieval images she had seen online, with fabric pulled through laces like that. So she rephrased her question.

"Should I wear this léine under the gown, to pull through the sleeves?"

Leitis looked at her léine, then at the kirtle, then at the open window where the air was calm in the setting sun.

"'Tis warm enough to go without. Might be too warm with the léine. Do ye wish to wear the léine?"

From the way she asked the question, Ailith had the idea that Ailith Gordon would not wear the léine.

She gave Leitis a slight smile. *Forget the léine*. Ailith rose from the chair. "Just the blue kirtle, if ye please, Leitis."

Ailith stepped lightly down the stairs, holding her full skirt high so as not to trip over the hem and tumble to the bottom. What impression would that make?

Leitis hovered behind her, making sure every unruly strand was tucked into the loosely braided coronet that Leitis diligently wove around her head. She had tucked beads and flowers, tiny heather, primrose, and wee bluebells the same shade as her gown. A few crimson tendrils escaped the braid, much to Leitis's chagrin, and tickled her bare neck and upper back.

The bodice was fitted enough so that her – or rather Ailith's – abundant bosom swelled against the neckline that tied down the front in matching indigo laces. Once fastened into place with the beautiful ribbons, the fitted sleeves ended right before her wrist. Leitis had slid the golden wristlet, which turned out to be an armband, up her right arm, just above her elbow, then helped Ailith tie the laces on her shoes.

From what Ailith could see in the mirror and when she looked down at herself, she appeared the penultimate medieval Highland lass.

When she reached the final stair, she took a deep breath, collected herself, then stepped through the archway to the main hall.

Those seated at the benches near her and milling about at this end of the hall paused as she entered and tried to gather her courage to walk through the hall. Their silenced awe did not go unnoticed by others in the hall, and quickly reached her brother who sat at the off-set table as she had presumed. Seocan rose and smiled at her with an air of condescension as if she was a little girl who obeyed her guardian properly. She didn't love the expression, but given her status as a single woman in the middle ages, it wasn't exactly *wrong*.

He gestured to where she hid. "Clansmen and women. May I present my sister and the bride-to-be, Ailith?"

Guests pounded on the table and shouted *huzzah* – not exactly what she wanted. She was unnerved enough as it was. To have all this attention on her? Leitis shoved her past the archway and into the main hall.

Plastering a fake smile on her face, she greeted those nearby as generically as she could. After several head bows and more than a few kisses to the back of her hand, the attention on her fell away and she was able to take a deep breath.

When she did, her senses were hit with the smells of roasted meat and heated musk. The din of men arguing, laughing, and shouting to be heard over the other two groups rang in her ears and made thinking clearly difficult. Servants added to the noise, yelling at each other to do one chore or another, and Ailith had to push through the chaos to focus.

She stayed by the wall, trying to avoid being the center of attention, and made her way to the hearth as she tried to figure out where she should sit. The fire in the hearth burned hot against her backside, and on a night like this, they didn't need the extra warmth. But what was a hearth for if not to burn logs? It provided additional light that the deer-horn chandeliers and torches did not. The number of bodies in the hall also did not help the stifling air.

Ailith sent up a quick prayer of thanks that the doors to the hall were open to allow the breeze to flow in and guests who needed fresh air to find their way outside. It also allowed those warriors and other guests who dined outside to feel included in the feast inside.

Men were already seated on long benches at tables both inside and out, eating meat and bread from wooden or bronze platters. Many didn't bother using their knives, instead using their bare hands to tear bread and meat and shove it into their mouths.

Several men from clans sat in chairs closer to the main table. Ailith presumed them to be other Gordons (she recognized Daniel and the young man Simon) and the MacDougals, her betrothed's clan, and perhaps those other clans Seocan had mentioned earlier. The only problem was Ailith could not tell one clan from another. Daniel had mentioned the Morays, and given how he spoke about them, Ailith guessed they were either sitting farther away from Seocan and other guests of honor or were seated outside.

Those at the tables inside busied themselves with wine and conversation, ignoring the food out of respect, as they engaged in heated discussion with Seocan. Ailith flicked her eyes to Mairi, who was resplendent in her own rich burgundy gown, a stunning contrast to her pale skin and shiny black hair bound by a golden circlet around her head. Mairi seemed to be taking in the conversation, evaluating the information as she surveyed the servants to make sure food, wine, and ale flowed freely.

If that empty seat at the end of the table was for Ailith, she could wait for her supper. She wasn't prepared to sit under those hawkish eyes while she attempted to eat.

Especially because she could hear the conversation and see Mairi's reaction to it, and Mairi didn't seem to care for what the men were saying.

As Ailith walked past, snippets of their harsh discussion filled her ears, of the Mad King Donald (*and she was more than familiar with that history!*), and talk of what the Grants and MacIntoshes might do to replace their slain tanists. More than one man commented that the death of the maniacal king would be a balm to them all.

At this, the light in Mairi's eyes slipped, her stiff and authoritative composure sagging. She didn't like what she was hearing, and with a quick glance at Seocan, Ailith understood why that might be. To attack a king meant a penalty of death, and any war risked the same. What wife in Mairi's position wanted her husband threatened?

Mairi, to her credit, quickly recovered and slid her hand to Seocan, who covered her slender finders with his.

To avoid Mairi's sharp gaze, Ailith continued her walk around the perimeter of the hall. Her hand reached out, gliding across a tapestry that hung on the other side of the hearth. She'd always enjoyed looking at the old tapestries before in her time, but those were falling apart, with washed-out color and fraying hems and not touchable lest they fall apart. Most hung in museums or touring castles behind velvet ropes. This and others in the keep weren't old–they were freshly woven, vibrant, colorful wool tapestries. The detail was astonishing and sadly lost under the heavy footfall of time.

Ailith moved slowly, hoping to recognize a face or hear a name in a conversation, anything that might provide her with information to help her present herself as Ailith, or that might help with finding and protecting the fungus.

Two men at a table near the open door mentioned something about Seocan Gordan. She hadn't heard well, straining to eavesdrop over the general din of the room, but she paused and pretended to straighten one of the Gordan banners that hung flat from a seven-foot wooden pole.

The conversation shifted to horses and Ailith pursed her lips, moving on in hopes of catching other tidbits from other clansmen. And maybe figure out which men belonged to which clans.

A hand snaked around her waist as a mellow voice spoke against her ear.

"'Allo, my love. Ye are a divine sight for sore eyes this eve."

Ailith spun, readying her feet and making a fist, prepared to strike her assailant.

Who also happened to be a strikingly tall man with wide shoulders, rich blonde hair brushed off his brow, and the most brilliant blue eyes she had ever seen on a person. How could someone's eyes be that blue?

And he spoke to her familiarly. She squinted at him. "William?" She held her breath as she guessed.

If this was her betrothed, then she was off to a good start. This man was the polar opposite of the grizzled warriors who populated the tables. He was a stunning image of a Highland warrior and nothing like any painting or replica she'd seen in her studies. No slender, pasty-faced man here – his slightly tanned cheeks and braw muscles under his fitted tunic bespoke a man who worked outside and was capable with tools and sword.

Her gaze dropped to his side, where said sword hung in a shiny leather scabbard.

He grinned at her, and before she could react, he wrapped both arms around her, lifted her off the ground, and nuzzled that handsome face against her neck. Her insides turned to liquid at his bold move, claiming her as his in front of the entire hall.

So much for austere medieval propriety. William did not seem to care who saw them making out.

"Och lass. 'Tis been far too long, and with all that has transpired, I have a need for ye."

A need . . .

Feck. Was he going to ball her on a table in front of all these people?

Thankfully, he half-walked, half-carried her to the edge of the hall, as far from prying eyes as they could get. Not far enough–Ailith noticed many voyeurs awaiting another show.

He pressed her back against the wall and nuzzled her jaw with a low growling sound. Her heart slammed in her chest. She wanted to push him off–the rational part of her mind was screaming not to let him touch her and encourage his amorous notions of loving her, but the primal side of her encouraged her to be putty in his calloused hands. And reminded her that she was his betrothed. Even if she had never really met him before, she had to act the enamored lover–which was easy given how her body reacted to him. She might not want to marry him, but he'd be a fun roll in the hay.

Literally.

Ailith closed her eyes and allowed herself to enjoy the moment, of his lips on the curve of her sweat-glistened neck, his hand on her rear end, gripping possessively through the fabric of her skirts, his animalistic growl that made her knees weak.

When he put his leg between hers, Ailith came to her senses. While they might be betrothed, they were in public, with her brother in view. Slipping out to the barns to enjoy the giant, blond Highlander might be fun, her brother would *not* appreciate the behavior, Ailith was certain.

She also thought she should get to know him a bit better before she let him between her thighs. Though one-night stands weren't her favorite, she'd had her fair share in her own time, she still preferred to know something about the guy before screwing strange men. It might also help her play the role of the beloved betrothed more convincingly.

Balancing all this only made this whole situation more complicated.

She placed her hands on his chest (*oh, his muscled chest–there was something to be said of a body trained in warfare and hard work*), and pushed lightly. William immediately took her hint and shifted back a mere inch. He was still close enough to tower over her and cover her body with his.

"Ye are a sight, lass," he said in a loving tone. "Are ye well? Ye dinna seem yourself, and Mairi has said the same."

She licked her lips. "Aye. I was feeling a bit fevered earlier. I'm well now."

William nodded, his wavy blond hair brushing against his face. She had to fight the urge to reach out and sweep it from his cheek.

"This sennight has tried a man's soul," he commented. "Has your brother spoken of it to ye?"

Ailith bobbed her head. "He made mention because of the other clans this eve, and Daniel said 'twas a slaughter."

William's sultry expression shifted to expose a pain behind his sky-blue eyes. Had he been related to or known one of those who were killed?

"'Twas, and the tanists for the Grants and MacIntoshes were both slain by the king's men." He lowered his voice. "Right now Lucas MacIntosh will likely have Ian's brother, Fergus, shoulder the task. As for the Grants, I dinna know. They are in a wee bit more distress after the loss of their men. I ken your brother prefers to keep much of this turmoil from ye, to protect ye, but as a lady in the clan and the chieftain's sister, I feel 'tis best that ye know."

A wash of relief flooded her. If nothing else, maybe William would be willing to share whatever information he had along the way. That was a welcome bit of knowledge.

"And how is your clan taking the news?" she asked.

At this, another man came up behind William, one who resembled William quite strikingly, if not quite as tall.

"They are despondent, to be sure," the man answered, then the shadow on his rugged face departed. "But as we are Highlanders, we shall overcome." He curled his lips to the side as he bowed slightly to Ailith. "Ye, lass, are a pleasing sight to behold, and enough to soothe any man's soul."

Despite the man's grim observation, amusement pulled at her mouth.

"Thank ye for the compliment," she replied.

William reached out and socked the man's shoulder. "Ailbert, get ye gone. Can ye no' see I'm trying to have a private moment with my betrothed?"

Ailbert, the roguish brother, glanced around the hall. "No' much privacy here." With a playful expression on his face, Ailbert turn back to her. "But I will take my leave at my brother's behest." He bowed again and this time a giggle slipped from between Ailith's lips.

William waved Ailbert away then shifted again, dwarfing her body with his. "Ignore my brother, *mo ruaidh.* As for me and our clan, we are devastated at this news. I could have used ye, lass. Naught can make a man whole again like the welcome of a lass. *My* lass."

He lowered his face to hers, his full lips pressing as light as a feather, so contrary to the restrained desire that wafted off his body in a tenable wave that coursed over her. His kiss was light and delicate, everything his body was not, and it robbed her of all her thoughts.

A loud cheer roused behind William, and Ailith had to force her lips away, even though she really did not want to. It would be too easy to let his lips slide lower, down her neck . . .

"I should go to my brother," Ailith gasped, her breath stolen by this man's kisses.

His face softened, while his eyes burned in a blue fire as he gazed at her. They slipped to her cleavage before returning to her face.

"Aye, but no' for long. Eat a bit and I'll come to ye soon. I need ye more than he does."

His suggestive comment made Ailith's heart flutter. *Stop it! Dinna act the fool! Ye dinna even ken the man!*

So what? Now she wanted to know him and know him well. *Grandmother Ailith, ye have great taste.*

As she tried to stop her legs from shaking, Ailith circled around the room, making her way back to the main table. She had avoided her brother and her sister-in-law long enough, and they might grow suspicious if she didn't eventually sit with them.

As she rounded the corner of a table, a rough hand grabbed her right wrist, surprising her and pulled her hard. With a mix of shock and fury, Ailith turned toward her aggressor, and with a basic move she had learned in martial arts, she twisted her arm away and slipped from his grasp.

Who was this man? What was he doing? Dismissing him, she turned to march away.

"Och, lass. Aren't ye a feisty one. Come 'ere."

His hand was on her arm again, higher this time, nearly touching the arm circlet, and too high to whip out of. He also grasped her harder and moved faster this time, yanking so she stumbled off balance and fell backwards, landing in his lap.

The man's sneering laugh boomed into her ear as one hand groped her breast while the other tightened into an iron grip around her waist.

"Give us a kiss, lass," the vile-smelling voice said in her ear.

His hands were nothing like William's, and Ailith didn't think, she reacted. In a practiced, nearly automatic move, her right elbow whipped back hard and fast, colliding with the man's nose, breaking cartilage and spraying blood. The hands locked around her waist loosened and she immediately jumped up, spinning around to face her attacker.

The crowd near them quieted and the man grabbed his nose with both hands and shrieked in anger. Ailith shuffled back two feet, bringing her hands up in a fighting stance, more out of muscle memory from her training than in any true desire to fight. Her skirts twirled around her legs, and she realized that she had never practiced or fought in a full gown before.

Crap.

The man's fists slammed on the table at the same time as he rose and shouted again in fury, getting the attention of the entire hall. Everyone had stopped what they were doing and craned their necks to observe the commotion.

Once again, the center of attention. *Feck.*

The man's fingers closed around the large meat knife lying on the table in front of him. Ailith swallowed hard – she had just avoided being grabbed and groped and was now in a life-or-death situation with a pissed-off, drunken warrior with a knife and no qualms about killing her. Her Jiu-Jitsu training never covered this type of threat, so she searched for a way to withdraw from the situation without getting stabbed.

A wooden plate sat on the table next to her. She grabbed it, flinging cabbage and meat across the room, as the plate smacked into the side of the man's temple, knocking him back a step and allowing Ailith to back away.

The only true winner of a fight is the man who avoids one, she told herself, repeating words her father had taught her which was oft repeated by her martial arts instructor.

The truth was, she wasn't going to fight a man with a big-ass meat knife with her bare hands while wearing a blue gown. She figured she could take him in a fair fight, on the mat, one on one, with rules, but standing in a crowded room with no rules unarmed in a full skirt? Well, Da didn't raise no fool.

And at the end of the day, she needed to attract less attention to herself, not more.

The angry man glared at her as he slowly raised his right hand holding the knife to his face. Extending his first finger away from the hilt of the knife, he touched his temple, and his finger came away with blood on it. His gaze moved from his finger to lock onto her with fury. He took a step forward, knife pointed in her direction, a snarl on his face.

Ailith backed up another step until the wall was at her back.

Oh, no.

In a flash, William strode in front of her, blocking her with his body.

"Back away, Moray," William said in a deadly tone. "Ye are here as an invited guest, but I'll slay ye where ye stand if ye lay a hand on my bride."

So he's a Moray, Ailith thought.

William's sword, crafted in the old Pictish style with a Celtic knot at the hilt, was still in its scabbard, but his long Seax knife was clutched backward in his hand. He palmed the hilt, with the steel riding up the back of his forearm, to hide the blade and not encourage or force the man into a fight. But he was prepared to act on it as necessary.

William's knife was at least eighteen inches of thick steel, from tip to end, a single-edge blade, unlike the more common double-edge knives. The back side of his blade was unique in that it had notches cut into it. It took her a moment for her shocked mind to realize it was designed to trap an opponent's blade. She'd never seen one quite like his, but had seen later versions called sword breakers, designed to trap blades in those jagged teeth. William's blade appeared to be an earlier version of that breaker.

The fact that William hadn't drawn his sword made little difference given the overall length of his blade. He might as well be holding a sword.

The Moray man froze for a second at the tone and seriousness of William's voice, but the scowl on his face didn't change. The man must have thought he now faced an unarmed man and lunged forward, raising his knife higher.

William wasn't having it. Keeping Ailith at his back, he flicked his wrist and his overwhelmingly large knife spun in his hand, like a magic trick, blade now out in front of him. Another man stood behind Moray and crossed his arm over his chest.

"I said, back away and dinna molest my lass. In fact, ye and the other Morays should take your leave."

"We are here as Gordon guests, MacDougal. Ye should ken your place, pup."

The air in the hall thickened and tensed. Ailith tucked herself behind William and looked around for help. The entire hall was transfixed on the two men before her, and several other men stood, ready to take action. Unbridled violence vibrated from ceiling to floor, and hands slowly moved for swords or knives.

She noticed Daniel on the other side of the room, whose deep-set hazel eyes watched her. His right hand came up and his fingers curled several times, silently telling her to move away from the two men facing off with each other. His face was a mask of worry about her getting caught in the middle.

The Moray man spat at William's feet. "Drawing weapons on an invited guest. We should have expected this from ye."

"Weapons because we cannae trust a Moray. Ye are the least trustworthy of them all, Craig, laying hands on a woman and insulting the Gordon's hospitality. Get ye gone." The final words were little more than a low snarl.

Craig Moray shouted "*sabaid cluasag!*" for his clansmen to fight as he dropped the meat knife and drew his sword in a cross draw that turned into a slash aimed at William's stomach.

A screech escaped Ailith's lips before she slammed her hand over her mouth. When had this gotten so out of control? Did chaos really happen this quickly?

William jumped back from the blade with more grace than Ailith would have expected, and out of the blade's reach. As the blade's tip passed him, William lunged forward to close the distance. The room exploded as men screamed their war cries, threw chairs, turned over tables, and drew swords and knives. The clash of steel rang loud and was almost instantaneous.

Ailith was trapped between the wall and a room full of men now trying to kill each other, with much of their violence focused on the Morays right in front of her. She controlled her breathing and told herself not to panic as she looked for a shield on the wall or something she might hide behind or defend herself with.

Remember your training!

Her eyes locked onto one of the banners. Lifting the banner out of its bracket, she ripped the banner from the pole, letting the cloth fall to the ground. She may not have been trained in the use of a broadsword or battle axes, but this pole would work towards her strengths. She was an expert with a bo staff, and this pole fit her hand just as well.

William slashed for Craig Moray's stomach, hoping for a quick end to the fight, but Craig managed to bring his sword back in time to smack William's blade away. Craig followed up with a kick to

William's leg. Other than taking a step back, William didn't seem to notice it much and pressed forward.

From the corner of her eye, Ailith noticed another large man edging around the table and moved for William's back, his sword out and raised. His eyes were locked on the back of William's head, determined to slay the distracted man while his back was turned.

In an immediate reaction, Ailith shot her right arm forward and her left arm back, bringing the butt end of the pole up and out and colliding with the man's face.

Blood shot from his now torn cheek, and Ailith followed up by jabbing the butt of the pole again into his face, aiming for the man's eye. As she destroyed one of his two eyes, the man swung his sword blindly with one hand as he grabbed at his face with the other. Ailith chopped down with her pole, striking the man's sword arm on the wrist and causing his fingers to open. The blade clanged to the stones. Twisting her upper body fast and hard, she brought the other end of her fighting staff around and down on the man's head. The unknown man slumped forward in a heap, unconscious.

As the man collapsed, another man standing behind him stepped up. His hard, raging eyes focused on her. Though she kept a steady grip on the staff, she had no chance at a free swing like last time. He came in fast, sword out in front, tip directed at her chest. His arm went up and back as he prepared to hack at her.

She knew she might block the blade's deadly arc, but unlike training in the twenty-first century, the man's blade was razor sharp and would slice right through her pole and down into her chest. She panted as she watched his lethal swing, bracing herself.

Suddenly Daniel ran straight into her, shouldering her to the side and into the wall to stand in the spot where she had been. His own sword rose expertly to meet the Moray man's sword.

Daniel pushed the Moray man's sword to the side, then stepped in to throw a hammer strike with the hilt of his own sword to the man's face. It was a solid if not a lethal hit. The man stumbled back, and as one of his clansmen yanked the injured man backwards into their cluster, another stepped up, sword out but unmoving. He didn't charge Daniel but seemed content to stand his ground and hold Daniel off.

Ailith spun around, searching for any other attackers, when realizing what she had been doing. She dropped the pole onto the ground.

Had anyone other than Daniel seen her?

I hope not.

William's blood burned under his skin as he struck at the man who had dared lay a hand on Ailith. *Feckin Morays.* Couldn't trust one as far as he could throw him. Inviting them to this celebration had been a poor idea from the start.

Craig Moray stabbed at William, who blocked the thrust then struck out with his left hand, punching Craig's left ear. The blow was not a killing strike by any means, but had the desired effect of causing Craig to shuffle back. Shaking off the hit, Craig grabbed a fat candle from the table and threw it at William.

It was a desperate move that William easily knocked away in midair with his knife, but Craig was already moving forward, slashing his sword. William didn't have time to block the slash, so he stepped into Craig, shoving the man off balance and causing the tip of his sword to hit the wall before it reached William. The two men had now traded places with Craig's back to Ailith.

"All I wanted was a squeeze and a kiss from the lass. Your women are known for lifting their skirts," Craig shouted, mocking William and his entire clan. Fury raged so hard inside him, hot and burning at the back of his throat. Only death was good enough for the likes of this Moray man. They weren't worth the time or effort Seocan gave them.

"Then you should've gone back to your village and cattle, like the rest of your clan," William taunted back.

Craig must have believed he had the advantage over William with his sword upraised, and he stepped towards William. Not waiting for the blade to drop, William leaped forward and drove a good six inches of the blade into Craig's throat.

With his arms still above his head and blood pouring from the gash in his neck, Craig's fingers opened, allowing his blade to fall to the stone floor in a clatter. Craig's eyes rolled back, and he slumped against the wall, dead.

Good riddance to bad rubbish, William thought before spinning around.

Two more Moray men approached William from behind. He spun to face them fast enough to hold them off and swept his sword to the side, ready for them.

As they stormed toward him, Ailbert's blond head appeared behind them with his own sword in one hand and a wall torch in the other. Blood stained Ailbert's face yet didn't appear to be his own. No injuries or wounds were evident on him. Ailbert drew his sword and torch out in front of himself, forcing the Morays to scramble back. One faced William while the other turned to confront Ailbert.

They kept their swords up and sidestepped together towards the center of the room to join the rest of the Moray clan, but they were severely outnumbered.

The Gordons had the benefit of men in superior numbers and allies in the MacDougals, Grants, and MacIntoshes. Their men had pushed the Morays together, like a group of sheep surrounded by a pack of wolves. A few other men lay on the ground, not moving, but whether as dead as Craig Moray or merely knocked out, William could not say.

He glanced around the hall, searching for Ailith. She stood near the hearth by Mairi and a few other clanswomen, wide-eyed and stricken by this harrowing turn of events. Mairi, so pale already, had gone white as milk, her eyes riveted on her husband as she clutched her hands into her skirts.

How frightened they must have been to see this all unfold! Satisfied that Ailith was safe for the moment, William turned his attention back to the center of the hall.

Seocan pushed to the front of the cluster of men. "Drop your blades or be slain like your kinsmen," he yelled out in a booming voice to be heard by the whole hall.

His own sword was in his tight grasp, but he was surrounded by his men. William did the same, moving to stand with Ailbert close to his uncle Cormag, just as he had with Ailith. If a Moray wanted to reach Seocan or any other chieftain, he'd have to get through four or five battle-hardened Highland warriors first, and only after they climbed over the tables that their men thought to overturn onto their sides as a makeshift palisade.

William's body buzzed as he waited for the Morays to make their next move. Most men in the hall bore evidence of the conflict with blood on either their faces or hands. The fighting had been quick and hard, but if the Moray men didn't do as commanded, more would die here tonight.

William sheathed his knife and pulled his curved-handled sword, stepping to ready himself for whatever the Morays might do next. One of the men in the circle finally realized the futility of their position and with a scowl, dropped his sword, then raised a hand, motioning for the rest to do the same. One by one, their weapons clattered to the stones.

"The egg-sucking coward who attacked my sister and started this folly is dead," Seocan announced. His face was red with fury and exertion as his gaze swept his hall. "I'll consider the matter done after ye are marched out of my tower and off Gordon lands. Make sure that when ye return to your clan and tell your version of what happened here today, ye include that it was one of ye who broke the peace, and it was I, Seocan Gordon, who allowed the lot of ye to live. We'll be keeping your swords. Mayhap my smith can turn them into plows. Pick up your fallen, be they dead or injured, and leave under guard and arms."

Several Gordon warriors, with the assistance of the MacDougals, Grants, and MacIntoshes, shoved the Morays out the double doors and into the bailey outside. William returned his sword to his leather scabbard and strode to Ailbert who stood near the doors.

"Ye did well," Williams said to Ailbert, without taking his eyes off the men in front of him. "Are ye hurt?"

"Nay," Ailbert answered, his gaze flicking around the hall. "The blood's not mine. How is Ailith?"

"She is safe with her brother's wife," William said, tipping his chin toward the buxom redhead who had stolen his heart when he was still a lad and had never let it go. If needed, he would have killed the entire Moray clan himself if anything had happened to her.

"Aye," Ailbert said. "I can see that. What was she doing with the banner? You might think she mistook it for a scythe."

William screwed up his face at his brother. What was he saying? Ailith had been shoved behind him, then taken under Seocan's and Mairi's protection. *What banner?*

"I should go to her," William said and clasped Ailbert on his shoulder.

He wiped his face with his sleeve to remove any drying blood before striding across the hall to Ailith. Best not to approach her with the remnants of death on his face.

Even after the bloody events of the night, in her rich blue gown and brilliantly red, woven hair, she was a vision of perfection. William's groin surged at the sight of her, and all he wanted to do after that surge of blood lust was flip those skirts up and sink his cock deep inside her.

But not the now, not when her face was pale and she stood forlornly next to the chieftain's wife, not when she was probably frozen in shock over the event of the night. He sighed wearily. Over an event meant to celebrate their union.

Poor Ailith.

He walked through the hall toward her, stepping over a fallen gold and blue banner along his way. *Was that the banner Ailbert had been talking about?*

Then he reached her, and without a word, he wrapped his arms around her waist and drew her near him. She must be dazed because she stiffened when he first touched her before curving into him. His poor lass, seeing such a fight. The world was too vile for the soft wonderment of women.

He loosened his embrace and gazed into her face. Her green eyes were less wary than he expected, intent as she searched his face.

What is she seeking?

Her rosebud lips quivered slightly, and he kissed her tenderly, hoping that his steadfastness might pass to her, calming her.

"Are ye well? He did no' injure ye at all, did he?" William asked as he brushed a loose lock of hair off her face. He didn't see any blood, nor did any stain her delicate gown.

"I'm well," she sighed. "He did no' hurt me, no' really."

William's hand curled into the skirt at her waist. "He touched ye. I killed him for that offense alone."

She shuddered under his arm, and he hugged her again.

"I'm pleased ye were no' involved in the violence at all. A scuffle like that is nay place for a lass. Ye should wash this night from ye and find your bed. The day always seems better in the morn. I had hoped to spend more time with ye this night."

The tone of his voice left no doubt as to how he wanted to spend that time. Even now his cock was rigid and needed to find solace after a heated battle. A man was never more hard than after a bout of blood-lust. But Ailith needed quiet and rest more than anything else.

He kissed her clear forehead, her hair tickling his nose. "But ye need to rest. I'll visit ye on the morrow, and mayhap we can resume our time together then?"

Ailith blinked rapidly at him, then a slight smile softened her lips. "Aye. Thank ye, William. I would like to see ye on the morrow."

Keeping his arms around her, he walked her to the stairs, and his gaze remained fixed on her as she climbed the stairs. When she was at the curve in the stairwell, she paused and looked over her creamy, smooth shoulder at him. Her skin was yet pale but her eyes burned into him as though she saw into his soul. How did she do that to him? Make him feel as if the world came to a halt with a mere look?

Then she turned back to the stairs and disappeared behind the curve. Knowing she was settled in her chambers under the protection of her brother, William took his leave, following his brother and the rest of his clansmen back to Drumoak Castle.

Leitis was silent as she aided Ailith in stripping from her clothes. She offered to help Ailith wash, but Ailith shooed Leitis back to her own chambers, claiming they all needed to find their beds, Leitis included.

With a pursed-lipped gaze, Leitis nodded and departed the chambers, securing the door behind her.

Only then did Ailith let out the tight breath that had been suffocating her all night. To meet the mysterious, and shockingly attractive betrothed, then to fight for her life and risk being seen fighting with a staff?

Yet she made it out of the event uninjured and had much to be grateful for, that Daniel had stepped in without question, that the Moray man who had assaulted her would never touch another woman again, and that it seemed William had no clue that she had knocked out a Moray man and held off a second with that banner pole.

That was probably the most important. Daniel might confront her about her actions or mention something to her brother, but she could play that off saying she grabbed the closest thing she could find to hold them off.

But if William had seen her using it as an offensive weapon, well, that would lead to a lot of questions, which might complicate her betrothal to him. While she had no idea about how time travel or physics worked in that way, she knew that her great grandmother many times removed had to get married and have children. If nothing else, she had to make sure she married this man so the Gordon legacy continued.

She finished wiping the grime and fight off her skin and donned the léine she had worn earlier. Exhausted, she blew out the tallow candle and flopped onto the bed, her mind on William.

Aye, she had to marry him, and if he had been an old, decrepit man, or missing most of his teeth, or a smelly drunkard like that Moray man had been, marriage might have been a more terrifying prospect.Wil liam MacDougal, however, was a paragon of the handsome, warrior Highlander, which made the idea of marriage that much easier.

Her body had finally started to calm as she had changed, and now her eyes were heavy. The next day was going to be a lot to handle, especially if anyone found the need to discuss tonight with her, but right now, as her eyes slipped closed, all she thought about was a tall blond Highlander with the brightest blue eyes she had ever seen.

Chapter Ten

Ailith's mind was more torn into conflict than she had realized, and her dreams tortured her for it.

The Romani woman, Eladon, appeared in a fuzzy haze, only it wasn't Eladon. It was a woman who looked like her, but younger, and dressed in clothing similar to what Ailith was wearing in the past. In her dream, the night spread out like a star-studded curtain behind the young Eladon, swirling around her as if she could control the very night sky itself.

The dream Eladon's mouth was moving, but the words didn't match her mouth and came from behind the dream Eladon, like a surround sound movie in Ailith's previous life.

Ye can find me, the dream Eladon's voice said. *Search for me as I come to ye.*

Who are you? Ailith asked in her dream. *Who are you?*

The question made no sense;Ailith knew who Eladon was.

Unless this wasn't Eladon?

The night sky swirled, and the voice spoke again.

Keeper of the knowledge . . .

That final word drew out in the dream, fading as the night sky in the background faded.

What knowledge? Ailith was screaming in her dream state. *What knowledge?*

Both Eladon and the sky disappeared, jerking Ailith from her troubled sleep. She sat up, panting and clutching at her plaid blankets.

What had the dream meant? Was Eladon trying to speak to her? Or wasn't that Eladon? Was it someone else?

Eladon's final words before she had fallen asleep that fateful night rang in her ears. *Pay attention to your dreams.*

That was fine and all, but what did she need to pay attention to? What did it mean?

Sweat covered her forehead and neck in a thin film, and Ailith kicked off the blankets. She padded barefoot to the shuttered window and opened it to see the real night sky. This one was cloud-covered, no stars peeking through, but the breeze was enough to cool her sweaty head. She perched on the edge of the window.

That the dream had come on the same night that she met William, her intended, and after a bloody fight between the clans could not be a coincidence–she didn't really believe in them. All things have meaning, that was what her father had often said, and her heart clenched as she heard his voice in her ear. She had rushed into this task, and while she was doing it for her father, that didn't make the pain of leaving him, of never seeing him again, any less.

Ailith sighed and scooted off the ledge and closed the shutter. Night still blanketed the world, and she had much to accomplish the next day, not the least of which was starting her search for the elusive, reddish-tipped mushroom. She had tried to burn its image into her mind, but it was the location, on the deep northern valley side of Dunnottar, that would tell her she had the right fungus. And other than this night, the summer appears to have been cool and damp. With any luck, the mushrooms would be thriving on that hillside.

She padded back to her bed, tucking her now-cold feet under the wooly covers. Finding them would be the easy part.

Then she had to figure out a way to save them for centuries to come.

That was the most daunting aspect of this task.

But that is a worry for another night, she told herself as she settled back into her pillows and drifted into a dreamless sleep.

Leitis's knocking pulled Ailith from her sleep. She wiped at her sleep-crusted eyes as Leitis entered, setting the platter on the trunk.

Despite the bloodshed the night before, it was business as usual the next morning.

"Good morn to ye!" Leitis said in her cheery voice.

How could she be so merry after all that happened?

"Good morn to ye, Leitis," Ailith replied, kicking off the blankets and rising from the bed. The day was a bit cooler this morning. The clouds' breeze from the night before must have been a harbinger of morning mists or rain.

Leitis shook out her blue kirtle, and after ensuring the night before hadn't stained or marked it, (shockingly, since Ailith had pretty much broken that Moray fellow's nose) folded it neatly to be returned to the trunk. The brown kirtle, however, did not receive the same response, and Leitis crinkled her nose at it.

"I'll take this to be washed. Is your léine still clean? Mayhap we should launder that as well."

Ailith sniffed at léine and her sour expression struck Leitis as comical, because the woman cackled as she wiggled her fingers at Ailith.

"Off wi' it." Leitis turned and moved the tray from the trunk to the chair. No more waiting on laundry, it seemed. She was a woman with a purpose.

A peculiar purpose. Why the focus on laundry after all that had transpired the night before?

Ailith pulled the léine over her head and handed it to Leitis, who had pulled a fresh one from the trunk along with a clean yellow kirtle. She then placed the blue kirtle in the trunk, along with the sleeves and the armband, tucking everything away.

Then she gathered up the dirty clothes, and with her arms full, she moved toward the door. "I'll return for the pot, aye?" she asked. Without waiting for an answer, she opened the door.

"Wait!" Ailith shouted as she tugged her head through the opening of the léine. "What about the hall?"

Leitis's brow furrowed as she paused at the door. "The hall?"

Ailith shifted from one foot to the next. "Do I need to hurry down to help scrub the hall?"

It had to be a bloody disaster, with platters and food and blood staining the stones. Though she hadn't fully registered the amount of damage and disrepair in the hall, from what she had observed, she knew it was significant. Surely three kitchen maids were not going to be the only ones cleaning it.

Leitis's brow softened, and her smile held a note of indulgence. "Och, lass. Several clanswomen arrived at dawn this morning. They brought several of their brawny lads, and the hall is nearly set to rights. Ye would never believe anything had transpired yestereve." Leitis's smile widened and she waddled past the door. "Now, dinna fash. Ye have been busy these past few days preparing for the celebration. Today ye must work on your own duties."

Uncertain of how to respond, Ailith just nodded as Leitis shut the door behind her.

Was the hall already clean? Mairi definitely ran the tower with an iron fist. And her own duties? What were those? She sighed heavily as she washed her face with the damp cloth, wiping away the final vestiges of her troubled sleep. Most likely, Mairi had a list of those duties ready for her.

Ailith pulled the new, pale-yellow kirtle over her head and fastened the belt around her waist. Flicking her gaze to the shuttered window, she opened the trunk back up and dug around for that hood she had seen earlier, and the plaid cape with the penannular brooch. Better to be prepared in case it started to rain.

Because she was going to do her duties in the morning, but after the midday meal, Ailith planned on escaping the tower and beginning her search.

Enough time had passed. Another saying of her father's flitted through her mind in his deep, resonant voice: *Procrastination is the thief of time, lass.*

And she had indeed learned just how big a thief time could be.

Fortunately for Ailith, Mairi's list was short. The woman's heavy green gaze squinted at her when Ailith had asked, and Ailith had the uneasy sense that she should have known what her own duties were.

To cover, Ailith added, "Before I begin my tasks for the day."

Mairi appeared to buy it, and her hard gaze relaxed. She nodded curtly and directed Ailith to take the broken crockery outside for disposal in the midden heap beyond the tower walls.

Ailith brightened at this chore, seeing the opportunity to observe the lands outside her limited view from the tower and try to figure out where exactly Glenbervie tower was.

The broken crockery from the overturned tables filled several hampers, and Ailith carried them one at a time past the main gate to the left several paces from the wall. The local crockery craftsman would be busy for a long time, replacing all these broken wares.

The Glenbervie lands were a mix of valleys, narrow glens, and wooded groves, from what she had managed to discern. The lands around the tower proper were clear of trees and brush for definitive reasons, yet thickets populated the hills and valleys farther on. Underneath the damp, cloudy skies, it was truly a paradise, untouched by the stain of modern man.

Ailith might not know where she was, but she knew that from the main gate, she could turn left and be on her way facing east.

East to the coast.

East to Dunnottar Castle.

Once at the coast, she would be able to determine if she had to go north or south, but that was a detail best saved for when she got there.

If only I had a horse.

It would make getting to the coast quicker, but she didn't know if Ailith had a horse, if she could simply walk out of the stables with one, or if medieval saddlery was different from what she was familiar with.

Maybe investigate that tomorrow, she thought as she entered the tower hall for her midday meal.

Set up in a cafeteria style, several large, bronzed platters of food were stacked on the repaired tables, along with pitchers of mead and ale. The platters held the remains of roasted pork from the night previous, pickled fish, bannocks with berry and apple preserves, cheese, and thick chunks of dark bread. Bowls were set next to a large cauldron of pottage filled with broth, barley, vegetables, and a meat Ailith didn't recognize.

Men and women came and went during the midday meal,Mairi evidently dispensed with formal etiquette when it came to midday eating, or she wanted the tower set to rights before another meal was hosted in the main hall.

As she filled her wooden platter with dried haddock and a bannock with honey, a figure came to stand next to her. After the events of last night, she stiffened, ready to throw an elbow punch at whoever was close.

"Ye did well yestereve, lass," a familiar voice said.

She turned to find Daniel standing next to her, a cup in his hand and a crooked-toothed smile breaking through his beard. Her stressed body relaxed and she returned his smile with a wavering one. How much had he seen? He had to have noticed something, coming to her aid as he had.

"Thank ye," she stammered. What else could she say? How could she explain away what she had done?

"If William taught ye that trick with the wood stick, 'twas smart by far. Too many dangers for us in the Highlands. Mayhap ye should keep a stick on ye all the time, aye?" Then he winked at her and for the first time since the harrowing events of the night before she felt fully relieved. He wasn't calling her to task on how she knew to use the staff – in fact he was encouraging it!

She bobbed her head. "Aye. 'Tis sound advice. I shall take it."

Daniel made a grizzled sound that resembled a laugh and moved on his way toward the main doors. Feeling light in her steps, she searched the hall, looking for a place to sit.

Gwen and Isa sat together on a bench at a table close to the archway to the stairs. Grabbing a final chunk of cheese, Ailith balanced it all on her square wooden platter, then dipped her horn cup into the mead pitcher, and joined the women by the stairs.

Both appeared pleased to have her sit with them, and Ailith had a flare of panic strike in her chest. Did she not normally sit with the kitchen maids? Or was she not supposed to? The day-to-day protocol of classes was elusive, and Ailith had the sense that she was going to make so many mistakes, the Gordons might believe her mad.

She thought about Mairi's hard eyes always staring at her. Perchance they already did.

Mairi had one more basket of debris for the midden pile. The skies had darkened slightly, and a misty rain kissed the leaves and grass, making them shine in an emerald glow. Before heading back outside, Ailith raced up to her chamber and retrieved that shoulder cover and hood with the dramatic fringe. With the volume of hair on her head, she thought it best to cover it. Otherwise, it would take forever to dry and she didn't exactly have a hair dryer.

Heading in the same direction as the midden pile seemed the best course to take. Not only was she familiar with that direction, she could use that midden pile and the tower as points of reference to find her way back.

The thicket of trees sprouted with saplings and leafy brush off the trail to the east, and Ailith decided to start there. Her plan, weak though it was, involved slowly heading east, searching for any evidence of the mushroom. She had tried to commit the image to memory when the scientists had shown her dad the photo, and later, she had pulled the image up on the internet. While she had not been sure of what she might need the image for, she was grateful she had studied before visiting the Romani woman.

The woods were not quiet – the twittering of birds and their rustling from branch to branch told her they were enjoying the misty rain and their chirping followed Ailith as she tried to keep on an eastward direction. She moved slowly, picking her way through tree roots and wet leaves, pausing to check the shady, damp areas of the vegetation. Mushrooms loved the wet and decay, so she crawled into the underbrush, searching for any hiding fungi.

A lot of creamy white and fleshy mushrooms, but none with the red-tipped caps and tiny fungus growths. The loamy scent of the earth became more potent as she dug under a bush, sweeping away the dead leaves and grass to see if any mushrooms were covered by the compost.

Dark brown dirt caked in her nails and between her fingers. She sat back on her heels and looked at her hands. They were filthy. Her eyes caught the front of her kirtle, which was covered with dirt and grass stains. She groaned to herself.

Leitis was going to kill her. All she did was make more work for that kind woman.

Ailith gathered her skirts to rise when she noticed the birds no longer tittered in the trees.

Why would they stop chirping? Because someone was in the woods, disturbing them.

Her chest heart skipped a beat as she shifted her movement to tuck herself under the brush she had been digging under. Who was in the woods? Was Mairi or Daniel following her? Or had the Morays returned to seek revenge for their fallen clansmen? That thought sent a chill down her spine.

The jingling sound of reins carried through the wood, and Ailith risked peeking out from between the leaves.

Her eyes widened when she saw William MacDougal atop a golden-brown steed. He wore a hood much like hers that covered his blond hair, but his hood was attached to a longer cape that protected most of his tunic and sword belt from the rain.

She tried to step out of the brush but slipped on the wet leaves and tumbled into the mud right next to him.

William didn't dismount right away. Rather, he remained on his horse, looking down at her with a humored smile on his full lips.

"Need a wee bit o' help, Ailith?" he asked in a teasing tone.

"Nay," she answered as she regained her footing. "I'm quite capable of standing on my own."

She did as she said and gave him an austere look as she stood upright in front of him.

"Ye are a fair mess, lass. What have ye been doing? Digging in the dirt?"

"Actually, aye. I have been doing just that."

His brow furrowed and he leapt off his horse. He strode to her and took her hands in his.

"Weel, no' the Ailith I am used to seeing as of late. Ye remind me of when ye were a lass and we tried to catch frogs in the mud puddles after a deluge of rain. We were covered in mud from head to toe and I thought my mother would have my head."

Ailith nodded as if she shared that memory. "Aye. We were a mess," she lied.

Before she could say another word, he pulled her close, ignoring the stains on her kirtle, and placed a warm kiss on her surprised lips.

William was the affectionate sort, it seemed. That was not something she had anticipated for the middle ages! When he pulled his lips away, he stayed close, near enough for his breath to warm her cheek when he spoke.

"Ye should have waited for me. I would have helped ye dig. What were ye digging for?"

Ailith tilted her head to the side. "I'm fine digging on my own. We're but a few steps from the tower."

A shadow passed over his face, so brief she barely saw it before it was gone. "Aye, but the Morays are no' going to let the slight against them pass. I'd no' have ye out on your own until we have dealt with them."

She wanted to ask how he planned on doing that, but the more pressing issue for her was her mushrooms.

"Fungus. Mushrooms," she explained to him.

His brow wrinkled again. "What?"

Her breathing stopped in her chest. What did they call mushrooms? What word – "Toadstools!!" Ailith shouted, then snapped her mouth shut and swallowed. "I was digging for toadstools."

"Toadstools? Och! Puddock-stools!"

Ailith had to force her mouth to stay shut, otherwise a huge burst of laughter would rush from her. Puddock-stool? *Oh, that's the most perfect Scots word.*

"Aye, puddock-stools."

His eyes shifted, looking at the ground around her. "There are all sorts of puddock-stools around here," he commented.

"Aye," she nodded. "But I'm looking for a special one. A puddock-stool with a reddish cap and smaller white freckles."

William looked around again. "I only see the yellow ones." His cerulean gaze returned to her face. "Why do ye need these red ones?"

Ailith steeled herself. Here it was, her first major opportunity to get William to assist her, paired with her first major half-truth regarding these mushrooms that she had traveled over the span of time to protect. She had been planning this part, tying several threads together in the hopes that she–small, nobody, Emilie-turned-Ailith–might save the most inauspicious of plants.

"For bad humours," she explained quickly. "The Norse and Danes use them for many illnesses and injuries, as did the ancient clans. Wet or dried, eaten or made into a poultice, these wee puddock-stools can do much for injuries or illnesses. They are verra useful."

"Aye. I've heard of puddock-stools used this way. Our clan has Norse connections, as ye ken." He pointed absently to his brilliant-blond thatch of hair. Of course, he had Nordic blood, his hair and eyes, and his height were testaments to that. "And I've heard my mother and sisters and cousins remark the same."

Ailith locked that information away, hoping she might use it later to obtain more information from him about the Norse and try to convince him that the Norse should try to settle on the coast, not invade and spike the king's violent ire. Perhaps that would be easier with his Viking connections. But how might she share that she knew these Vikings were on their way? The rain increased slightly, changing from a mist to a gentle rain. William didn't seem to notice.

He grinned widely at her. "Perchance ye can use it on your illness ye've had as of late." He tugged her hand. "Come. We should get ye out o' the rain."

She didn't move. "What illness?"

William reached his horse and tugged again, pulling her close. "Leitis and Mairi commented that ye had no' been yourself these past days. I noted it yestereve. If these puddock-stools can relieve any humors ye have, then I am willing to search with ye for them."

He looked at her expectantly but she could not move. In the history she had studied of Highlanders, from the time of the Caledoniis to present day (*her present day*), these men were presented as rough, wild, nearly barbarian warriors. They had been one of the only people to stop the spread of Roman colonialism, and in the future, they would throw off the mantle of the oppressive English, if for a short while. To have this giant Highland warrior, with his strong jaw, defined muscles, and sword on his hip speak to her as a love-sick puppy, was contrary to all the presumptions she'd had about these men.

About *this* man. She had assumed that Ailith's betrothed was nothing but another ruthless warrior, and she had braced herself for that. Ailith had no safeguard for a man that stirred her heart and loins. How was she going to keep him at arm's length? Then again, with a man like William, a tender warrior, mayhap she didn't need to.

As it was, with his deep blue gaze on her, she had the sense she didn't want to. The side of her lip curled into a tiny smile against her cheek. Maybe marrying the man was what she should do. It suddenly seemed like a much more tempting prospect. She tipped her chin to his horse.

"Might we ride around a wee bit?" she asked as she let him guide her to the beast. "I'd like to see if we might search this area before the rain gets worse?"

He turned his face up so the small drops splashed on his skin. "What? This? 'Tis naught but a fine Highland day." Then he lowered his face and regarded her with blue intensity. "Mayhap 'twill be a reward for your dear betrothed for helping ye?"

My dear betrothed. Ailith's heart fluttered under her breast, and she giggled nervously. "Mayhap a wee gift." She wasn't quite ready to bed a strange Highlander, though she was getting close.

With one hand under her foot and the other taking liberties against her backside, William boosted her into the saddle, then swung up behind her with ease. It had been a while since Ailith had been on a horse, and never had she ridden double like this. The beast shifted under her thighs and she gripped the edge of the saddle to hold on. William's legs cradled hers in the saddle, holding her in place. The heat and pressure of his body against her back were enough to make her forget what she was supposed to be doing.

The mushrooms! Focus!

He leaned closer, placing his lips by her ear. "And I have a favor to ask of ye." His breath was warm on her skin, and another shiver, for a different reason, coursed down her spine. "When ye plan on going out again, call for me. As your betrothed, 'tis my job to protect ye."

"Do ye fear the Morays will try to exact some measure of revenge?"

He nodded against her hair. "Aye. They are no' the forgiving sort, and the clan chieftains fear that they're too aligned with the violent king to be trusted. I shall escort ye."

If anything, that was exactly what Ailith needed. He had a horse and familiarity with the area.

She'd find her mushrooms much more quickly if William was helping her.

She'd just have to find a way to fight her growing desire for the rugged blond Highlander.

With his strong arms around her, time passed quickly as he reined the horse through the woods, picking their way through the underbrush and searching for the mushroom.

"I've heard that the puddock-stools only grow farther east, closer to Dunnottar."

William reined the horse to a stop, and she twisted around to question him.

"Weel, we won't reach the coast before this rain increases, so we cannae go today. And I hesitate to be searching that close to the king –"

Her stomach dropped. "I have to reach the coast! The pud-dock-stools are there!" she protested like a petulant child.

He held up his palm to quiet her. "I did no' say we would no' go. I would rather be better prepared and no' soaked by this fine Highland rain. We can try again on the morrow, aye?"

A grateful smile parted her lips.

Nay, he was nothing like she had assumed.

"Aye. On the morrow then."

She waited, ready for him to turn his horse around and head to the tower, but he didn't. His blue eye bit into hers, staring deeply until her insides quivered.

"What?" she asked. What was he waiting for?

"My reward for helping ye?" he asked, a sultry grin on his lips. He had such surprisingly full and soft lips for a hard man.

What was he expecting? She thought in a moment of fretful wor-ry. But he didn't move–he remained still, with only that blue gaze touching her, growing more intense and deeper as the gaze lingered. Almost like he was gazing into her depths, trying to caress her heart.

That gaze, so full love, was too much for her. Loving this blond warrior was not on her agenda, no matter how much she desired him. Shifting her eyes from his to break that profound hold, she lifted her palm to the curve of his jaw, defined but overly sharp, and smooth. He tilted his head slightly into her palm and his eyes narrowed. Turning to better situate herself, she leaned in until her lips caressed his in a soft kiss. His arm snaked around her waist, bringing her closer, but his kiss remained soft, tender. Too tender. Ailith decided to take the lead.

She grew bolder, and when her tongue brushed across his lips, urging them open, he growled low in his chest and his arm clenched, holding her tight.

It was like a chained animal lived inside him, growing more aggressive and savage the longer they kissed.

And if she didn't stop now, they wouldn't stop at all, and as long as he didn't look at her with that burning blue gaze, she was fine with that. His cock had hardened as she kissed him, his hard length pressing boldly against her hip, showing Ailith how much he desired her.

Then a snap of thunder in the distance made her jump.

As she did the night before, she rested her hand on his tunic-covered chest and pressed herself away.

His raving lust was evident on his face. "'Twas a fair reward." He adjusted her in front of him and dug his heels into the horse's ribs to resume their trot home. As they rode, he leaned close to her ear again. "Next time, though, I'll want more."

Chapter Eleven

William held Ailith's hand as she dismounted, then stood with his back to his horse while she mounted the steps. She glanced over her shoulder at him before she entered the tower, a masked look under her soggy hood, crimson tendrils curling around her face. Then she stepped through the wide doors, leaving him alone in the rain.

Something was off about her – he'd have to be a fool not to see it. Nothing significant, yet Ailith while not quite Ailith. He still burned for her, and from what he could determine, she burned for him, though something tempered it, as if she was afraid of what their passion was. They had lain together several times before, and Ailith's passion with him was unbridled. When he loved her, whether it was a tender kiss or joining with her, it was wild and uninhibited. It was only the two of them.

Yestereve and today, something else was present. It wasn't just the two of them–something was drawing part of her away from him. Was it the Morays and their threat on her the night before that was causing her distance? Nay, she had seen violence and battle before. And her odd request about the puddock-stools. Did that have something with her distraction? He rubbed his hand across the back of his damp neck, made tight by his concerns so close to their wedding.

Today, she could barely look him in the eyes. That was unusual, disturbingly so. How many nights had they laid beneath the stars and gazed upon each other? And his words of love had little impact on her. Instead of crushing into him under his passionate attentions or his tender proclamations of love, she seemed to pull away.

Ailith hadn't said anything about it, but he would be a fool not to feel the change in her.

For a couple in love that was to be wed, this didn't sit well with him. And William loved her too much to let it go unaddressed. If something was bothering her, then he'd make sure to remove that irritation so he might have those loving looks return to her face.

Och, *a Dhia*, but he missed it. Even if only for a day, he missed it.

He mounted his steed and made his way in the rain toward Drumoak castle. He didn't care what her irritation was–as long as she was still his, that she was marrying him, that she loved him and no other, William would do whatever it took to resolve that distraction. He would do anything so her heart and mind were clear.

Even if it meant searching for wee puddock-stools.

Several men were gathered in the main hall when William entered. His father, his uncle Cormag as chieftain, and Brian, his tanist and second in command, sat at a long table at the front of the cavernous hall. As a full castle, the main hall was separate from the keep proper and had been constructed to withstand any sort of invasion. William's grandfather made sure of that. The man, rumor claimed, did not trust anyone, least of all kings who proclaimed to work for the clans and instead coveted that power for themselves.

Given the present situation in the Highlands, William didn't blame him.

Other kin and clansmen and some warriors from other clans, similar to the collection of men from the night prior, stood along the walls or sat erect and irate at tables facing Cormag. William had walked into a type of war meeting it seemed.

War against who? The Morays? Their allies? Against the king himself? Overthrowing a king – now *that* was a problem.

Ailbert lifted a hand at William who joined him along the wall, not far from their father. Another familiar blond head was next to him, his cousin, Robb, Brian's son. His shock of white-blond hair, similar in coloring to William, was pasted against his skull, and he appeared the water-logged Viking of his heritage. If Robb was here, that meant other Dane and Norse Viking kin and clansmen were also present, and William spied those blonde and light brown heads and full, grizzled beards with ease. He also noted Ailith's brother, Seocan, and his man, Daniel, sitting on a bench near the front.

William shoved his leather hood off his head and leaned toward Ailbert. "What are we here for?" he asked in a hushed tone so as not to interrupt his uncle or draw attention to his tardiness.

"A few issues. Of course, that dispute yestereve with the Morays. Everyone is on edge at how violently they reacted."

"Mmm," William mumbled with a nod. He had been thinking the same. "Any notion as to what set them on that path?"

Ailbert pointed to Robb. "Uncle Brian believes the problem has several roots. That the Morays are in the king's pockets far deeper than we anticipated. That they will no' speak for the clans. And if the Morays collude with the king . . ."

"Then so do the Keiths," William finished for him, cursing under his breath. Donald as the mad king had done more to cause a schism between the clans than any foreign invader.

Robb stood stiffly against the stone wall. "Father has had word from kin in Norway," he spoke up, keeping his eyes fixed on the men in the hall. "More settlers want to come, but Father fears the king's response."

William's lips thinned. Aye. Most of the clans understood Robb's meaning. Dane and Norse settlers formed alliances with local clans, and the strength of the clans threatened the power of the king. It was no mystery that King Donald fought against any Danes or Norse who attempted to settle the eastern seaboard. After years of bloody invasions by the Vikings, attacking any incoming Norse or Danes had become his standard reaction when dragon prows landed on their shores.

Cormag said something that had the hall up in arms, arguing and shouting loudly enough to echo off the stone walls. Cormag stood and waved his hands over his head. His plaid cape swirled around his body as he worked to regain control of his hall.

"Aye. We all share the same concerns. But now we must discuss what this attack and Clan Moray mean for our clans, for us and the Gordons and Grants. For all of us."

Chieftain Lucas MacIntosh rose, his tall, portly frame and pock-marked cheeks telling the tale of distress that he and his clan had experienced as of late.

"I agree with Cormag. Morays are wolves at our gate, ready to drag us to the King's feet to meet our demise – the demise not just of us, but of so many Highland clans. The Highlands are the clans. We must show the king that one man is not all of Alba. We must rally the clans and work together in a force of numbers so he does no' feel he can crush us under his bootheel."

Cheers and huzzahs erupted as the banging of cups and fists on the table lauded MacIntosh's words.

"But no' all the clans are with us. Ye've already spoken of the Morays and the Keiths. How are we to challenge the king if he has an army of our own Highlands clans, men willing to suck at Donald's saggy teat in hopes of meager scraps?"

"Here, here!" a few warriors shouted in agreement.

As Lucas sat back down, Brian stood and looked pointedly at Cormag, then at his Viking kin. "The Norse and Danes who have settled here years ago have become part of the Highlands clans through marriage, through oaths, through bairns. Whilst I ken that a good number of ye, especially those clans farther inland, dinna have much cause to trust this fresh blood. Weel, we know we cannae trust the mad king. We can build and strengthen our clans against the king and his sycophants. What have we to lose?"

Men grumbled, and Cormag stood again, moving close to Brian. A show of support, William presumed. The two were as thick as thieves.

"My brother has the right of it. We reach out to other clans who've been the victims of the mad king, and to the Viking settlers. If we convince them to ally with us before the Morays and the king can sink their claws into them, it can garner the strength we need to confront the king. We can let him know under no uncertain terms who retains power in the Highlands."

The hall erupted in a cacophony of cheers and pounding on the tables. William huzzah-ed along with them.

But as he shared a cautionary look with Ailbert, a darker thought crossed his mind. How many clans and warriors might join them? And if they did, the clans might have a show of force numbers, but what exactly were they going to do to put the king in his place? He knew of only one way to temper the power of a tyrannical king.

Execution.

Chapter Twelve

Ailith spent several days with William, traipsing closer to Dunnottar, but not all the way to the stronghold, yet. She had to play as though she only had a general idea of where the fungus might grow. If she pointed him directly to the slopes near Dunnottar castle, he'd ask how she knew exactly where to go. Her falsities about the Vikings would only pique his curiosity and lead to more questions.

Questions she couldn't answer.

Each night she ate her evening meal at the keep under the watchful glare of Mairi, and was practically asleep by the time she reached her chambers. She had drifted asleep in the low, wide tub that Leitis had brought up for a bath. Weary though she was, Ailith was more than grateful for it. Warm water and a hard ash soap scented with rosemary and heather cleaned several days of digging in dirt and under plants off her skin.

She was weary not only from her efforts, but from the mental fatigue of each day's pretense. Her language and word usage had shifted, so she at least sounded more like she belonged here. But it was all so much work. Keeping up her daily facade tried her brain, and today a headache had formed behind her forehead. Mairi's glare hadn't helped at all.

Another, equally pressing concern had sprung into her mind after the day's quest with William. Before bringing her back to the keep, he kissed her again, each kiss more passionate than the last, until rational thought was gone, his face was pressed between her breasts, and his hand so high on her thigh that his fingertips brushed against her woman's curls.

She had gasped and snapped backward. William caught her before she fell into the damp, leaf-covered dirt. His pink-cheeked, quizzical face rose above hers as he panted and studied her face. Ailith had the sense that she and William had been intimate before, and now he couldn't understand why she was essentially rebuking him.

Ailith dipped the cloth in the cooling water and wiped at her throbbing forehead. Eventually she was going to have to bed him–she was marrying him, after all. And while he was handsome and attentive enough to make the prospect of sleeping with him more than acceptable, exciting even, she struggled with the lies and half-truths that came with it.

Having sex with him wasn't the issue, but getting pregnant *was*.

Ailith might have no idea what she was doing in this time, trying to save a plant that might make it to the 21st century and save millions of lives, yet she knew she was not ready to bear a child.

As she reclined in the bath, letting the rich scents of rosemary and heather swallow her senses, she placed the cloth over her face and considered her options. Not sleeping with him wasn't an option, not based on what she knew about hand-fasting and betrothed couples in the Highlands. And once she was married, he'd expect her to perform what people here called "wifely duties." There was the three-day method, but again, he'd expect to lie with her a lot more than that, and how might she begin to explain the science behind the rhythm method?

And she didn't even want to think about how often that method outright failed.

A form of birth control then. What did women use in this time? Barriers-oils and wee bits of cloth.

Honey. Ailith recalled that honey was often used but mixed with something else. An oil? What was it called?

Fern. Worm fern.

Feck. Honey was in ample supply, but where might she find worm fern? And who would she ask? Not Mairi for certain.

Mayhap Leitis could help me out?

She didn't realize she'd fallen asleep until Leitis opened the door, and the squeaking hinges woke her.

"Och, milady. Lounging in the bath. Do ye feel washed?" Leitis asked as she bustled into the room with a long linen cloth to use as a towel. Ailith blinked and wiped the wet cloth across the back of her neck under her pinned up hair. Then she hung it over the tub's edge and stood, her skin pimpling against the chill as she wrapped the linen around her. Using buckets, Leitis scooped then dumped the water out the window until the tub was mostly empty.

"I'll shove this to the hall then send up a lad for it. Ye should find your léine and your sleep. Ye appear drawn, milady. I had hoped that your illness might have abated by now."

Ailith had donned her léine and sat on the bed, unpinning her hair. "Illness?"

Leitis's lips pursed briefly before she spoke. "Your fever? Many of us have noticed ye seem a bit, weel, off. And now with ye running away every afternoon –"

Ailith sat up straight. "I'm no' running away. I'm . . ." What was she doing? Searching for mushrooms? That sounded like something an ill person might say. Flirting with William . . . that sounded like something a bride-to-be would say. And if that were the case, then asking about worm fern might not be a stretch.

"May I ask what ye are doing?"

"I'm spending the time with William," Ailith announced boldly with a lift of her chin.

Leitis paused and she slowly set the bucket down. Her head turned to Ailith, and a knowing smile curled her lips into her apple cheeks.

"Och, spending time with your handsome mannie. No wonder ye are away every afternoon!"

Stifling a satisfied grin, Ailith set the last of the pins atop the linen and worked her fingers through her thick curls as she considered the best way to ask Leitis about the worn fern.

"Do ye have something ye need to ask, milady?" Leitis stretched tall and looked directly at Ailith. Direct and to the point. Ailith loved that about Leitis.

"Aye. We are no' married yet, and with everything that is going on in the Highlands, I would prefer, that is to say, if I can avoid getting . . ."

She was not as direct as Leitis and licked her lips.

Leitis spoke, thankfully, and saved her from having to ask more. "And ye want something to stop him from putting a bairn in ye," she stated with certainty.

Ailith bit her lip and nodded. Is this how conversations about sex and birth control went? Her mother had died when she was young, so she'd never had the opportunity for the sex talk with her, and her father had left those conversations up to the school and her friends. A community of experienced and knowledgeable women was not in her wheelhouse.

"Aye," Ailith answered with hesitancy. "Do ye ken something that might work? At least until I'm wed and these threats are gone."

Ailith might be hesitant, but she was no fool. She understood the impact of religion on the Highlands. Not as rooted as it was in other places, like England and populated cities and towns, but gaining a foothold.

"I've heard of honey and worm fern oil, but I dinna ken where to find worm fern."

Leitis glanced at the door before stepping past the tub to Ailith and leaning in close.

"Let me finish here, and I'll return with a wee pot of fern oil and honey. Dip a bit of cloth in the mixture and place it inside ye, far up." Her eyebrows crinkled at Ailith. "Ye ken what I mean, inside?"

Ailith nodded quickly and Leitis exhaled. "Och, aye then. I'll bring it up. Make sure ye have it in place before. Dinna let him see ye use it. And make sure ye hide it well, in your trunk. No' all men are understanding of these things."

Nay. Nay, they are not.

Ailith smiled at Leitis, a slim, grateful smile. Leitis patted her hand. "Och, milady. No wonder ye've no' been yourself. Ye've had a lot on your mind." She stood upright and held out her hand. "I'll take the linens and send for the lad for the tub. If ye are asleep when I return, I'll set it under your kirtle there on your chair."

While not intended, Leitis's motherly tone wrenched Ailith's heart. It was nice to be taken care of amid all this craziness, even if it was just for a little bit.

Ailith climbed under her blankets and arranged her hair on her pillow. She left her candle lit for when Leitis returned, in case she was asleep. She never heard the door open and close again that night. Sleep took a hard hold on Ailith and did not let go until morning.

It wasn't a restful sleep. Ailith tossed and turned, squirming under her blankets as her mind churned, filled with a jumble of thoughts and worries. No images, no activity, only a swirl of color. Her dream mind saw it as tie-dye

A soothing voice called out to her from the nether, cutting through the turmoil burning in her head. *Keep your course.* It sounded like Eladon's voice. *Follow Ailith's path.*

Ailith tried to speak to the invisible voice, but nothing came out. Something gold flickered in that flow of lights. Gold dots. What were those dots? Ailith struggled in her dream, trying to make them out.

What path? What was Ailith's path? What course?

Then the light was gone.

Ailith shot up in bed, her heart slamming in her chest, sweat in a film on her skin. She knew that the voice had come from the Romani witch, while at the same time Ailith had the sense it wasn't her. It was someone else. The other Eladon.

The gold dots – those weren't dots, they were circles, like gold coins on a scarf.

Donning her yellow kirtle and leather shoes, Ailith stepped into the bailey where William waited. She paused on the stone steps that led down to the dirt and grass yard, her eyes on William's long, muscled

form as he held out his short-handled dagger to Simon. Her younger brother looked upon William with shining eyes full of admiration.

So she wasn't the only one who was charmed by the blond giant.

William grinned at Simon, said something to him that Ailith couldn't hear, then spun the *sgian-dubh* in the palm of his hand with barely a flick of his fingers. Simon's open-mouthed awe mirrored Ailith's. He did it again, then he cupped Simon's hand and placed the dagger in the lad's hand. With his larger fingers, he guided Simon's, showing him how to flick the knife the same way. After a few practiced tries, William took the bog-oak handled weapon back and tucked it into his belt, where he could easily grab it.

He tousled Simon's deep red locks before sending the boy on his way and turning toward the tower. His entire face brightened when he saw Ailith where she waited on the stair. She was frozen where she stood, the tenderness of William's behavior with Simon keeping her transfixed.

Such an enigma, William was. Hardened warrior on the outside, soft hearted and beguiling on the inside. Her heart trembled in her chest.

Be careful, Ailith! She instructed herself. *Stay the course.* And that course was to find the mushrooms and protect their growth.

"Ailith!" he called as he reached her.

He leaned in to kiss her hand, and the rich scent of the man, earthy with a touch of musk, enveloped her–a scent she had come to know as uniquely William, one that made her heart flutter even harder.

He kept her hand in his, and his thumb brushed over the back of her hand, sending shivers up her arm. But his sapphire eyes were narrow and questioning. What had she said or done this time?

"Are ye well? Ye seemed stuck on the stairs. Did ye see something that made ye feel amiss?"

Oh, laddie, ye have no idea.

"Aye, I guess I did."

William looked over his shoulder to where his steed fidgeted, tapping his foreleg. "Something in the yard?"

A slender smile tugged at her lips. "Aye, but 'tis of little matter. Shall we go?"

With his free hand, William swept his hand toward his horse. Ailith lifted her creamy yellow skirt and stepped off the last stair. William fell into step with her, transferring her hand to his other one.

As he boosted her onto the horse, she spoke up. Today was the day.

"I'd like to investigate the lands directly around Dunnottar castle today, if we may."

She made the statement sound like a question, but from her tone, he'd know it was not.

William sat up and gathered the reins slowly. He didn't answer right away, and Ailith knew he was figuring out what to say to her. That did not bode well.

"Lass, how important are these wee toadstools?"

Her back stiffened slightly. "Verra important. Why do ye ask?"

From behind her, she felt his head fall forward as he led his steed, whom William affectionately called Lugh, through the main gate to the dirt road. The horse ambled along as she waited for William to answer.

"Because I dinna want to take ye there. *A Dhia!* Ye dinna ken what ye ask."

She shifted slightly in the saddle so she could see his troubled face from the corner of her eye.

"Why? What do I ask?"

Clouds were patchy in the sky, allowing peeks of sunlight to burst through and making William's hair as shiny as a Highland sunrise.

When he dipped his head, his hair formed a halo that resembled paintings by a classic artist she couldn't name. Then he lifted his face to hers.

"As ye have seen, we are in conflict with the Morays. I had thought ye might recall the reason why?"

"The king." It wasn't a question. She knew the history of mad King Donald. Yet she also knew that as a woman in the middle ages, it might be dangerous to share how much she knew.

"Aye. Ye've heard Seocan and my uncle Cormag. The king's grab for power is bringing the Morays along with him."

"And ye dinna want to get too close to Dunnottar Castle because ye dinna want to encounter the king."

"Or the Morays. More than that," he said as he guided Lugh easterly off the beaten path. His arms tightened as they rode into the woods. A trail wove through the trees, underused, and evidently, more direct. "The reason for the Morays' unwavering support of the king is partially due to their clan lands. We will have to ride through a narrow stretch of Moray lands to reach Dunnottar. And if the king is there, I can vow that Morays will likely populate the castle grounds itself."

Stay the path.

How, Eladon? How if Gordon enemies littered the landscape like lice?

"Can we try?" she asked in a timid voice. The worst he could say was nay–she'd then have to try and locate the valley slope on her own. Not the best option . . .

He huffed out a deep breath that blew against her hair. "If I dinna take ye, will ye go there on your own without me?" he asked in a dejected tone. He already knew the answer to his question.

Ailith bit the inside of her cheek to stop the guilty smile that wanted to appear. She faced forward again. "Aye. I have to do this, William."

William huffed again. "Lass, I dinna ken what has come over ye. Yet I appreciate your desire in this." His lips shifted closer to her ear. "Ye've always been passionate. I just miss your passion for me." His tone was low, husky, and full of need.

Ailith let out a shaky breath. She'd been at Glenbervie for a fortnight, and in all that time, she had kept her emotions for William at arm's length. If they'd had a lustful relationship before her, then her lack of passion now must be frustrating him.

"Take me to Dunnottar. If I can find a measure of peace having found the mush – toadstools, I have the sense that my passion might be found, too."

He kissed her neck where it curved to her shoulder. "Och, Ailith, ye do try me. 'Tis a good thing I love ye as much as I do, driving me to the brink of madness as ye have."

He loved her?

Well, of course he did. He loved Ailith – he was marrying her after all. But would he love this new Ailith? This *odd* Ailith, the one who drove him mad?

Oh, the unseemly business of playing with this poor man's emotions! He had agreed to a marriage to a woman who was now someone completely different. Could he love this new, changed Ailith?

And would she ever be able to love him back?

They rode to the edge of the wood, and William narrowed his eyes at the clearing. The broad expanse of the sea was the backdrop, gray-blue waves kissing gray-blue in a marriage of sky and sea. The outcropping jutted into the sea as if challenging it, stone meeting bright green grass and brush as it rushed to the sea.

Dunnottar Castle rose off that outcropping, clinging to the edge of the land in perfect positioning for defense. With only the narrow strip of cliff-like land joining the curved outcropping to the mainland, the keep was surrounded on three sides by cliffs and churning sea. The only means of land attack was that slender strip of land, a death funnel if the stronghold was adequately guarded for battle, which William presumed it was.

He reined the horse to a halt, before they exited the woods into the clearing that unfolded before the outcropping. A tapering, well-traveled path extended north of the woods, passing over the strip of land, and ran right up to the first palisade wall. The wall itself was singularly unique in that the main castle entry was accessible only by a series of tunnels cut through the rock.

Truly a marvel in military defense.

Perfect for sequestering an overreaching king who was despised by his own clans.

Tightening his arms around Ailith, Lugh chafed under William's tense grip, pawing at the ground. Moray ground. His horse did not want to be here either.

He leaned close to Ailith so her hair tickled his cheek. "Are ye certain 'tis the only place ye ken where these puddock-stools grow. Are they that important to ye, lass?"

"Aye," she answered in a strained voice.

Rising tall in the saddle, William scanned the clearing. No movement from the road or the castle itself. It seemed safe enough.

If anything regarding the Morays or the king can be construed as safe.

"Where then? Where did your Viking friends say this wee plant might be found?"

Ailith pointed to the north ridge of the castle, where the land fell away mere feet from the road.

"There, I think."

William squinted, searching in the direction she pointed. He didn't see anything, but if the toadstools were small enough, he'd not be able to see them from this distance.

"Weel," he breathed out, "here we go."

He leaned into Ailith and kicked at Lugh's ribs. The horse moved like an extension of his own body, galloping into the clearing, crossing the path, and heading straight for the north facing valley slope. Curving more north before cutting back on the slope helped him avoid the steepest aspect, and once they were below the rim, he could tuck the horse against the slope and he would not be visible from the road, or hopefully from the castle as well.

Lugh picked up a bit of speed as he crested the slope heading downward, and Ailith pressed her body into his as they raced down into the valley at the edge of the sea.

Without slowing, William shifted to his right, leaning into the turn as he pulled on the reins. Ailith audibly gasped as he rounded the valley and reined Lugh to a walk at the base of the sheer valley wall.

Ailith was panting, breathless from the wild ride. William halted his horse with one hand, sliding his other around Ailith's waist to reassure her.

"We made it. Now, let's find your puddock-stools."

He slid off the horse first, then held his hand up to help her off. Her entire body trembled under his hands, which he thought was peculiar. He'd taken her on wild rides through the glens before, usually at her urging, her crimson hair blowing in the wind, against his face and making his excitement for her rise. Finding these toadstools must be consuming her. For that alone, he'd make sure he helped her find them.

Not that he was even sure what she'd do with them later. The MacIntosh healer had plenty of her own herbals that quite satisfied her. Ailith's obsession did not make strong sense. Mayhap 'twas part of her recent illness, this obsession.

Though she stood on her own two feet, she was shaking enough that he didn't remove his arm from her waist.

This part of the valley slope was heavily shaded, rarely seeing sunlight even at sunrise where it might slip over the sea to brighten the sheer face. Nay, this curve was eternally blanketed in shadow. Green moss grew as thick as fur and covered nearly every surface, blending in with the patchy grass and obscuring the summertime rockface.

The perfect place for puddock-stools. Ailith had been correct about that. He could even see a few white heads peeking from the grass, fat and oblong and fleshy. He pointed them out to Ailith.

Her face lit up with a brilliance that rivaled the sun itself in the shade of the outcropping. His heart surged in his chest. That was the cheery smile he knew.

"Are these the ones?" he asked as she left his side for the toadstools.

Gathering her skirts, she crouched close to the white plants, leaning in close to study them. In a smooth movement, she rose and shook her head.

"Nay. The ones we are looking for have a reddish pink head, white gills decorating the top, and they are verra, verra small."

"'Tis understandable why they are difficult to find." He tilted his head at her. "Gills?"

Ailith licked her lips and briefly averted her gaze, and he tried not to read too much into her evasive manner. After a moment, she reached down and plucked one of the white stools and returned her shining green gaze to him. She came close and showed him the plant.

"The underside of these have these ridges. They are oft called gills like ye see on a fish. See how flappy they are?"

Her hand held up the plant for him to have a better look, leaning against him as she did so. His entire body flared in immediate lust. Did she not recall that it had been over a sennight since he'd last lain with her? Did she not understand what she did to him when she was this close, when she touched him?

Nay, she must not, because she expected him to keep his eyes on the fat puddock-stool and not on her generous breasts that swelled over her kirtle to entice him.

William cleared his throat and shifted his eyes to the white flesh. "Aye, I see it."

"The toadstool we see has a small version of these on the reddish top, like freckles. And the ones we seek are small, like my little finger." She wiggled said digit at him, and in a burst of lust, he wrapped his lips around her finger and sucked.

Ailith froze, her green eyes wide. Her breasts heaved as he slowly dragged his lips up and off finger.

His lips then found hers. He crushed her to him, trying to touch and kiss as much of her as he could. At first she was stiff, then as his lips slanted over hers, pressing them to part so he could taste her tongue, she relaxed into him. Her arm slipped around his back and gripped his tunic, clinging to him, and his cock flexed under his braies, searching for her heat. He needed her, longed to feel that closeness with her.

He wanted her here and now, on Moray lands –

His entire body reacted, pulling his head up from their kisses.

Nay, no' on Moray lands. I cannae drop my guard.

"Ailith," he rasped. "I want to toss up your skirts and take ye now, but we are yet on Moray lands in the shadow of the mad king's keep. Let's find these wee puddock-stools of yours and find our way back to safety."

She nodded, a stricken look on her face, and he despised the king and his clan confidants even once again for robbing him of her body. For frightening her.

"Aye," she agreed, and grabbed at her skirts as she moved away. Her gaze shifted to the grass and moss, her eyes searching. "We must look in the crooks of rock, at the base of plants. They like to hide." She glanced over her shoulder at him. "So I've been told."

He did as she instructed, kneeling under the overhang of the valley's edge, peering into every tight, shadowy space he could find.

"What has made ye so interested in these stools as of late? Ye've never had an interest in plants or healing before."

Ailith was bent over, her fine backside facing him, and her hands held her loosely banded hair from her face as she studied the grass. "Aye, 'tis a sudden interest. When I heard it mentioned at some gathering, it piqued my interest. I dinna ken why. Ye ever hear something that ye just cannae put from your head?"

"Your voice," William told her.

Ailith popped up straight, her pale hands clutching her hair, and her shocked face staring at him. She stared at him for the space of heartbeats, then her rosy lips lifted in the most tender smile.

"Ye say the most loving things," she said with an odd lilt to her voice, almost as if she didn't believe it.

He shrugged and resumed his searching. "Why would I no'? I love ye, after all."

"I presume I did no' realize Highland men could be so affectionate."

William snorted as he brushed a plant to the side. "Surely ye jest. Ye recall your mother and father? They were the most affectionate couple I had ever seen. They had no qualms being that affectionate before others. The Christian God ordains that man is to love his wife, to sanctify her." He lifted his head and gave her a wicked grin. "I'm only doing what God ordains."

Ailith tittered. "Aye. I'm certain 'tis the only reason." She flapped her hand at him. "Regardless, I wanted to thank ye."

"Thank me? For what? Loving ye?"

She didn't answer right away. Finally, she looked directly in his eyes. She regarded him for a moment, then nodded.

His heart swelled heavily. Her statement moved him in a strange way. She was thanking him for a feeling he couldn't control? Of a fate he was bound for since he was ten?

He couldn't stop himself. He stepped over the plants to return to her side, and with a gentle hand on her arm, he turned her to him. He used his finger to lift her chin so her eyes, as dewy green as the moss under their feet, had no choice but to look into his eyes.

"Thank me for bringing ye here to this mad search for a puddock-stool. Thank me for protecting ye from the Morays. Thank me when I bring ye a gift. But dinna thank me for loving ye. Ye might as well thank me for breathing. Ye and my love for ye are a part of me as much as my mind, my heart, or my breath. I could no sooner no' love ye than no' breathe or blink or bleed. From this life to the next and for all of my days, ye are part of me, bred into my bones, and I will always love ye."

He kissed her again, a light kiss this time, one that sealed the vow he'd just made.

This time, she didn't stiffen or act hesitantly. This time her hand curved around his neck, pulling him closer.

"Lass," he spoke into her lips. "As much as I want to keep ye here in my arms, we really must press on."

She stepped back, tossed her head to throw her hair off her face, and cupped his jaw. Her eyes remained fixed on his.

"That type of love deserves thanks," she told him in a thick voice. "'Tis familiar to ye, but know this. The type of love ye profess is a rare gem indeed."

They returned to their search, his words of love tethering them even as they searched separately. William had begun to think this was all for naught–that Ailith had an odd quest but this puddock-stool didn't exist –

Then a hint of pink peeped through the blades of grass.

Nay –

He crouched low and brushed the blades of slender grass to the side. An entire cluster of wee pinkish freckled caps, no larger than his little finger, hid in the grass on this side of the valley slope.

By the gods, she'd been right. The wee fleshies had been here all along!

"Ailith," he called out. She turned her head to look at him. "I think I've found it."

The expression on her face grew serious. How were these wee plants something to take so seriously? He might indulge her, but he didn't understand a lick of it.

She lifted her skirts as she picked her way over the plants and came to kneel next to him. He held the blades of grass to the side to expose the pinkish plants. Dozens of them were clumped together around the patch of grass, extended to the left and upward. William released the blades and pushed another set of strands to the side. More puddock-stools. So many hiding in this one spot. If he hadn't been searching for them, he'd never have seen them. They were so unfamiliar, he did not believe he'd ever seen them before.

How had she been so confident that they'd be here?

William peeked at her in a side-long gaze, taking in the look of awe and wonderment she had at seeing these tiny plants. How did something so small bring her so much joy?

"Are there more?" she asked. He crept forward and pushed more grass apart. More pinkish caps. To the left, more pinkish caps. It wasn't until the mossy grass thinned where it met the stones that the toadstools ended.

Ailith sat back on her heels, her hands pressed together under her smiling mouth.

She appeared so pleased with herself.

"What now?" he asked, moving back to her. "Do we pick them –"

"Nay!" she shouted, then coughed lightly. "My apologies. No' yet. Dinna pick them yet."

He reached his hand back. "Weel, then. What are we to do with them?"

Ailith's eyelids slid down, squinting with consideration as she studied the plants tucked among the grasses.

"I dinna ken. No' yet. I have to think on it."

What was there to think about? If the plant was useful as an herbal, shouldn't she want to collect it, dry it, and add it to mead or put in a poultice? Why leave it here?

As he looked upon her studious gaze, he knew she would not tell him. At least not yet.

Still the odd Ailith, but he had to admit, he liked this fiery side of her. She'd always been bold, now she was bold with purpose. And that was a powerful Ailith. Give him a powerful woman over a fragile one, any day.

Aye, contrary though it seemed, he not only loved Ailith, he liked her as well.

His cock surged again.

And he'd show her, once they were off Moray lands.

Chapter Thirteen

I did it, Ailith thought as William took her back toward Glenbervie. *I found them.*

But that was only the first step. Now she had to figure out how to save them.

Keeping the king from razing the land, of course. But what else? She tapped at her chin as William guided the horse deeper into the woods. Could they be replanted? She had propagated lots of different plants on her father's farm but never mushrooms. Spores were in the gills – those could be planted. And if there were filmy roots attached to the base of the mushroom? That usually worked with other plants, setting those roots into the dirt. Mayhap it could work with these fungi as well.

She pressed back against William, a flush of satisfaction warming her. Those were tomorrow problems. She had found them, and for now, that was all that mattered.

And she had a today problem to deal with.

William and his shockingly ardent affection. It was one thing to sleep with a man–that was just physical. William made it feel like he truly loved her.

Fool–of course he did. He loved Ailith.

Which made sleeping with him more difficult. What if she couldn't return his deep affection? He must have noticed it already.

The horse shifted, and his strong thighs tightened against her. Not that she didn't want him. In fact, the more time she spent with him, the more she found herself *craving* him. Physically, he was an ideal man–more muscled and defined than any other man she had bedded. But he was also emotionally attractive. And that went a long way in helping her make this decision.

That and the fact he hadn't pressed the issue overmuch. He could have. As her betrothed and in reality, he could have forced her against her will. It wasn't like that wasn't socially acceptable in the tenth century.

But he hadn't. He wooed her, even though he already had her. And oh, did he woo her.

She rested her hand on the leather pouch hanging from her belt. She had placed the small corked pot in the pouch, along with a small swab of cloth. Leitis had been true to her word, leaving the kit on the chair under her kirtle. That morning, Ailith had put the pot and a few pieces of cloth into the pouch. The rest of the patches she had put in a separate pouch in her trunk.

Not that she had planned for anything to happen between her and William, but only a fool would ignore where their time together had been heading. And now that she knew him better, bedding him would be an easier task. Mentally, that was.

Physically, she was already there. He was a sexy blond Adonis, with intense blue eyes, strong hands, and muscled thighs. Yeah, she was already there.

Balancing on the saddle, she reached into the leather pouch and, keeping the wee bottle inside the pouch so as not to be seen, she doused the tiny swath of cloth with the honey and fern oil mixture. Stabbing the cork back into the pot and keeping one hand on the saddle, she reached under her skirts and pressed her finger with the swath deep inside her sheath. She tried to keep as still as she could, so he would see what she was doing or question why she was moving so much.

It wasn't perfect, and she had to hope it was in the right place as she wiped her hand on her léine then adjusted her skirts.

With William's legs tight against her thighs, Ailith inhaled deeply, gathered her courage, and rested her leg on his thigh. High on his thigh.

Her insides quivered for him, but not her heart, and she worried that sleeping with him would send the wrong message. Fearing any overt gesture on her part might send the wrong message, she wasn't ready to be bolder than that in invitation.

She didn't have to be. William immediately reined back the horse and stopped in the middle of the woods.

With a deep, guttural groan, his arm snaked around her waist, crushing her back to his chest, and he pressed his lips to the curve of her neck. His lips were warm, ardent, and the touch of his tongue on her skin sent a shiver down her back and a heat built between her legs.

Oh yeah, she was there.

And he needed no more invitation.

William reined the horse into a thicker copse of trees, well hidden from even the narrow trail through the woods. He moved with purpose, heated, as if she could feel his need buzzing off him like a live electric wire. And his palatable desire drove hers. Her heart slammed inside her chest as he slid off the horse and threw the reins over a low-hanging branch.

Then his arm was around her waist again and his lips crashed onto hers, driven by the raging need she saw in his face and in his movements. His lips ravaged her lips, her jaw, her neck, and his hand cupped her breast, gripping it through her kirtle. Everywhere he touched her, she burned until her mouth kissed and bit and ravaged as much as his.

She shifted under his grasp, leaning forward to give him better access. His hand moved and slipped past the square neckline to her loose breasts, cupping one and dragging his thumb over the already hardened nipple. He groaned into the skin under her jaw–no, it was more like a gnarling, huffing sound of a man completely lost in his own raw desire.

That sound kindled her passion more, strung her higher like a soaring bird rocketing toward its zenith. How long since she'd been with a man? A man that drove her to the brink with his kisses and touch? Too long. And William was hitting every mark to drive her lust.

Her lust for this man.

William's gnarling became a snarling groan, and he lifted her from the ground and spun, lowering her into the spongy grass and leaves that carpeted the ground. Her hair spilled from its bindings in a dark vermillion pool against the green. He hiked up her skirts over her thighs to the ruddy cinnamon curls between her pale thighs. Instead of rushing to satiate his need that made itself known at the front of his braies, he paused a moment with his fingers digging into her fleshy thighs, staring down at her enticing entrance.

Keeping her gaze lowered to his chest, Ailith lifted onto her elbow. "William?" she asked in a raspy whisper.

"Beautiful. Every part of ye is beautiful, your wild red hair, your eyes as green as the glen, your breasts that make me lose my thoughts. But here, where ye welcome me into your body, 'tis the most beautiful because 'tis here where I do more than look at ye or can touch ye. I become part of ye, sharing that beautiful body. 'Tis the part of ye that takes me in and gives me all of ye, makes us one. Sometimes 'tis all I can do no' to stare and let the mere thought of it consume me."

She closed her eyes at the power of his words, letting them wash over her like the warm surf. His finger left one of her thighs and brushed over the curls, his finger dragging between the cleft. Her head fell back and she lowered herself to the ground, losing herself in the sensations he stirred deep in her belly.

He touched her intimate folds once more then shuddered and shifted over her. "I cannae wait, lass. I cannae –" he rasped as he freed his engorged cock from his braies. The whetted tip swept over her inner thigh before finding home – the inviting opening between her legs. Without another word, he sunk deep and she arched her back to accept his length, all of him, filling her completely. His cock was as long and thick as the rest of him.

Her fingers dug into the damp ground as he shoved himself to the hilt. Then he paused, holding himself over her, his blond hair falling across his closed eyes, and he uttered the most animalistic groan.

They were silent, with only the wisp of the wind in the trees and the crinkling of the cool leaves under her backside. He rocked against her hips over and over, his thick cock reaching deep inside her, touching her most intimate parts, and flicking over the most sensitive spot as his staff dragged out.

She moaned, breaking their silence and her hands moved to his hips to pull him closer, drive him deeper. The shocking tingle of her own orgasm built low in her belly, a titillating sensation that crept through her body, up to her breasts, down her arms, until it enveloped her mind in a haze.

William's thrusts increased, slamming against her hips as his need grew more wild, more desperate, slowly losing control. He growled and grunted as he dove into her, deep and out, in her sheath and dragging over her swollen folds until she arched again, driving her hips to meet his frenzied movements, and cried out in a series of breathless puffs. Then she found her moment, soaring as high as she could. Her nails dug into his buttocks as she came, chanting *Oh God,* as her moment of release engulfed her.

Och, he was good.

Through slitted eyes, she noticed his own blue gaze boring into her, and she slammed her eyes closed. Once she arched her back, William did lose control. His thrusts became unpaced, slamming into her with wild abandon as he chased his own heights. His cock spasmed inside her as he froze, his body hanging over her as he grunted with each flex as he spurted into her.

He exhaled harshly, and his eyes refocused on her face. The love that shone from his was as tangible as his staff inside her, and it made her heart clench in her chest. He kissed the tip of her nose, disarming her emotionally conflicted thoughts.

"Dinna make me wait a fortnight to be inside ye again, *mo muirninn*," he said breathlessly (*My love?* she thought, trying to translate with her swirling mind). "I cannae wait that long."

Then he kissed her, a long tender kiss, before he sat back on his knees, pulling his sated cock out. A sensation of emptiness caught her unaware, as if removing his cock also removed a part of her, as if she lacked a part of her that could only be filled by him.

She sat up as well and looked him up and down. She had the sense that she should say something, fill the quiet. What would Ailith say in this moment? But she had nothing, and what if she said something that gave her away? She felt so open, so exposed after this intimate moment. Better to remain quiet until she could understand the leap she had just taken with William without the fear of revealing herself or making him think she was even more *fevered* than he already believed.

And in a way, she was in a state of shock. If nothing else, this moment in the woods made it real for her that she was going to have to marry this man. This wasn't a casual relationship, and she had never considered marriage, at least not in her twenty-one years. To have it right here, directly in front of her, to a man she'd only known a couple of weeks? A light sweat sprung out on her forehead, a sweat unrelated to her sexual escapades with William.

What if he learned who she really was? What she really was? The shock of it all robbed her of her words.

William held out his hand and helped her rise, then walked her back to his horse.

"I'd rather remain here and spend the afternoon between your thighs, but your brother and his wife would have my hide. Best to get ye home."

She turned to him before they mounted, finally finding her own voice. "Can we return tomorrow? I'd–"

William grinned widely. "Och, lass. As long as I can bed ye in the wood again, we'll ride anywhere ye want to go."

His words somehow managed to light a fire of desire deep in her belly and curl around her heart, and she leaned into him as they rode back to Glenbervie.

Mayhap marriage to the man wouldn't be so dire a thing, she thought.

Chapter Fourteen

If William noted Ailith's quiet behavior on the ride home, he didn't make mention of it, thankfully. Leitis gave her a sly side grin when she entered Ailith's chambers to help her undress. That good woman had to notice the leaves in Ailith's hair and the dirt stains on the back of her light gown, yet she kept her words to herself.

Though many of Ailith's thoughts were on William and her budding relationship with him, her future husband (*that* was a prospect she was still trying to wrap her head around), the image of those wee mushrooms was always at the back of her mind. Leitis chatted idly before departing, and Ailith only gave her half-interested responses. She had too much on her mind as it was.

The urgency behind the mushrooms eventually drove the titillating memory of William from her mind, and as she washed her face and neck (*the neck William licked and sucked on*), her mind worked on the mushroom problem.

She could do her best to protect the mushrooms under the ridge, but the Vikings were going to invade one day soon. No fence or one woman was going to stop the king from razing the land.

Stop the invasion? That would be ideal, but again, what could one woman do against a mad king? Prevent the Vikings from attacking Dunnottar Castle? Again, one woman against a horde of Viking invaders? Nay. Those were not solutions.

Again, the thought of speaking to William and encouraging him to have the incoming Viking settle and not attack Dunnottar entered as an option, one she immediately dismissed. If she mentioned the upcoming Viking arrival, he'd want to know how she knew, and that was a conversation she wasn't ready to have. Not yet.

So, replanting. But that took so long, and she might not know if the mushrooms took root or if she planted them far enough away until it was too late. She wracked her brain, trying to recall the map on the Dunnottar tour that showed the area razed and destroyed by the king in his fury. Was Glenbervie within that area? She didn't think so, yet . . . what if it was? Where would it be safest to plant the mushrooms then?

She dropped the cloth next to her bowl and climbed into her bed. She hadn't had an Eladon dream lately. Maybe she'd have one tonight, telling her the best way to keep these mushrooms around.

Ailith woke the next morning, dreamless. Pale sunlight filled the cracks around the window shutter. Either sunrise or a gray day, or both. It didn't matter–rain or not, she had to do something about the mushrooms she'd found.

Out of options, replanting around the Highlands, wherever she could, was her only choice for the moment. There wasn't anything she could do about the Morays, but the more mushrooms she planted, the better chance that razing the coast would not destroy them all. Not a perfect solution, but it would keep her busy, and it was a start.

After she dressed and ate Leitis's breakfast, Ailith headed downstairs. She had a few basic tasks to complete–gathering eggs and Mairi had asked her about weaving. Ailith hadn't woven before, not as far as she knew, and if the old Ailith could, there was none of that muscle memory in her fingers. Ailith hoped to duck out of the keep and avoid Mairi before she asked again. Sneaking out of the tower and keeping herself busy in the barns and stables, or in the kitchens with Leitis, had worked thus far in avoiding her brother's wife.

Plus, that woman's hard gaze unsettled her. Her brother didn't look at her like that, so if Mairi had concerns about Ailith, she hadn't shared them with Seocan. Or if she had, Seocan hadn't paid those concerns much attention. That put Ailith at a bit of ease.

Daniel and Simon hadn't looked at her crossways since the night of the confrontation with the Morays. Ailith had half expected him to ask her again about that night of the fight, about how she defended herself, but he had kept his questions to himself and remained the same kind and humorous man who had helped her with the tables. She didn't know what type of relationship Daniel and Ailith had before she arrived, but she appreciated the one she had with her brother's second-in-command.

Simon was oblivious. But since he was a younger lad, that didn't surprise her. He was too busy chasing the local crofters' daughters or picking fights with other young lads to pay much attention to his older sister, for which she was grateful. He was the one person she could be more of herself around and not have his eyebrow raise at something she said or did.

Adjusting the neckline of her kirtle, she ducked around the edge of the stairwell. With no rear door by which to escape the tower, she had to cross the main hall to reach the double doors, or sneak down the stairs to the kitchen level, and leave out the door tucked next to the pantry. From the sounds carrying in from the hall, the kitchens seemed the best option.

She had just stepped into the space of the arched doorway that led to the hall, lifting her foot to rush toward the kitchen, when a voice spoke loudly from her side.

"Are ye rushing off to spend more time with William?" the terse voice asked.

Ailith froze, one foot at the edge of the top step, and groaned inwardly. Almost made it.

Flipping her rope of crimson hair off her shoulder, she turned to Mairi with a huge smile.

"Nay. I have to attend to my duties," Ailith said, hoping Mairi would believe her.

Mairi's stiff expression never changed. "One of your duties was weaving with me. Why have ye no' met me in my chambers for that?"

Ailith licked her lips. She had no good answer. None at all.

"Are ye off to meet William again? Are ye skipping your duties to meet him?"

That worked as an excuse. "Aye. He's to meet me."

"A wee bit early, do ye no' think? He usually meets ye after noon-tide." Mairi's head tipped ever so slightly, and Ailith knew she'd been caught. There was nothing that happened in this castle that got past her discerning eye.

"What are ye doing with him in the afternoons? Other than the obvious? No matter how infatuated he is with ye, it cannae take that long."

Ailith's cheeks burned at Mairi's coarse assessment of her interludes with William, but what other answer did she have? She could not tell her brother's wife about the mushrooms. William might indulge it as a flight of fancy for the woman he loved, but Mairi – nay. She'd require a more pragmatic answer.

"We talk," Ailith answered in a timid voice.

Mairi's eyebrows rose a wee bit on her forehead. "Och? For hours? What do ye talk about?"

So many questions. Why was the woman so concerned with her romantic interludes with her intended? Was something else troubling her?

Ailith blurted out the first thing that came to mind. "Our wedding."

"Your wedding. For hours." She said it like a question, but it was more of a statement, one she did not believe. Ailith had the sudden realization that weddings in the Highlands in the middle ages were simpler affairs, not the expensive, protracted events of her modern age.

Mairi didn't believe her. That much was clear. She presumed Ailith was up to no good.

"And our life together," Ailith added quickly.

"Ye've known him since he was eleven. I dinna think 'tis anything left for ye to talk about."

Doubt colored every word that fell from Mairi's lips, and again, Ailith had no answer for her. Why was she so worried about Ailith's comings and goings?

Mairi stared at her for a moment longer, her light green eyes blazing. Then she tilted her dark head to the ascending stairs. "Come. Ye've been avoiding weaving for too long. I ken ye hate the work, but it must be done."

Oh thank God, Ailith released the breath that had been trapped in her chest. Ailith hated weaving. 'Twas as good an excuse as any to want to avoid it now.

Mairi walked up the stairs without so much as a look back, and followed her.

It was like she was walking to her doom.

The heavens must have smiled upon Ailith, or Eladon managed to reach out across time and work some magic because all Ailith had to do was carding. The complicated-looking loom stood unused in the corner of Mairi's cavernous chambers. One level up from Ailith's smaller rooms, Mairi's chambers she shared with Seocan boasted a carved, four-poster bed, a pair of arched windows that bathed the room in sunlight even on the dimmest days, and a large hearth was built into the wall, opposite the bed.

A tall wardrobe of rich dark wood was tucked into the corner, next to the loom. A brown wool rug covered the center of the chambers near the hearth, and two overstuffed gray-blue chairs sat atop it. A cradle was next to one of the chairs, where a squeaking baby rested. Mairi and Seocan's son, Morgan, whom Ailith had only seen in the main hall once before. Mairi was oddly overprotective of the lad, rarely bringing him out and keeping to her own chambers with him much of the day. Perhaps some of those terse looks Ailith received were a result of being over vigilant or sheer weariness regarding the baby.

Aye, she had servants and clanswomen to help with the bairn and visit, but what a lonely existence. A flare of guilt lit in Ailith's chest. But until this moment, how was she to have known this?

Mairi sat in the chair next to the cradle. She gave the baby the first smile Ailith had seen on her face and then rocked the cradle with her toe as she picked up her carding boards. Ailith bent over the cradle and smiled at the baby, too. A pink, healthy babe, chubby, with a swath of red hair. Definitely Seocan's son. The Gordon stamp was all over this lad.

"So handsome," Ailith complimented, and Mairi's tender gaze turned to her son again.

"He looks like his father, aye?"

The pride and love in Mairi's voice was unmistakable. The woman adored the babe and his father.

Would she feel that way toward William one day?

Ailith nodded, collecting her thoughts. "Aye," she answered truthfully. He would be the spitten image of Seocan one day.

She moved to the empty chair, and under the guise of adjusting her skirts in the seat, she watched Mairi work the carding board. It was hard, tedious work, the cards flattened and wove treated wool into a weak fiber, a roving, that could then be spun into yarn. Mairi selected different hues of wool from her baskets between the chairs and her forearms bulged as she dragged the teeth on the cards back and forth. Once she had a length of roving in the right shade, she moved on to more wool.

A new expression crossed Mairi's face, one of contentment, as she rocked the cradle and carded the wool.

Ailith slowly gathered her items and did her best to duplicate Mairi's movements. She was shocked at just how much arm strength it took to card the wool. Once she felt she had the movements down, she glanced at Mairi.

"Do ye enjoy weaving?" Ailith asked, hoping to find a safe conversation. Anything to prevent Mairi from asking more questions.

"Aye," Mairi replied, her arms moving in a steady rhythm. "'Tis something peaceful in working the wool, deciding the color, and knowing that eventually, it will become part of a beautiful kirtle or a fine plaid. And the peace is welcome in these troubling times."

Ailith cleared her throat. She alone in this time knew how troubled these times were, and the upcoming wrathful battle with the mad king played a large role in those troubles.

She didn't have it in her to lie to her sister-in-law about the precariousness of the situation, or offer hollow words of comfort. She tried a different approach.

"Weel, we can hope that the clans will no' abide these troubles much longer. If the clans remain allied, I'm sure the power of the king can be brought to heel." Ailith said it in an off-handed way so as not to sound like she knew too much about Highland politics.

Mairi paled to the color of skim milk at this, and Ailith immediately regretted saying anything about the Highlands. Mairi dropped the cards she was using as if her skilled fingers forgot how to function.

"Dinna say such things. I have asked your brother, begged him, to remain neutral and not ally with the clans against the king." She blinked rapidly and picked up her carding tools. "But he is a proud man who will do what he believes is right, even it if means refusing to listen to reason."

Her reasoning, Ailith surmised. But Mairi's tone was strange. Not authoritative but desperate.

"My brother but lives by his honor. He –"

Mairi slammed the carding paddles against her lap and sat up tall. "Damn him and damn his honor!"

Ailith forgot to blink with the woman's outburst. It was the most emotion she had seen or heard from Mairi since her arrival. Her controlled, stoic sister-in-law's reaction was so out of character that Ailith's tongue froze in her mouth.

Realizing the effect of her outburst, Mairi glanced at her lad to make sure she hadn't disturbed him, then smoothed her skirts as she picked up her carders again.

"I need your brother. I need him to live. He has a family, kin. Me, our bairn, even ye. I cannae have him lying dead on some battlefield on account of some misbegotten obligation to clan and honor. I cannae lose him."

Her last words were barely a whisper, and Ailith had the sense that it was a difficult admission for her, that she didn't want to reveal her weakness to Ailith.

The moment drew out, and Ailith wracked her brain to think of something to say, something appropriate that wouldn't bring up any more painful thoughts or admissions. Despite Mairi's stern ways, Ailith realized she was still a woman who loved her husband. Of course she feared losing him.

Mairi gathered herself and resumed pulling the wool between the carders. "This wool won't card itself. Let's focus on our work here," she said, her strong tone having returned.

Thankful for Mairi's regained composure and change of subject, Ailith copied Mairi's movements with her own carders.

"Do ye do this often?" Ailith asked, keeping the focus on weaving. Better to focus on weaving than to make anymore offhanded comments about the Highlands. She hoped that question wasn't foolish or gave her away.

Mairi nodded. "I try to do a wee bit every day. Some days I cannae. Too much to do in the keep or we're preparing for a gathering. But most days."

They worked the wool for a while when Mairi spoke up. "I understand why ye dinna care for it. Ye have always preferred more active pastimes. Outdoor pastimes. I should no' have been surprised ye have left the keep with William more as of late. Even with your fevered behavior, at least ye have not lost yourself that way."

Ailith let the words hang in the air. That was at least something–her departures from the keep weren't overly disturbing or different. And Maira sounded more like she understood than accusing her of nefarious intentions. A type of apology, perhaps?

Finally, Mairi asked the real question that had been on her mind. "Are ye feeling better? Or are ye still unwell?" Mairi's face had stiffened again, the contentment gone.

Ailith's gaze remained fixed on her work. "A wee bit. But I rather feel 'twill take a bit of time for me to be my old self. If I ever go back." It was a partially honest answer, and Ailith felt Mairi deserved that.

Mairi's eyes narrowed, however, as if she didn't fully believe or care for Ailith's answer. Their conversation dropped, and they worked the wool in quiet occupation.

After another hour, Mairi leaned over to survey Ailith's work. She clicked her tongue. "Better, but ye need to be more consistent in the coloring." She glanced at the large window, then back at Ailith.

"I've kept ye long enough, and we have a good pile of rovings. Off with ye, lass."

Ailith didn't have to be asked twice. She felt as if the worst, longest interview ever had just been completed, and she didn't even care if she got the job.

She peered into the cradle once more where the ruddy baby slept, then she gave Mairi a small smile and left the chambers, closing the door behind her. Mairi's hawkish gaze followed her until it disappeared behind the door.

Though it was supposed to be a quiet morning with her sister-in-law, it had felt more like a test. And Ailith wasn't sure she'd passed.

William arrived shortly after the midday meal, a bright spot in cloudy, gray skies. When he saw her, the hard lines of his face softened, his eagerness to see her chipping away at the warrior mask he wore. Sliding off Lugh, he tossed the reins over the saddle and rushed to Ailith, sweeping her into his embrace and off her feet. The kiss he planted on her lips was just as eager as his embrace.

Ailith couldn't help but smile to herself. A wee bit of sexy time and he was vigorously amorous. For lack of a better word, she thought it was cute.

"Have ye made a decision regarding the wee plants?" he asked as he set her down and walked her toward his horse.

She held up the leather satchel hanging on her arm.

"Aye, I must replant them. I must go back to Dunnottar, pick as many as I can, and plant them all around the Highlands."

"*We*, lass. We must plant them."

She paused and grasped his arm, eyeing him before reaching for the saddle. "How do ye have the time to spend your days chasing puddock-stools with me? Surely a man such as yourself has duties ye must attend."

Her gaze shifted around the yard to the Gordon clan milling about, digging in the gardens, getting water from the well, tending animals, hanging laundry, carrying baskets of food or supplies–so much activity to keep a castle running, and that was just out here. It didn't include all the duties inside the tower, or the duties those in power had to attend. Politicking, settling disputes, ensuring the clansmen and women had all their needs met.

While William wasn't a chieftain's son, he was the nephew. Surely that granted him some measure of clan duties?

William wrapped his arm around her to boost her up into the saddle. "Aye, but sword practice and discussions with my father and uncle can be done in the mornings and evenings. And my clan encourages my time with ye. This alliance will do much for our clans. Did ye ever wonder why your brother never put a stop to your outings with me?"

Ailith reached the saddle and stilled. *What?* Her mind went to the past week, where she had been given free rein of the keep, with few obligations. Only Mairi had called her out on it. Ailith had believed that she must have always been a bit of a wild child–comments from others supported that idea. Not once had she considered that her brother and clan chieftain was permitting that behavior to the clan's benefit.

Women in the middle ages were oft treated as chattel. Why should it be no different for the sister of the chieftain? That put her perspective of marrying William in a different light. Had this been arranged, or had William and Ailith really wanted to marry?

What difference does it make? she asked herself. Marriage to William was an inevitability. Why care if it was arranged or not? But with how snugly William fit his body against her backside and how tenderly he had treated her over the past several days, she had to believe that there was more fondness in this betrothal than mere agreement or politicking.

He guided the horse to the main gate.

"Truthfully, I had no' given it much thought."

"Thinking about your wee stools?"

Her lips thinned and she turned profile to him, nodding.

"And mayhap thinking about our wedding? My uncle and your father would prefer it to happen sooner. What say ye?"

Ailith looked ahead at the path that disappeared into the mist that had started to gather. She sniffed the air. Rain soon?

"What does your uncle say? When would he prefer we marry?" Since she had no idea when her wedding was actually supposed to take place, that seemed a better reply. Why hadn't Mairi mentioned it? Maybe she wasn't happy with the arrangement?

"Cormag and your brother only mentioned performing the ceremony soon. I had the sense they would prefer within the month, or even a fortnight if possible." Ailith's stomach dropped. *A fortnight?* William kissed her neck before continuing. "The sooner the better for me. I cannae wait to have ye in my bed every night." His sultry voice was like a velvet ribbon slipping over her skin.

His bed. At the MacDougal keep? *Oh no.* Another thing she hadn't considered. She felt like she had allies in Leitis and Daniel. How could she leave and live in a castle where she knew no one, again? Especially when she was supposed to know those people?

How long might she feign an illness to cover herself at Drumoak?

"If Cormag and Seocan wish it, then it should happen as they command."

He shifted behind her. "Aye, we are at the whim of clan politics. But what do ye wish?"

Ailith's breath was heavy, and she was sure that he could feel her bones shaking. How to answer that? She had given up any real control of her life the minute she laid in the Romani woman's bed. How could she have any say in it now?

And more than that, what did she wish? A single woman in the middle ages was a dangerous proposition. A man like William, one who indulged her whims and drew blood in her defense, one who was a powerful, handsome Highlander and a romantic poet at the same time, might be the perfect way for her to do what she needed to.

But it still felt like lying. Was it fair to lie to William this way?

She sighed quietly. What other choice did she have?

"I wish to marry ye," she said quietly, not quite feeling the truth in her words. Resignation. That was what she felt. "And aye, sooner would be best."

William had led the horse into the woods, taking the shortcut through the Moray lands as he had the day before. Today, though, he seemed distracted by her. He held the reins with one hand and his other touched her–around her waist, brushing over her thighs, caressing her arm and neck, sweeping the loose braid of her hair off her neck so he might kiss it. He was making it difficult to focus on anything–mushrooms or weddings–with his tender touches.

"Mayhap if the weather holds, we might dally in the woods on our way back?" he asked, sweeping his tongue over the tender skin behind her ear. She shivered. A flare of lustful excitement bloomed low in her belly. Before she could answer, William stiffened at her back and tall in his saddle. He tilted his head as if to listen to the air. Ailith heard nothing.

No chirping birds, no skittering animals, nothing. The warmth he had kindled in her cooled instantly. She knew what that silence might mean.

She opened her mouth to ask, but he held up a finger, halting her speech. His face was hard again, his jaw set and his eyes narrow as he studied the trees. William slowly pulled back on the bridle, stopping Lugh in his tracks. She felt William's head moving from side to side, tracking movements, and she knew they were not alone. She scanned the trees, but as dense as they were here, she could not see anything other than branches and leaves.

She had that overwhelmingly fearful feeling a woman had as she walked to her car in a parking garage by herself at night, but somehow knowing she was not truly alone. When she felt the pull to either leave the garage the way she came or run for her car. What they were to do next was up to William, as she sat in front of him like an apprehensive observer with no control over the situation.

The horse smelled something and felt his master's body tense because he pawed at the ground and lifted his head with a snort. Leather cracked as Williams snapped the reins tight between his fingers. His left arm snaked around her waist and up to her ribs, pulling her back into himself, like a seatbelt, and Ailith willingly leaned into him. She might know her martial arts, but this was the middle ages, and as she saw with the fight at Glenbervie just a few nights ago, these men had no compunctions of killing, which made any conflict so much more dangerous.

With the slightest movement to the reins, Lugh's head shifted to the right, and the horse turned around in a half circle, facing back the way they'd come.

Good call, let's leave the garage, Ailith thought, her mind numb with fear.

A twig snapped off to the right, then another horse snorted somewhere off to the left. William's chest started to heave at her back, bringing in deeper breaths of oxygen into his lungs. Ailith would call it the fight or flight response, while he would call it readying himself for battle. William's heels tapped gently into the horse's flanks and the horse stepped forward. The bushes to their right rustled, and William pulled her tighter while leaning forward a few inches at the same time. A second ago everything was going so slowly, like a sick waiting game, but now time sped up in an avalanche, coming at them.

A horse and rider burst through the trees ahead of them and off to the right. William shouted and kicked Lugh hard. The horse leaped forward, and as his front legs slammed down to the ground, the beast was already in a full run. Ailith's hair whipped around her face as they raced away from the wood.

Two more men on horseback broke through the trees ahead of them–*three of them!* Ailith thought in a panic but Lugh was at a full sprint now, and they raced the men before they had the chance to react.

William held tight to Ailith, and she white-knuckle gripped the edge of the saddle. But even with William's strong arm around her, she still bounced around uncontrollably. She felt herself starting to slip but managed to stay on the horse, only thanks to William yanking her back.

The rider of the first horse was on their heels already, and with his mount only carrying one rider, he managed to come along William's left side. The man struck out, swinging his reins at William's face. Instead of letting go of Ailith and blocking the man's swing, William took the blow on his cheek. The man yelled and forced more speed from his mount, then swung to his right, colliding his horse into Lugh.

Neither horse fell but Lugh slid to a stop and reared up on his hind legs. His front legs kicked at the rider on the other horse, knocking him from his mount. William took advantage of the opportunity and dug his heels into Lugh again for a burst of speed.

Even with William's arm around her, Ailith shot forward when Lugh landed and tumbled over the horse's neck, falling over the horse. William was unable to stop Lugh or grab Ailith in time to stop the mishap, and she struck the ground. Despite the shock of the fall, she managed to keep her wits and tuck with the fall to prevent herself from breaking her own neck, but hit her head against a rock.

The shock of the fall and striking her head hindered her faculties and she took a moment to gather her wits before she got to her feet. Once she was standing and had wiped her hair from her face, she regained her senses as the other two riders passed her, going after William and nearly running her down.

William pulled hard on Lugh's reins, spinning the horse around to return for her. With Ailith no longer in front of him, William drew his sword and charged the two on horseback riding his way.

A noise came from behind her, and she whirled around, her hands clenched. The man Lugh had knocked off his horse stood in front of a bush, a dirty, barrel-chested man not much taller than she, and before Ailith could react, he backhanded her in the face. A sickening crack exploded in Ailith's head as she spun in a circle and fell to the dirt. She rolled with the hit and climbed to her feet, and the man stepped up and backhanded her again with his other hand. She again fell to the dirt.

This time, her senses remained intact as she didn't get right back up but looked over her shoulder and, when he moved forward to strike her again, struck with a savage sidekick. Her foot collided hard with the man's kneecap, and he screamed in a mix of shock and pain as he stumbled back, barely managing not to fall himself.

Fear left Ailith as anger replaced it. If this man wanted a fight, he was going to get it. She was no milkmaid to be smacked around. Women of her century were not used to being slapped without retribution. She sprang to her feet, taking up a fighting stance, calmly planning her next move as her sensei had taught her. It was time to put her skills to real use, not just sparring, and with his man's fury painted on his face, she didn't care if William saw her.

The man screamed at her, and he stumbled forward despite his injured knee. He aimed a punch at her face. She slapped his fist down and away with her left hand and stepped forward throwing a quick right jab at his nose. The man staggered back, grabbing at his face.

The punch was not powerful enough to break his nose but designed to cause watery eyes and fear.

The man's eyes watered but he stumbled forward again without any fear. He still saw her as a helpless woman. And she noted he lacked any good use of his right knee. Ailith kicked out a straight kick to the man's chest between his outstretched arms. The top-heavy man fell backwards again and with only one good knee, this time he tumbled onto the leafy earth.

As he bellowed and struggled to his feet, the metallic taste of blood filled her mouth from the two slaps the man landed. Raising a hand to her face, her finger came away with too much blood to be just a bloody nose. Her face felt sticky-wet and her hair stuck to her face and head. She must have cut her head in the fall from Lugh. Her adrenaline helped her hide the pain, but it was now starting to creep in, and what would happen if she lost too much blood?

The brute found his feet, his hand wrapped around his sword handle, ready to draw. Now she had a real problem.

In the microsecond it took for the brute's muscles to tighten as he slid his sword from its sheath, Ailith's mind flashed back to her Ju-Jitsu instructor and her weapons class.

When your opponent goes for a weapon, you either attack, and fast, or you die.

With her instructor's words loud in her ears, Ailith did not wait for the man's steel to clear the leather. In a flash, she shot forward, grabbing the man's shirt with both hands and snap-kicked his shin.

The man grunted but managed to free his sword. Her right foot snapped forward again, but not to kick, instead she snaked her foot behind his left ankle and used all her strength to yank it back. The heel of her foot struck and pulled his good leg forward as she shoved him back, releasing his shirt. Off balance, the man toppled like a felled tree. He landed hard, his sword flying into the damp leaves a few feet away.

The man was down but not out and, panting heavily, rolled onto his knees, yelped as he put weight on the ruined right knee, then tried pushing up with his hands and uninjured knee. Ailith didn't waste the opportunity his clumsiness gave her. Though it wasn't part of her training, she danced around behind him, took careful aim, and kicked as hard as she could between the man's legs, destroying whatever size balls he boasted to once possess. He lost all color and crumpled onto his face. She thought the brute looked just like a fish her father caught once and dumped on the shoreline, its sickly pale mouth opening and closing in silent protest.

Ailith wiped her sleeve across her face, then moved quickly to the man's sword that lay in the dirt and picked it up. She held it with both hands in front of her, pointing the tip in the man's direction as she backed away from him until she hit a tree. He made no attempt to rise, and his only movement was to vomit onto the ground right in front of his own face and to curl his legs into the fetal position, trying to recover the family jewels she had robbed from him.

Ailith wanted to yell at the man but she needed to catch her breath. Though she tried to control her breathing, she was panting from both the physical exertion and the rush of adrenaline that kept her moving. The clashing of steel from behind her made her turn to look around the tree. William was off Lugh, facing off with one of the men who almost ran her down. The third Moray attacker was face down in the dirt, sword still in his grasp and blood pooling at his neck, his fighting days done.

William had to focus on this Moray *greadadh* before he could reach Ailith. As much as he hated it, he had to put thoughts of her from his mind so he could destroy this man and save her.

The well-kept Moray man swung his finely-hewn sword at William's head. William blocked it with his own Pictish sword, but was forced back a step. William knew he was the better swordsman of the two–it was a skill he prided himself on, but he was also the more tired of the two. He'd been forced to fight both Moray men at the same time on horseback yet had only managed a lethal cut to the first man's throat because they were not trained to fight together. They'd each repeatedly charged him, getting in each other's way, horses colliding with each other more than not.

Fools, William thought when he impaled the first man's neck. When that man fell into the dirt dead, William spurred Lugh into the other man's horse, knocking the rider off. To the man's credit, he had charged before William had fully dismounted. With a sweep of his sword, William had blocked the man's forward thrust before pressing his own attack.

The Moray raised his sword high and stepped in, chopping down. William swung his own sword in a lazy arc, deflecting the blade as he sidestepped the man. He followed this by bringing his Pictish back with a slice as he stepped away and carved his blade through his opponent's left arm. The man spun around to face William just in time for William's sword to slice down and across his chest. Blood gushed from the man's arm and chest, and he stumbled backward, looking down at himself, his face a mask of shock.

William and his opponent both knew that he was beaten.

With a final step forward, William drove his sword deep into the man's stomach, face-to-face with the man as his sword exited the man's back. William gave the man a hard shove as he pulled his sword free, and he fell to the ground dead.

William then spun around and looked for Ailith, ready to slay the man who had chased her. He was praying that he wasn't too late when he saw Ailith holding a sword she had managed to find with both hands, staring back at him with concern written in her wide green eyes. The left side of her face was covered in blood.

He ran to her, taking her in his arms. The blood was from an open gash in her head. Her lip and cheek were also bruised. At her feet a few paces away was the final Moray man, the one who had given her chase, moaning and struggling to get to his knees.

Rage boiled inside him, taking over his mind and his sword.

The Moray on the ground was the one who caused her to fall from Lugh. He was the one who had marked her face. He was the one who put the look of shock and fear in her eyes.

And he would be the next one to die.

William kissed Ailith softly so as to not put pressure on any of her cuts or bruises. As he kissed her, she pressed her bruised face into his chest. William sheathed his own sword as he kissed the top of her head and his right hand snaked down and along her arm, ending at her hand. He gently pulled the sword from her fingers.

"Look away," he whispered to her as he stepped from Ailith and towards the man who was struggling to get to his feet.

William strode over to the man and waited patiently until he had eventually, painfully, managed to get to his feet. The man bent at the waist and held his balls. William moved behind the man and kicked out, catching him behind his knee and causing the man's legs to buckle.

The Moray's knees struck the ground, but William grabbed him by the hair with his left hand before the man could fall forward and held him upright. William reached over the man's shoulder while pulling back on his head and forced the man's chin upward. Then William dragged the man's own sword across his throat. Blood bubbled and poured freely down the man's chest as William sliced so deep he nearly decapitated the man.

The man's body jerked a few times in dying, then William released his hair, and the body fell face-first back into the dirt. William opened his hand, and the man's sword dropped freely to the ground next to its owner.

Neither would harm Ailith again.

Chapter Fifteen

William rushed over to Ailith, grabbing her upper arms. "Are ye well, lass? Were ye wounded at all?"

He looked her over to see if he had missed any of her wounds. He peered again at the gash on her head above her right eye, partially covered by her loose tresses that fell in her face and covered the wound. It disguised the wound, crimson on crimson. He gently brushed her hair off her forehead with his forefinger. The gash didn't appear deep, but it was fairly long, near her hairline, and bled horribly. Her cheeks were red as well, either from her falling or her fight with the Moray, and her lower lip bled as well. But that appeared to be all. Nothing dire, no mortal wounds. The bruises and cuts would heal, but the look of her bloodied and bruised face made his blood boil again. It took everything side him not to leave her to go stab the vile Moray once more.

"How did ye get the sword? What were ye thinking, attacking him like that? Ye should have waited for me." His voice was tender but tinged with concern.

Why had she done that? What made her think she could fight a huge man? And how had she bested him? He wanted to say it was impossible, but here they were, three dead Morays, one brought low by Ailith's own fighting skills. Her shock at the incident wore off. Color pinked her cheeks, and her green eyes blazed at him.

"I could no' stand back and watch ye take a beating and perchance lose with three on one! No matter how mighty a warrior ye are, those are no' good odds! How could I stand back and watch ye be slain!"

He clenched his teeth, his jaw twitching. "Do ye think I cannae protect ye?"

"Ye killed two men!" she shouted, her brow furrowing. "Of course, I trust ye to protect me! But if I can do something small to aid ye, make sure ye survive, then I will!"

His mind boiled. What was she saying?

"How did ye even know how to fight like that? I've never seen ye do such a thing!"

Ailith stiffened, and her eyes leveled at him. "Ye may no' have seen something yet it does no' mean it doesn't exist. I've scuffled with my brothers. And as ye recall from the gathering, I've had to fight off men before. 'Tis a frightening prospect, a woman who cannae fight off a burdensome man."

His mouth worked hard at her words, which held so much truth. Her logic, as frustrating as it might have been, was shockingly sound. He leaned closer until their foreheads touched.

"I would ask that ye no' do it again, but I can see from your vehemence that ye believe yourself to be some Viking shieldmaiden."

Truly that was what she had reminded him of, with her tensed muscles, bloodied face, and dark red hair loose and unruly, she was like Queen Boudicca come straight from the wild tales of ancient legend.

He briefly wondered if her hesitancy with him as of late was due to her fear that he might not protect her in these uncertain times. As quickly as the thought entered his head, he dismissed it. Nay, she had seen him fight for her and his clan in the past, even today, and knew he would fight to the death to protect her.

"Ye would know," she interrupted, her lips pressing into a thin smile.

William licked his lips, which twitched to smile back. His gaze flicked to her wound then back to her blazing eyes.

"I do ask, as my betrothed, try no' to put yourself in that position. 'Tis a small gash now, but it could have been so much worse." She opened her mouth to speak, and he pressed his finger lightly against her rosebud lips. "Yet if ye are in such a position, let me take the lead and kill who I can. I'd no' risk ye. Only if I am dead, or no' by your side to protect ye, then ye might fight your way out. Can ye honor that as my wife?"

She squinted at him as if measuring his words.

"Or if ye are losing or about to be killed," Ailith added and lifted her hand to cup his tense jaw. "I'd protect ye as much as ye protect me. If I can do the smallest thing to aid ye, then I will. But I will only act in the most dire of circumstances. I shall honor that as your wife."

She tipped her head at him, waiting. William dropped his chin to his chest. What choice did he have? And it still didn't answer how she knew to move her body in such a way to take a full Moray down as she had. Shaking his head, he lifted his eyes to her determined face.

"Aye. Agreed. And I shall honor ye and this peculiar skill ye have." He glanced at the dead Moray a few feet from them. "Ye learned how to do that tussling with your brothers?"

Ailith looked at the dead man and nodded.

"Well, then, his fault for trying to harm ye in the first place. Come," he said, standing upright and taking her hand, "let us get ye to Drumoak and treat your wound. 'Tis closer than Glenbervie, and I'd rather treat the wound before returning ye to your brother and receiving a tongue lashing for your injury. Mayhap we can tell him ye bumped your head?"

He settled her into the saddle, and she watched as he swung up behind her.

"'Tis better than telling him I fought off a Moray. Aye, let us wait on that bit of news."

***

The horse galloped as fast as William was willing to go, and Ailith was thankful he didn't push Lugh. Now that the adrenaline rush of the fight was over, the wound on her head throbbed, and each pound of Lugh's hooves sent a fresh bolt of pain through her right temple. She was sure she also had a fair-sized bruise on her cheeks from the backhanded strikes the man delivered. What she wouldn't give for an ibuprofen right now.

Mayhap a peppermint tea might take away the ache a wee bit.

Drumoak's heavy stone gate appeared out of the mist, rising out of the gray, followed by the taller stone edifice of the main tower. An imposing structure, surrounded by a tall stone wall that defended the entire castle structure. As they rode past the gate, Ailith could see another stone building that extended from the tower, forming an *L* inside and attached to the wall. To her right, a barn and stables, also made of stone, were set into the east-facing wall. In the southwest corner, a small church, more a chapel, also made of stone.

A true castle, larger than Glenbervie tower, this stronghold was more than prepared to withstand any attack and defend against fire or a raid. The MacDougal keep was the epitome of imposing security.

A trait that spilled over into Drumoak's warrior son.

The main door to the hall was not in Drumoak tower, it was in the longer part of the *L* at the back, far from the main gate to protect the entrance into the castle building. Arched oak double doors, as imposing as the rest of the structure, led to a cavernous main hall, larger and longer than the one at Glenbervie, with several roe deer horn chandeliers hanging from the beamed ceiling, tapestries and MacDougal banners hanging with pride, covering large swaths of the stone wall. Window slits provided narrow rays of light into the room, shining on several rows of tables, chairs, benches.

No need for outdoor seating here, she thought as she took in the sheer size of the hall.

Ailith tried not to gape at the castle, walking through living history as she was. She didn't need to give William another reason to question her.

"Muire! Sine! Help me please!" William shouted into the echoing depths of the keep.

A servant near the doorway at the far end that must have led to a hall jumped into action, racing away into the darkness.

William sat her at the closest table and peered at her wound. His worried face was close enough that his breath warmed her cheek. Her worried expression pulled on her heart in an odd way – one that ached and throbbed nearly as much as her head.

"I'll be fine, William," she tried to reassure him.

"'Tis still bloody. Wet bloody." His lips pursed as he moved her hair off her forehead. He stood and flicked his intense blue gaze to the arched hall entrance. "Where are Muire and Sine?" he huffed more to himself.

"Brother! What has ye coming in here, shouting and scaring puir Jeanne? She's fit to start crying. Ye do realize how frightening ye can be, aye?"

"Muire, please," was all he said, his voice strained, and from the corner of her eye, Ailith saw a young woman rush to her side.

"Och, lass! What happened to ye?"

The woman had blue eyes similar to William's, with thick brown hair that was braided and wound around her head. Her kirtle was a checked plaid, brown and blue, and Ailith wildly wondered how long it took to weave such a pattern. Muire went to work pressing against the wound, making Ailith hiss under her ministrations, and pursed her lips with the focus on her work. That lip pursing reminded her of American friend Angelina. Maybe it was the shock of the attack and her head wound, but she had the irrational wonder if she might become a friend with this woman.

Which would be a good thing, given she was to be this woman's sister-in-law. Not the best way to meet Muire, but then, this wasn't really the first time she'd met this dark-haired woman.

"Ailith, what have ye done to yourself?" Muire asked in a low tone, one that was almost conspiratorial.

She opened her mouth to answer, but William spoke up. "We were set upon by the Morays. We-I managed to subdue them, but Ailith was somehow struck on the head."

"I think 'twas when I fell off the horse," she said with a direct look at William, who dipped his head almost imperceptibly. They had their cover story, and as long as William was okay with it, he was right that it was better to keep the full truth from everyone else.

"Well, ye did a wee bit o' damage, 'tis certain. But ye'll live. And William's a lucky man," she added, patting Ailith's shoulder and half-turning. "Any scar will be hidden by your hairline and no' ruin the beauty of your face."

"As if anything could ruin that beauty," William corrected.

Muire snorted and smacked her hand against his chest.

"Ruin what beauty?" a voice called out. Ailith twisted her head a bit toward the hallway to see another young woman, this one the spitting image of William and about as tall as Muire, enter. "Ailith? Are ye injured?" she shouted and raced over, noting the blood staining Ailith's kirtle.

Ailith glanced over herself, her muddied and bloodied kirtle, her dirty léine, the scratches on her hands. She was a wreck, and Leitis would have her head over another ruined outfit. It wasn't like she could just run to the mall and buy another. She sighed inwardly–she'd owe more weaving time to Mairi after all this.

The younger sister fell to the bench next to Ailith and grasped her hand.

"No need for dramatics, Sine," Muire lectured. "She's fine. But we could use a bit o' honey, wine, and a small piece of linen if ye can find those for me?"

Muire's tone softened as she asked for her medicinal items, and with a pat on Ailith's hand, Sine, rushed off in a swirl of brown skirts.

"A fine lass, but her heart has always been bigger than her good sense, hasn't it?" Ailith realized that Muire was speaking to her and smiled weakly.

"Aye, a grand heart, that one," she agreed.

Muire returned her attention to her brother. "What happened with the Morays? Were they on MacDougal lands? Father and Uncle will need to know if there's been another encroachment."

William leaned his bright head close to her dark one. "We were in the wood and must have crossed into Moray lands unknowingly. Three came upon us and attacked."

Muire's eyes widened and her eyebrows flew to her hairline. "Three! Ye are lucky to have walked away with only a scratch! A fine warrior ye are, taking on three!"

William had the good sense to appear sheepish as he shared a quick glance with Ailith, who bit her bottom lip to hide her smile.

"Weel, Ailith managed to distract one, which gave me time."

"Falling off the horse will do that," she commented. William let the misconception pass.

It was better that way.

"And I won't ask what ye were doing in the wood," she continued, this time with a sly grin on her lips.

Again, they let it pass. The story of a pre-marital tryst in the woods was far better than the truth. And wouldn't it have gone that way eventually, had they not been interrupted? Aye, she told herself, it would have.

Sine returned with the necessaries, and Muire went to work on Ailith's forehead. She had a light touch and tender bedside manner.

I hope she's the clan healer, Ailith thought as Muire wiped away the wine to clean the wound and began spreading on a thick layer of honey to prevent infection. *Pus* as they might call it. She would have made an excellent doctor or nurse.

Once she was patched up, Muire and Sine walked with her and William to his horse. The women had offered to have her stay at the keep, but Ailith wasn't quite up for dealing with new strangers in a strange house. William appeared crestfallen but nodded in agreement.

Ailith looked at him from the corner of her eye as they walked. Maybe he understood more about what she was going through or was more accepting of her odd illness than she had presumed. If she was acting surprisingly to him, she could say the same, for he surprised her at every turn. Muire and Sine watched until William reined the horse back to the main gate back toward Glenbervie.

Chapter Sixteen

They arrived as the evening meal was being served. Mairi's piercing gaze fell on her hard, while Daniel and her brother lit up at her appearance. After brief words with William, Seocan resumed his supper as if everything was normal. The man masked his emotions well. Before leaving the tower, William swept Ailith into his arms.

"Are ye sure ye are well, *mo ruaidh*?" He peered at the wound hiding in her hairline. "I am worried for ye."

My red. He had called her that before. A pet name for her? Her chest fluttered at the endearment. She patted his muscled chest. "I'm well. 'Tis little more than a scratch."

He leaned forward and kissed the scrap of linen covering the wound that had finally stopped bleeding.

"I am sorry that ye have been embroiled with these Moray demons. Their destruction knows no bounds, it seems, not even for women or families."

"Can ye tell me what is going on with them?" she asked, risking the question.

She had heard and seen only bits and pieces, and she knew it would benefit her to know what was going on, to know if the invasion that was going to destroy the mushrooms was happening soon, and how much time she had to replant the mushrooms.

"'Tis apparent they are in leagues with mad Donald. The king is trying to divide the clans to weaken them, and some clans have fallen into step with him, feeding off the scraps of power he throws at them. The king has started to attack his own people, most recently the Grants and MacIntoshes, as ye know. Our clans, we share kin with the Grants, and these massacres have changed our discourse about the king." He lowered his head to press his forehead against hers. "I'm not sure what Cormag and Seocan and the other clans have discussed behind closed doors, yet I have the sense that something is rising. Ill winds blow from Dunnottar Castle, and I fear for what the future holds."

Ailith wrapped her arms tightly around his waist. *Ye have no idea*, she thought gravely.

He kissed her forehead again.

"Enough of these dark thoughts. Ye are alive and mostly well. We are together, and God willing, will be wed before the fortnight is out. All in all, I believe we fared well this day."

Ailith nodded her agreement. "Aye, it could have been so much worse."

"I do hate to leave ye, Ailith," William told her, his voice deepening with the emotion behind his words.

"Aye. I will see ye on the morrow?"

The side of his mouth curled upward. "We have a bit of planting to do on the morrow, aye?

Her face lit up at him. "Aye. We have to make up for today's lost time. I'll keep ye quite busy."

That curl of his lips rose higher, becoming more of a wolfish grin. "Och, I hope ye do, lass."

Thankfully, the next day when they raced to Dunnottar for the ridge shadowing the fungus, they encountered naught but the salty breeze and the fine mist that covered the Highlands. Not a full rain, but enough to make her dark crimson hair sparkle like silver and diamonds adorned her tresses, and not just raindrops and woolen string to bind most of her locks back.

Under the outcropping, William squatted with Ailith as she showed him how to delicately tug each cluster of pink and white toadstools from the ground. She encouraged him to make sure the tiny mycelium roots at the bottom remained intact where they could, but if that did not happen, or if the stool didn't have any, not to fret. She gently touched the under cap and showed him how the spores from the cap could also be planted.

"They'll just take longer," she reassured him when he yanked out another stool with no thread-like roots attached.

They worked side by side, collecting as many mushrooms as they could in Ailith's sack. With her hands in the dirt and the quiet comfort of William by her side, Ailith relished this rare moment of contentment. For the first time since she'd started this journey, her heart wasn't racing nor was her mind working hard to blend in and make this crazy plan work. It was she and William and the rain and their presence with each other, and it made her feel comfortable.

Once her satchel was full of the tiny, priceless plants, William assisted her onto Lugh, and they took another frenzied race across Moray lands. She had wondered why the king didn't have guards overseeing the lands, but the ridge was on the far side of the land bridge, and he believed he was subduing his people. Why have guards surveying one's own subjects? If there were any guards, Ailith had the sense they were watching the sea for invaders, not their own clans. Especially since the Moray lands buttressed the castle, and from what William had said, that clan was in the king's pockets.

William pushed Lugh past the Moray lands to the edge of Gordon lands shared with the MacIntoshes.

"Where, lass?" he asked, leaning into her ear.

That was a good question. Very little light. Wet. A lot of wet. And thick leaves or grass – that's where the mushrooms had been on the ridge. She had to try to replicate that same environment.

She shared that information with William. "Is there a place in these woods like that?"

He slowed the horse and sat silently behind her. Ailith studied the woods as he did, both for a place to plant the mushrooms and with a modicum of fear that another set of Morays would burst through the trees at any moment.

"I've got it," he said and yanked on the reins. Ailith gripped the front of the saddle as he swung Lugh around, heading into a thicket of trees.

On the other side of the thicket were several large stones, almost like a large cairn, on the long side, about four feet high and under a dense arch of trees. The north side of the stones never saw the light of day if she used the thick carpet of moss on the rocks as any measurement.

A slow smile slid over her lips.

Perfect.

William dismounted, then helped Ailith off the horse (*I really need to learn to do this myself,* she chastised herself). She eyed the shady pocket created by the stones, sweeping her hand over the damp smoothness of the mossy stones. Gathering her skirts around her knees, she crouched to the bright green grass, leprechaun green it was so bright, and pressed her fingers between the blades to the earth. Spongy, wet, and cool. Perfect.

"Aye. This will work. Here, I'll show ye how we need to plant them."

She started digging with her fingers when William flicked a small knife handle toward her.

"Take my *sgian-dubh*. 'Twill be quicker."

Accepting the knife, she showed him how to plant either the thread-like root end or the cap as needed, and he joined her, using another knife to dig alongside her.

For that moment, Ailith again was at peace. She could be in her garden at home planting morel mushrooms. She knelt in the misty forest, carefully digging a small hole with her knife, and placed a mushroom's thin rooted base into the hole and covered it with soil, patting it down gently. She planted several in a row before leaning back on her heels to survey her work. She smiled to herself, feeling a sense of accomplishment. If this worked . . .

Those pinkish rows were a chance. A chance for her father and Ashland. A chance for Eladon's grandson. A chance for the future.

If it worked.

But their job was far from over. They had dozens of mushrooms to plant, each one requiring the same careful attention. She moved from one spot to the next, planting and patting down the soil until all of the caps and roots were in the ground.

With the last one tucked into the black soil, Ailith sat back on her heels and wiped the sweat from her brow with the back of her muddy hand. She took a deep breath and smiled at William, who smiled back.

Now, all she could do was wait and see if her hard work paid off. Her heart raced at the prospect as she gazed around the woods. This was but one location, and if anything happened to these too . . .

They'd need to plant more.

She glanced at the blond warrior digging in the dirt next to her. She wanted to laugh at the sight of this giant Highlander jabbing at the dirt like a tow-headed lad. He had finished his last one and was wiping his knife against his pant leg. She handed him the *sgian-dubh* back.

"Are ye satisfied?" he asked, tucking his knife in his waistband.

"Aye, for now," she answered. She dropped her gaze to her dirty hands and picked at the soil under her fingernail. "But I need to do more. I'll need to plant more. And I'll need help protecting it, making sure they grow."

"*We* need to do more," William emphasized, his intense blue gaze fixed on her. "Why this plant, lass? Ye mentioned its benefits as a medicinal, but 'tis much work for a wee herbal. And how ye are about it, as though life itself depends on it." *Oh, William, it does,* she thought, but remained quiet. "What is it about this plant?"

She cleared her throat as she considered her response. "'Tis a very important plant in so many ways, mayhap ye could say life does depend on that. It can be used for illness, a cough, for breathing." Her eyebrows rose on her head. "Oh, 'tis useful to keep blight away from other plants! Very valuable for crops or gardens."

William crept closer to her as she spoke. "How do they do that? Did your Vikings tell ye? Ye see, many Norse and Danes have settled with the MacDougal clan, bred with us and became MacDougals themselves, as close to the coast as we are, and I've no' heard so many accolades over one plant." His eyebrows were high on his forehead.

Feck. He was calling her bluff. Ailith licked her lips and tried to ignore the heat wafting off his body and making her feel overly warm even in the cool mist.

She pointed to the mushrooms they planted. "Aye. See the red tops, and they stand out noticeably, but these little white pieces, as they grow, they disguise the puddock-stool, so it blends in with other stools and plants. Sneaky, aye? Then its roots cling under the soil and take over. They are good for getting rid of weeds or plants ye dinna want, or other, poisonous stools, because the red stool sneaks in and takes over. Then ye have a lot of these useful toadstools and no plants ye dinna want."

He didn't answer. Instead, he stared wide-eyed at her.

It was like lightning struck William's head and he froze, staring at her dewy skin and green eyes as bright as the moss surrounding her. Something she said – the puddock-stools disguise and take over. They are sneaky. His mind turned over her words as he realized that this same ploy might work with the mad king. More Norse settlers were supposed to be coming over the summer. Their dragon prows would distract the king, because he would surely attack them to prevent them from invading or settling. As Brian and Cormag had said, the last thing the king wanted was more support for the clans, and these incoming Norse were just that.

And these Norse, who were also mighty and violent Vikings, would fight back. While the king was busy attacking the Norse on the seafront, the clans could sneak in from the land bridge and strike from the rear.

They would have the king believe one thing that was really another.

"William, are ye well?" Ailith asked, narrowing her eyes.

He launched himself at her, excitement pumping through his entire body, and he kissed her deeply as his cock throbbed painfully under his braies. Then he yanked his head back.

"Aye, lass," he answered in a low, growling tone, "more than ye know."

Then he kissed her again, shoving her backward onto the spongy ground.

"William!" Ailith cried, and he paused.

"Do ye want me, lass? Tell me ye want me," he rasped.

The curve of her breasts pressed over her square neckline. He kissed one swell, then the other.

"I'll stop if ye tell me, but ye have ensorcelled me, even here, in this wood. I see ye in the mist and I cannae–"

"Ensorcelled? What? Talking about puddock-stools?"

He lifted his face and grinned at her. "Aye. Paddock-stools. Your passion, lass. I've never met the like, and the more I am around your passion, the more passion I feel. 'Tis like ye create more love and desire in me with every moment I am with ye. I had no' known such a thing to be possible, yet here ye are, concerned about a wee plant, and the passion ye have echoes inside me."

Ailith rested her hand on his cheek, scruffy with the day's growth of beard that made him appear more dangerous, but the fiery lust and love in his eyes tempered that danger.

He hated to admit it, but he was smitten by her. Rumors of her supposed fever or even her being touched by the fae had made it rounds in the clans, when it was this passion – just more of it. Ailith was willing to show her passion more, and if others believed it to be an illness or a curse, that was on them.

"William, I—" She stopped herself.

He lifted his chin, waiting. When she didn't continue, he kissed her forehead, her cheeks, and finally her lips again.

"If ye are telling me to stop, that 'tis too rainy or ye are sore or ye dinna want to, I'll stop, but ye must tell me know. If we go any further, I will no' be able to control my need."

"'Tis no' that, William. I want ye."

Her voice was heady and breathless, and his cock surged even more. He growled.

"Then if ye are telling me ye love me, spread your legs and show me, while I show ye my love for ye."

She squeaked as if confused. He waited, hovering above her, searching her face. His cock trembled–hell, his entire body trembled with his desire for her.

Then she shifted, slipping her hand between them, and hiked up her skirt. Her eyes never left his, and they shared their gaze, looking into each other's souls as their bodies moved. She parted her tender thighs, and William reached between his legs to release his staff. Ailith's hand reached his before he unfastened the laces.

He groaned his disappointment. *She's stopping me* --

Her fingers rubbed against his pulsing bulge under her wool braies.

"Let me," she said, and the rush of excitement in his groin shot to his head and removed all conscious thought. There was only one directive in his mind. To have Ailith. To sink between her thighs.

He rolled slightly so she had better access to his braies and unleashed his leather belt to pull it off. With deft fingers, she unraveled the leather lace holding his braies on hips, and shoved his pants down so his cock sprung free, searching for Ailith's warm sheath.

Expecting her to move her hips to welcome him, he shifted again, but her hand didn't move.

"Uh-uh," she breathed. "Not yet."

She wrapped her dainty hand around his thick, throbbing manstaff and squeezed. He groaned and dropped his forehead to hers.

"Remove your shirt. I want to see your chest."

"Lass," he begged.

She smiled and her hand moved, touching him intimately, sliding up and down until his engorged head pulsed. William gasped and shuddered under her hand's tease.

He whipped his shirt over his head and looked down at her again. With her free hand, she pressed her palm against the pale hair on his muscles, sinking her fingers into his skin.

"Please, Ailith," he begged again.

"Tell me ye want me," she said. His cock flared again. He wasn't going to hold out long enough to come inside her."

"I want ye, Ailith. All I want is ye."

"Do ye need me, William?" Her hand continued its tortuously erotic movements. His cock begged for release as much as he begged to have her. What was she doing, teasing him like this? And by God, why was he letting her? Why did this make him want her more? His gaze bored into her mirthful green eyes.

"I need ye more than breath itself. Now release me before I force your hand."

Her eyes narrowed slightly, and she released him. In that moment, he thrust forward with a snarling groan, sinking into the hilt with another shudder. Then his hips moved without his awareness, his need taking on a life of its own. Her fingertips dug into his shoulders, and he tugged at her kirtle and léine, releasing her ample breasts from their confinement to his deprived eyes. He hadn't seen her naked form in more than a sennight, and it was tearing at his soul. He gripped one breast as he thrust and she arched under him, as if offering more of her body to him.

Her hips moved with his, a frenzied dance of need and desire, of love and lust, his blue gaze clashing with her green one as he used his cock to show her just how much he loved her and craved her. And she used her womanhood to show him her love and desire for him. Together they gave and took and gave until his mind was gone, and his cock was as stiff as his sword and his bollocks clenched, ready to burst.

Then, with a hard cry of "Ailith!" he did burst, pouring his essence into her.

Once he was empty, he collapsed atop her welcoming breasts.

William kissed the one pink-tipped nipple, then the other, before pushing himself off of her. Ailith watched every movement he made--his muscles flexing and bulging as rolled over. He still wore his boots and braies, but with the laces untied, they were lowered and exposed the long, taut stomach and that sexy expanse of skin that led to his pale cock, still half erect.

On impulse, she ran her hand down that length from chest to belly and lower, relishing the feel of his body. It was the first she herself had seen it in full, and it was something to enjoy. Days of sword practice and a medieval diet crafted his body into something that young men in her time killed themselves at the gym for. And here he was, walking around the Highlands like that.

Sexy indeed.

He closed his eyes as she patted him, indulging himself in the feel of her fingers caressing the light hair on his chest and the lines of his belly. She brushed her fingers over his cock, and it twitched against her fingertips, readying for her again. His skin not exposed to the sun was pale, his blond body hair making his skin look like burnished gold.

Ailith rolled over so she was on top of him, her soft breasts pressing against his hard chest. Most of her tresses had come loose as they always seemed to and cascaded around them in a dark red curtain. His arms went around her waist, holding her in place. She stared into his eyes, tender and so blue, and kissed his full lips, biting the bottom one before she released him.

"I ken that I have no' been myself as of late, and these toadstools are a part of that. Once I understand more of this, I'll tell ye what is going on in my mind. For now, I am thankful ye have no' set me aside because of it."

His eyes squinted slightly as she spoke.

"I could no sooner set ye aside than I could tear my heart from my chest. I have loved ye for over ten years. Ye dinna think that ye've changed in that time? That I have no' changed? As long as ye vow to love me back, act as ye must. My body and my sword and my heart will be there all the same."

Her mind thought about the invasion she knew was happening soon–the invasion she couldn't breathe a word of without creating some real problems for herself. She had tried to drop hints, but how far could she go in mentioning it? Better to plant seeds of information and ask vague questions than risk it. She was already fortunate that William was willing to offer information about the politics of the Highlands as it was.

"Even if it means me doing more with the stool? Defending them with my life as necessary?"

His face tensed slightly, but enough for Ailith to notice.

"Why would ye need to defend them with your life?"

She shrugged one shoulder. "I dinna ken. I'm presupposing. Should such a thing happen?"

His gaze roved across her face, then the side of his lips twitched. "Then I presume I have to be there with my sword defending ye, so ye might defend these wee plants."

Ailith moved her hands to cup his cheeks. "Ye are a good man, William." She leaned forward to kiss him again, but the light blue of his eyes darkened.

"Nay, lass. Never think that. I'm a rough man, raised that way, to protect three things. The Highlands, my clan, and ye. Ye may be able to stand on your own against a single man, but know that I would do the darkest, most depraved things to protect ye and my lands."

She stared at him for a moment, evaluating his words. Did he not know that those two things were not mutually exclusive? At least, they weren't to her. If he helped with her plants, defended her, and continued to love her, then she could readily accept the rough version of William as well. She kissed him.

"Then, ye are a good man for me, William. 'Tis all I need."

William narrowed his gaze at her, an expression Ailith had seen turned on others, but never on her.

What had happened in that mere second to shift his entire visage?

He sat up abruptly, setting Ailith to his side in the damp grass, and turned away from her to fasten his braies.

"William?"

His broad shoulders hunched at her voice.

Her blood turned to ice and her dirt-encrusted nails gripped the grass. Was he angry at her? He had just vowed himself to her again, yet everything in his body now appeared to claim the opposite.

"William?" she tried again.

He huffed out a loud breath.

Is he pouting? Or trying to control his anger?

That sent a bolt of fear through Ailith. She had done so much that frustrated him already. Why now, in this moment, right after a romantic interlude in the grass?

"Can ye no' say it?" he replied in a ragged voice.

Ailith stiffened. What was he talking about?

"I know 'tis no' your way. That ye use touch as your way to show your love, but I do need to hear it, Ailith."

Ailith. Not *mo ruaidh. That is not a good sign.*

"I tell ye I want ye, I need ye, I love ye. Hell, ye just made me beg with those words. Yet I have naught but '*ye are a good man for me*'?"

Her lips parted slightly, inhaling a thin breath as if to speak, but nothing came from her. Ailith's tongue was as frozen as her blood.

Why hadn't she said it? Everything he had done and said for her was enough to make any woman swoon! And the way her body responded to him? The chemistry was remarkable. Impossibly so. She had never felt this way toward any man in her life.

So why didn't she say it?

He spun around, turning those blue eyes filled with hurt directed at her. It was enough to make her heart clench.

"We are to be wed, aren't we? Yet ye dinna discuss that with me. And ye dinna tell me ye love me. Why can ye no' tell me? Is it that ye dinna love me?"

His voice broke at that, and Ailith had no answer. Nothing.

Because to tell him the truth, that she was falling for him and did care for him – more than she probably should – meant telling him her darkest secret, and she wasn't prepared to do that. He wasn't ready for that.

Ailith cleared her throat and braced herself. She'd tell him what he wanted to hear if it meant that much to him. He was not wrong, after all. For all his declarations, she'd said nothing to him of her heart.

"William, I–"

He shook his head and held up his palm at her, cutting her off mid-sentence.

"Nay. I dinna want ye to say it because I request it. Or ye feel obligated. I want ye to say it because ye feel it and want me to know. I want ye to say it because ye love me and wish to wed me."

He dropped his hand and along with it, his gaze.

There it was again. Marriage. The death of her freedom cloaked in the trappings of love. Marrying a man who didn't know the person he was taking as a wife. William claimed to love her, wasn't that enough? Though she had known she was treading on this inevitable path toward the altar with William, she had tried to push it off as far as she could. Yet this wedding had remained fixed and now the moment was here. Not just the wedding, but telling William that she did love him and was going to commit her life to him. In this time, that would make her essentially his property, and he would have to learn about who she truly was.

There seemed no good solution to this predicament.

They sat in silence for the space of several heartbeats. Ailith searched her mind for a word, a sentence, something that might mend this suddenly broken moment.

Then he lifted his gaze and his eyes were soft again, his full lips pulling into a slight smile. He shook his handsome blond head as if to clear it and rid himself of his emotional outpouring and resume his hardened warrior appearance.

"My apologies, lass. With much going on, I should no' have added to your worries. Ye are here with me, sharing your body, accepting my words. If ye show your love differently, I should no' make demands."

Then he rose and reached down for her hands, helping her to stand. Surprisingly he didn't release her hands. After such a hard conversation, that he still wanted to touch her, be close to her, ran contrary to what Ailith knew of relationships and lovers' spats. Instead of pulling away, William leaned back in.

William had exposed himself to her in a way that was difficult and gut-wrenching for most people, Ailith included. Yet he had done it while she remained the ice queen, staring at him in silence. Yet he was still loving her, even as he ripped open his chest and showed his weeping heart to her.

Ailith squeezed his hand as he led her back to his horse, silently thanking him for his steadfast love. She hadn't realized just how much she had come to rely on it. His love had become a foundation for her in this strange time.

Life with William was suddenly more complicated, and she vowed to find a way to fix it.

Chapter Seventeen

Leitis clicked her tongue again when she came up to take Ailith's clothes for laundering.

"Please, Leitis. Leave them. I have no' helped with the washing at all and these filthy gowns are my responsibility.

Leitis snorted loudly. "No' all your fault. William has a wee bit of blame for the condition of your clothes."

"Leitis!" Ailith shouted as she gathered her blankets to her chest. Was this what the keep was gossiping about? Her escapades with William?

Not that they were wrong . . .

With a flap of her hand, Leitis draped the léine and kirtle over her arm. "Och, lass, ye are to be wed in less than a month. 'Twould be more peculiar if ye weren't with him."

She was glad that most of her clan was making that assumption. She was even more glad that she'd had the forethought to put the oiled fabric inside her before leaving the keep that morning. Given how lusty William had been with her in days previous, it seemed prudent. With everything going on, including her recent gut-wrenching conversation with William, she didn't need to worry about a pregnancy as well.

Ailith pursed her lips, then huffed as she flopped back into the bed. Her hair was still damp, so she spread it out on the pillow, hoping the thick curls would dry by morning.

"But Mairi might be more inclined to ye if ye did help with the laundering and other chores. Ye might be leaving the tower when ye wed William, and I feel she wants to get as much work out of ye as she can."

"I do feel badly. I've barely spent any time with her or the bairn."

Not that Mairi tried to spend too much time with her, time that wasn't weaving or carding, that was. Still, William's words about her cold nature rang through her head. They didn't understand, they *couldn't* understand why she had been so reticent with them. Something like a fever had been an easy excuse, but as her behavior lingered, she worried they might consider her touched in the head or a changeling in their midsts. Neither would be acceptable to her family or the clan.

Ailith flicked her eyes to the clothing in Leitis's arms. She was going to have to do more weaving with Mairi, otherwise she'd have no clothing left by the end of the week. The léine she'd been wearing during the attack had to be burned, as stained as it was with blood and grime.

News of the attack had *not* gone over well with her brother. Seocan had been livid, even after William had tried to temper the actual events. The entire encounter had fueled Seocan's fury toward the Morays, and word was another small gathering was going to happen at the MacDougal keep and Ailith had heard they were planning to discuss the Morays and the problematic king.

"Easily solved," Leitis said offhandedly. "Visit her every morning before ye leave or attend your own duties. A simple good morn to mother and bairn might go a long way."

Leitis left the candle lit by the bed and shut the door as she left for the night.

From the way Leitis spoke, it seemed Ailith had not been very close to Mairi anyway. It was a sound solution to maybe break the ice with Mairi and stop that hawkish glare whenever they were together.

At least her apparent snubbing of her brother's wife was not seen as odd behavior, a thought which made Ailith wonder what she had been like before. That was how she had come to think of her life: Ailith before, and Ailith after, when she was really Emilie. And often she wondered what Ailith before had been like – what she had liked or how she had behaved. Even something like her relationship with William. When he slipped between her thighs, could he tell the difference?

If he did, he didn't seem to care. What he cared about was if she loved him. And how could she share her heart with him when she couldn't share the truth? It didn't seem fair.

But if he needed the words, she would tell him.

After all, her feelings for him had blossomed, and what she felt for William was as much love as she'd felt with anyone she'd said the words to.

Nay. More. There was more to her relationship with William, and maybe that was what was throwing her off. With all the changes and having to adapt to this new life, she had pushed those feelings to the side.

Maybe it was time to bring those emotions to the fore.

Ailith blew out the candle and closed her eyes, her last thoughts on William and his toned, strapping body, and all that blond hair.

Dreams of William welcomed her to sleep until the image of William changed, and her dreams became that familiar expanse of starry night sky. The younger version of Eladon, small as if seen from a distance, appeared in a burst of light against that dreamy night sky. The woman was walking along a shoreline, a green hill rising in front of her. Was that the shores of Britain? Was this her way of telling Ailith that she was in Great Britain? Or Scotland? Was she on her way here?

That didn't make sense. Even in her dream state, Ailith recalled that the Romani diaspora did not reach Europe until the thirteenth century. How could she be here? Was she traveling alone for another reason? Was she not traveling with a larger band of her people? Why not?

Ailith's dream mind made plans to find her and meet her, to see what it was this young Eladon wanted to tell her. It had to be important to seek her out, especially if this young Eladon traversed the dangerous breadth of the European continent to get here.

In her mind, she asked young Eladon if she was here about the fungus.

The dream-Eladon lifted her head, pale like the moon and noticeable even from a distance. Her words carried on the wind to her ears.

Marry the man.

Ailith's heart raced, both in her dream and in real life.

What?

Marry the man. He will be who ye need, and it continues your line. The future only happens with the two of you.

Why? Dream-Ailith shouted. *Why?*

Her emotions roiled in her mind. The entire focus of her voyage here and her dreams had focused on the mushroom. Now it's *marry the man*?

'Tis no' right to him. He's marrying a lie, Ailith countered in the dream.

Dream-Eladon turned to face Ailith directly, and her eyes were black pools of obsidian, darker than the night sky.

Then dinna marry him. Let him go and release him to marry a woman who does love him.

A shock shot through Ailith's chest. Release him? Having William by her side–he'd been her rock in this time-shifting storm.

She couldn't . . .

The dream-Eladon smiled.

She knew.

Ye dinna want to let him go?

Ailith shook her head. She opened her mouth in her dream, but no words came out.

Why not? dream-Eladon asked. *Say the words. Tell me why not. Say it.*

This time, the words flowed with ease. *Because I love him.*

The dream woman grinned. Then the sky swirled around and dream-Eladon disappeared in a flash.

A flash woke Ailith. She shot up in bed to a dark room and rain pounding against her shutter.

Why were the dreams so confusing? Why did they leave her with more questions than answers?

But it did answer one question. Ailith's internal struggle over marrying William, that he would be marrying her under a lie, continued to weigh on her. Though dream-Eladon's statement that she marry him was what Ailith needed to hear, it was still an overwhelming realization. Yet, having her admit that she loved him, that William was the person Ailith needed, assured her that marrying William, even under a pretense, was the right thing to do.

Somehow, the man who had been her rock had slipped into her heart, creating within her a love she didn't know existed.

And she would tell him the truth – that she did love him, in her own way. She just had to find the right moment.

She turned over and closed her eyes, thinking she'd never fall back asleep. She was wrong.

William stormed into MacDougal hall, loose leaves clinging to his hair and his tunic. He brushed them away as he found Ailbert in the narrow, window-slit lined hallway leading to the tower chambers. He was speaking to their younger brother, wee Brian, and when he saw William storming down the hall, he slapped his hand on Brian's slender shoulders and sent the boy off.

"William, what has ye so bothered?" Ailbert's blue gaze roved over William's disheveled appearance. "I cannae imagine time with your betrothed has ye in such a state. Are those leaves?"

Ailbert reached to William and plucked an oak leaf out of his hair.

"Where is Uncle Cormag? Or Father? Something happened today –"

"Och, 'tis evident," Ailbert teased with an easy smile.

"Nay, no' that. God's blood, Ailbert. Keep your mind off the lass-es!"

"And what else is as interesting and rewarding? Highland politics? The conflicts with the clans? Och, if life is precarious, let me die between the milky thighs of a lusty woman."

William shook his head at Ailbert's lack of seriousness. After his foolish words of pained love to Ailith, looking like a love-sick fool, he did not require any commentary from his brother.

"Ailbert, I have something I need to share with Cormag. Where is he?"

Ailbert leaned against the stones, crossing one booted leg over the other. "At the Grants. He returns early on the morrow for the meeting with your betrothed's kin. Even though naught has changed since our discussions a sennight ago, I have the sense that something is rising in the clans, that they will no' let the king and his lackeys continue their abuse to the clans, and they are trying to find the best route to accomplish that."

"Ye have the sense? Ye mean ye overheard," William commented before letting it pass. It did not matter how his brother learned anything. The idea that struck William earlier today with Ailith's causal comment about the puddock-stools might be exactly what Cormag and their allies needed.

Ailbert shrugged. William looked past him through one of the window slits.

"Either way, meet me at Cormag's solar when he returns in the morn. I would have ye there as well. Better than having ye eavesdrop."

With a barking laugh, Ailbert slapped William on the shoulder, just as he had done with their younger brother. "Ye have reaped the benefit of my overhearing information for years. Dinna complain until ye've tried it."

Ailbert strode off toward his chambers, but William paused a moment in the dim hallway, leaning on his hands near one of the window slits. Clansmen and women scuttled around the yard, finishing their chores for the evening before retiring to their eventide meals. He let the details of the day roll around in his mind.

Ailith's words struck a speck of fear in his chest. True, she had been behaving differently, oddly, but nothing that was overly bothersome. Ailith had always been a woman who knew her own mind–William attributed it to being the only daughter of a willful chieftain. Her father, Tamhas Gordon, had been known for his iron will. Why should Ailith be any less?

She had been overly cautious as of late and more standoffish, and that had worried him. At first, he believed she might have wanted to call off their betrothal, but nay. She was still as passionate about him as he was about her.

Some of her statements as of late. Her comments about these plants and what they would do. Her questions about the mad king. More of an interest in Highland politics than she had previously–yet that might be attributed to her marriage and the added benefit of solidifying alliances with their union.

Then his harsh words about her behavior. That had been careless. He was a hardened warrior. What did her words of love matter to him? He had enough love for them both.

Perchance once they married, she might feel more comfortable sharing her heart with him as readily as he did. Until then, he was content with what she did offer him – her trust, her small touches, and welcoming him between her thighs – as her way of telling him she cared. He made a promise to himself to drop the issue. They had more to worry about than if his future wife said three simple words.

As long as he ended up married to her, that was all he truly cared about. That and getting this tyrannical king off their backs. And oddly, if it wasn't for Ailith and her strange behavior as of late, he might not have had the idea. So if anything, and if they were able to pull this off, then the clans owed her a great deal of thanks. That was the most peculiar thing of all. He pushed off the wall and headed toward his own chambers.

The following morning, William was already awake and eating parritch in the main hall when Cormag and his father Bernard strode into the keep, damp from the morning rain. The mists from the past few days had turned into rain, and everything seemed covered in mud.

Cormag whipped his sodden cape from his shoulders and tossed it on a nearby table. Bernard followed suit, removing his leather hood and cape. Brian MacDougal emerged from the hall to meet them.

"Any news? Any more issues with the Morays?"

William noticed how his father's eyes cut to him. William shook his head.

Brian sat on the table and rested his feet on the bench. "Nay, no' since William's encounter two days past. What have the Grants said?"

"They are on our side," Cormag replied. He sat on the bench near Brian. "And they suggest the MacIntoshes and Hays are as well. But like the Morays back the madman, as do the Keiths."

"Och, we ken the Morays, but the Keiths are a sorry loss. Are ye certain? Who would have thought they'd sell their souls to the madman?" Brian commented. He flicked his gaze to Bernard and back to Cormag. "Did they say they had an idea of what we might do to avoid the division of the clans?"

"Division of the clans will mean a division of Alba, and 'twill ruin what Kenneth MacAlpin worked to achieve," Bernard intoned.

Cormag nodded at him. "They do have several concerns. Primarily, how we might counter the king to begin with. Dunnottar Castle is iron clad, even if we did have the warriors for an army. And when such an attack might happen. We have no sound strategy for that."

As they spoke, William pushed his wooden bowl to the side and moved to a bench across from the speaking men.

"And they also question if we are discussing completely removing the king from this world, or merely displacing him from his throne."

"The former, preferably," Brian commented with an air of authority. "Suffering him to live would mean he'd try to reclaim the throne, and if the clans are threatening to divide now . . . " he trailed off, letting the men present provide the obvious answer.

The Highlands would never recover, William thought. Keeping Mad Donald on the throne would mean the death of any Highland unity. What would Alba be then?

"The third concern was, of course, who would replace him," Cormag finished.

Brian sat up tall. "I presume Caustantin, son of Aed, his cousin. His bloodline appears more rash, if he is older. Age also brings wisdom and patience, two things King Donald lacks entirely," he answered.

Cormag nodded his agreement. "Aye, I told them the same, and the Grant Chieftain said he would send an emissary to Edinburgh to see if he is willing to support the cause of the clans."

"Aye," Bernard added. "'Tis no love lost between those cousins."

William leaned toward his uncle and father, his bright blond hair sweeping against his cheeks as he looked at them.

"What if we could solve one of the Grants' concerns?" William asked.

All three men looked to him with passive interest and raised eyebrows.

"What say ye, son?" Bernard turned toward him.

"Ailith spoke yesterday about her wee plants, and she made a comment about them that struck me hard. 'Tis a thought that we can use to start planning an invasion at Dunnottar."

Cormag rose from the bench and moved to William and sat next to him. "What thought is that? What could the lass have said that gave ye an idea?"

"Weel, the idea only works if we can know when our Norse kin will cross the sea. If we can know that, then we might use their arrival against the king."

Cormag and Bernard looked at Brian, who had the most Viking blood kin. He shrugged. "At best, I might presume close to now, at midsummer, while the North Sea is relatively calm. They land at Dunnottar because the outcropping is easy to see and use as a landmark for the boats. We might look for dragon prows on the horizon. If we were ready to act–"

"Act on what?" Cormag asked William.

"Ailith said her wee plants hide and blend in, and once they blend in, they take over. She said sneaky."

Cormag's brows furrowed. "Sneaky? What did your lass mean?"

William shook his head. "Nay, 'twasn't what she said, but how she meant it. The Norse who arrive are coming as settlers, aye? No' to invade?"

"Aye. Our kin has no' invaded in years," Brian answered with a measure of force.

"Will the king believe that?"

Silence filled the hall. Brian looked down at his hand, and Cormag cleared his throat.

"Likely, nay. He's been fighting invading Norse and Danes for decades. And he'd no' want more Viking kin supporting the clans. He'd likely try to slaughter them as they arrive."

It was a harsh truth that few had wanted to acknowledge, as if speaking the words would make it come true.

"What if we might prevent that fate, and use it as part of our attack on Dunnottar to overthrow the king? What will the Norse do if the king attacks them as they land?"

"A Viking," Brian answered, though William already knew the answer. Everyone in the Highlands and all of the isles did.

William narrowed his eyes. "Aye. A Viking. They'd go berserking against the king, swords and axes drawn, and they'd give the king a fair battle. But they'd no' succeed because the king is preparing for their arrival and will surprise attack. The odds are stacked against them. But what if while they are a Viking, we use that opportunity to creep in, sneaky, and take over while he's distracted?"

Cormag sat upright, his mind working, and he rubbed at his beard. "The mad king is prepared for an attack by the sea, but he'd never suspect an attack from land, no' buttressed by the Morays with only that thin land bridge leading to the outcropping."

William dipped his head to his chieftain. The man had a sharp mind.

"Sound strategy," Brian interjected. "And our Norse kin will be at the ready the moment the king mounts his attack. While this is a sound idea," Brian said, nodding to William, "my chieftain, ye have spoken of the very thing that will put this all to shambles."

Cormag slid his gaze to Brian. "The land bridge."

"Aye, the land bridge."

A series of tunnels, William knew. Many had seen it before and walked through those hellish gates. The path leading to the main gate, then from the main gate to the small excuse of a castle, was a series of tunnels and low walled walkways dug into the earth. It permitted only a single line of men and no horsemen – horses had to be walked through the tunnels. The entry, and thus the frontal defense of Dunnottar Castle, was indeed a military marvel. If men hadn't seen it, they had heard the rumors of it.

Cormag shifted his head so his gaze landed momentarily on each man. "We have a strategy for now. When at the gathering, we will share this information and see if any Gordon or Grant has a solution to the land bridge problem. And we will coordinate with the clans to have horsemen near the coast, watching for dragon prows. We must be ready to move at a moment's notice."

William nodded silently. Privy as he was to this secret meeting, he did not want to overstep by saying anything more. Yet his mind worked of its own accord and one part of his mind flashed, wondering if Ailith had another bit of odd wisdom to help in this matter. Thus far, though she might be fretful over her illness, as some had called it, those slight oddities had been nothing but useful.

He lowered his face to stare at his hands. Och, more of a shield-maiden than she realized, he thought with a grin.

Cormag pounded his hand on the table and rose. "We must prepare for tonight. We have much to discuss with the clan."

The cavernous hall at Drumoak was brightly lit, more so than when Ailith had been here midday earlier in the week. She again wore her bright blue kirtle, the one with the translucent fitted sleeves, and her hair was unbound tonight, a red cape around her shoulders with only her gold circlet to hold it in place. Her curls were wild in the evening air as her horse galloped through the gate, her first time being on a horse alone since she had arrived.

She'd had a flicker of trepidation when she mounted the cream-colored pony near her brother's stable. Once she was settled, though, her body seemed to know what to do. She silently thanked William for taking her everywhere on his horse and giving her a fair amount of practice.

A flutter in her heart made her catch her breath at the thought of William. That had been happening more as of late, for which she was grateful. Perchance marriage to this stranger would be a happy outcome now that he wasn't so much a stranger. And the fact her body responded to him so well only helped with that prospect. So much so that she was excited to see him this evening.

Was that love? The type of love William had for her? She wondered as they rode up.

As a result of this gathering, she hadn't been able to leave the tower, and she had spent most of her day in the laundry with Leitis, as she had promised.

In front of her, Seocan rode next to Mairi who, in a rare treat, brought wee bairn Morgan with her. He was strapped to her breast as she rode, and only his bright shock of red hair showed above his bunting sling. Ailith didn't miss how Mairi's gaze never lingered far from Seocan. The woman was enamored with her husband.

Simon rode next to his brother, sitting as tall and proud as his pubescent body could. One day he might be as broad as his brother, but today his dark brown tunic gaped at his bony shoulders, and his belt hung loosely about his boyish hips.

One day, though, she thought as he dismounted.

Stable lads lead the horses to the stables, and when she turned around to see which one might help her down, she saw Daniel there, his thick hand outstretched and his hazel eyes shining in the flickering torchlight. A wee bit of sunlight kissed the earth in shades of pink and orange amid the darkening clouds, yet the torches were lit for their welcome.

She took his hand, and with a wide smile, he placed his hand on her hip and guided her off the horse.

"Ye look the image of the old goddess Danu herself, lass."

Ailith patted his hand as she gained her feet. "Ye look like all the fierce Highland warrior yourself, Daniel." Her eyes flicked over the fur collar at his thick neck and the weapons on his belt, including his pride and joy – a beautiful sword with a silver Celtic tree etching in the hilt, trimmed in gold. If anything, Daniel looked like an ancient Celtic warrior from the northern hills of Caledonia.

"My da had the saying if ye are always prepared, then naught can take ye by surprise. I've tried to live by that my whole life," he explained as he placed her hand in the crook of his arm and escorted her to the main hall.

His words reminded her of those spoken by both her father and Master Park, and the side of her lips curled up at the tender memory.

"Sound advice, I believe," Ailith told him.

"Aye, and one that ye seem to have adopted as of late. In these times, 'tis a good piece of advice to have."

She didn't answer but looked at Daniel with a sidelong gaze. She didn't understand what he might be implying. That he accepted her and her new, odd ways? That he hoped she was always prepared, given their recent conflicts with the clans and king? Or had he seen her fight the Morays the night of the Gordon gathering?

It didn't matter. Daniel had done nothing but show that he was someone she might count on, and if he was giving her advice, she would take it under advisement. God knew she needed all the advice she could get.

More clansmen and women arrived, a larger gathering than the Gordon's, with wives and children in attendance as well. Some tables had been set up outside, with a piper and a drummer positioned by the open hall door so those both inside and out might enjoy the strains of notes. The outdoor tables were not for overflow, as she presumed, but evidently for those who cared more for drunken revelry than refined conversation, given the barrels and horn cups arranged on a table near the hall steps. A few of said revelers already lounged at those tables, drink in hand.

William met her at the door with a smile as bright as his hair and eyes. His tunic pulled taut over his muscled chest, a grayish blue fabric that complimented her gown and made his eyes even more blue, and in that moment, she realized that he had dressed for her. Another flutter in her chest.

He smiled at her. A true, brilliant smile that warmed her to her core. If he held any lingering ire over their conversation or her inability to tell him what he wanted to hear, he didn't show it. He looked as eager and in love with her tonight as he ever did.

Ailith, ye are a fortunate lass, she said to herself. She glanced around this hall. This was not the right time or place. Too many people were present for her to bare her soul, so poor William would have to wait another day for his words.

But soon, she vowed again.

He kissed her cheek as Daniel handed her hand to William, and she lifted her skirt to climb the steps and follow him into the hall.

She paused and tugged his hand. "William? All is well between us?"

His smile faltered a wee bit, but his eyes blazed hot. "'Twas a moment of weakness on my part, *mo ruaidh.* I should no' have placed such a burden on ye."

Ailith pursed her lips. "Nay, ye should have. The weight of love is not something one man alone should bear. And I would speak with ye about that." She glanced around the hall. "But not now, or here."

Something in William's face shifted, and tension he yet bore from his moment of weakness, as he called it, softened. "Aye. No' the now."

Then he slid her hand up to his elbow, holding her as if she belonged there, by his side.

The heat of their conversation had cooled, but it still trailed along with loose ends that they would have to deal with.

But not the now, as William said.

Every candle and torch flickered within, from the wall sconces to the horn chandeliers to candlesticks with long tallow candles on each table. The hearth burned as well, driving away any remaining chill and adding to the light and the ambiance. The tables themselves were laden with platters – this one duck, another pheasant, and more with mutton, roast pork, and tripe. Smaller trays of oysters and haddock, cheese, bannocks with preserves and honey, neeps and scotch eggs. Mead and honeyed wines in pitchers sat with carved horn cups at each table, and near Cormag's head table, a small barrel of what she presumed to be rich, amber *uisge-beatha* was ready for those who craved a more heady drink.

Several clansmen and women had taken their seats in swirls of color and chatter, the clang of knives and clanking of cups, and it was all so much that Ailith tried to look everywhere at once. How different this gathering was from the smaller Gordon one, which only bespoke the need for the Gordons to form these alliances and build their small clan.

It was no wonder the Gordons were nearly wiped off that map, she thought sourly. Her need to protect her mushrooms suddenly seemed too small an effort compared to her sudden desire to protect her clan, her people, her legacy. So little of the Gordon clan, lands, and history remained, and here she saw an opportunity to not only save those in the future of a dire illness but also save her own clan.

In that moment, she understood the staunch loyalties of the past, the force behind a clan of people and what drove them to behave as they did, because, as Ailith stood in that brilliant hall with William on her arm, standing in a moment of history, she felt the same.

William led her directly next to the head table, one with carved high-back chairs instead of benches, and pulled her chair out for her to sit. She swept her vibrant blue skirts close to her legs to sit and noted that William's eyes burned as he watched the movements of her hands. Once he sat next to her, she leaned over to him, offering her cleavage to his view to tease him, and rested her hand on his arm.

"Thank ye. 'Tis good to see ye, William." Then she lowered her voice. "I have missed ye this day."

William swallowed visibly, and his hand crept under the table to rest on her skirt-covered leg. He leaned in closer, letting his gaze drop to the view she offered.

"Be cautious of what ye say, lass, lest ye find yourself tupped behind the stairwell when I cannae control myself."

Ailith grinned to herself and sat upright, evaluating the feast on her table. William had just poured her a cup of wine when Cormag stood in front of his chair with his wife Caitir on his right. His man, Brian, sat to her right, with William's father, Bernard, next to him. On his left sat Seocan, then Mairi and Simon in their seats of honor. Daniel and William's brothers joined her table, offering well-manned nods as they took their seats.

"Ye are a bonnie sight for weary eyes, lass," Ailbert complimented her. Ailith blushed at his audacious boast. "Are ye sure ye want to wed this one? Ye can have your pick of men. Myself included." He wagged his blond eyebrows at her.

Ailith giggled at Ailbert's tease, then outright laughed as William punched his brother in the arm.

"Watch how ye speak to my betrothed," William cautioned.

The way Ailbert teased William reminded her of a class clown she knew back in her secondary school days, a young man who was always looking for an opening for a joke or a laugh.

Ailith leveled an earnest smile at Ailbert and patted his hand. "Thank ye for your kind welcome. Ye look quite well yourself."

Ailbert grinned at his brother before settling in his seat.

Cormag banged his fist on the table to quiet the room. The last notes of the piper fell away, and Cormag opened his arms wide.

"That ye for your attendance! Enjoy a night of feasting, music, and discussion on this fair summer night."

Discussion? Ailith wondered. That seemed to be the true nature of gatherings, she was learning. An opportunity for planning and strategy.

This night did not disappoint. From her vantage point with William next to the head table, she heard the heated conversation between her brother, the MacDougal chieftain, and the chieftains from other clans.

William was sagely quiet, but she didn't miss how he only picked at his food and drink as he listened to their words. More than once he flicked his gaze at her as he listened, and she narrowed her eyes at him. What was he doing? Did he expect her to do or say something? Or did he want her to pay attention to their conversation as well?

Ailith took his hint and leaned slightly toward William and closer to the head table.

They were discussing a plan to attack the king. To attack Dunnottar Castle.

"Ye speak of treason. Of killing the king. And even if we all agreed that 'tis the best course of action, it cannae be done," the Grant chieftain said with certainty.

He shifted his shoulders to face Cormag, his dark brown beard catching the firelight. Lines etched his eyes, making him appear downtrodden. This was a man abused by the ravages of the mad king, and Ailith's heart went out to him.

Seocan nodded. "Aye. Removal of the king has merit, that I cannae doubt, and ye have my sword and support. But the land bridge entry is far too narrow to bring an army to attack the king, even if the Vikings invade from the sea. A single guard could pick us off one by one as we pass through the narrow gate," Seocan added. Mairi sat stoically next to him, her hand on the sleeping bairn's back, her eyes downcast. Ailith had the sense his wife did not agree with him.

Ailith's mind worked trying to understand those dynamics and the point of the conversation. And why William seemed to want her to listen. Or had she misread that, too?

As if he read her mind, William leaned so his mouth was against her ear. "I got the idea from you. The idea for using the Vikings to distract the king while the clans overtake the mainland of the castle." He raised a blond eyebrow at her. "Sneaky, aye?"

Ailith stared at him for a moment. Sneaky? The idea came from her? What could she possibly have said to William to have him think of a way to usurp a king? She wracked her brain and recalled a few days earlier when she was telling him about the mushrooms, and he suddenly froze, then drove his cock in her with abandon.

What had she said? Oh, that the mushrooms blend in, then take over. How he had used that to come up with a strategy to defeat a king was all on William. She could take no credit for that, and she told him so.

"That was all ye, William. I was speaking of plants."

"But this strategy and a real opportunity to remove the mad king never would have happened without ye speaking of plants."

Ailith turned slightly to Cormac, then returned her gaze to William. She took a deep breath. "Why do ye seem to want me to listen in? Is there something I must hear?"

He lifted her hand to his lips and kissed it lightly. "Ye have a way of looking at things different than most. As unconventional as that might be, as a warrior, I find it valuable to consider alternate visions. We yet have issues and concerns in our dealing with the Moray clan and the king. I'd have ye listen."

Ailith knew that women, while often skipped over in the history books, had a voice in many political and military arenas. Yet, she was still surprised to hear William say it so plainly, especially since some people like Mairi eyed her with distrust. William threaded his fingers through hers and returned his attention to his chieftain.

"We've all agreed that treason, inasmuch any action against a mad sovereign can be called treason, is the only way to save our clans. Donald will kill us all if we dinna take action. So let us put our minds to work and see what we can do to attack Dunnottar."

Ailith thought back to her tours to the castle she'd taken with her father. Dunnottar, as a full castle, would not be completely built until nearly the twelfth century. In 900, it was called a castle, but much of the great tower and main hall did not exist – it was not a full castle in the sense that Drumoak was. More a glorified abbey, small tower-like manse, and living quarters, the stronghold had been built along the south-eastern edge, with stables that ran through the walled bailey to the northern part of the wall.

Yet the tunnels through the land bridge were there, improved upon as the castle became a full keep. In her time, most of the castle was crumbling, and little of the original buildings from the 900 remained. Most of the stones were covered in creeping plants and stunningly brilliant green moss, making the entire castle seem like it was bathed in green in the summer, in blue with the snows in winter.

Of the ruins she had toured regularly for most of her life, the lower kitchen of the original building yet remained, as did the low door to the outside to allow for nets of fish, barrels of mead, and sides of mutton and beef to be easily brought to the kitchens from the barns. Those storage areas, set into the top of the rocky outcropping, were part of her Dunnottar tours, as was another part of the early stronghold that was supposedly constructed long before 900 CE. Ailith sat back in her chair as she remembered it, recalling crawling on the dry dirt through the door as her father watched.

"Creep through here, Em," her father said as he shoved the door open.

It twisted, exposing a breath of daylight to the dark, moldy ruins of the pantry storage. She got on hands and knees and crawled through like a child.

Jack laughed and followed her through, ducking low to exit the stones into the misty, gray day, made mistier by the crash of waves from the North Sea below.

"Now come here, lass. Have ye seen this one?"

She stood upright, brushed the dusty, nearly ancient pantry dirt from her jeans, and joined her father as he walked behind some ruined stone remains – a sort of outbuilding? Maybe an old barn? – to the wall behind it. The wall didn't quite look right. It didn't match the rest of the decaying stones and appeared to have gaps large enough to stick her hand through.

Jack muscled the wall to the side, moving it like he'd move a stuck closet door, and Em's jaw dropped. A slippery, dark-stoned set of stairs, barely wide enough for a single person, descended the treacherous sheer cliff of the outcropping.

"Always have an out," her father said as he kept a strong hand on her shoulder while she leaned down to look at the camouflaged stairs. "Every good monarch had to have escape options."

"All strongholds have a weakness," Brian was arguing as Ailith blinked, bringing her mind back to the discussion at hand. "We may no' know it, but we can find one."

"We dinna have the time. What if the Norse arrive on the morrow? What good will our plan be then?" the Grant chieftain countered.

William felt her shifting and leaned on his elbow to her. "What is on your mind, *mo ruaidh*?" His tone was light as if he knew that her mind was laboring on the questions posed by these warriors. He seemed to like it. Was she reading that wrong?

"Ye believe these Norse are coming as settlers?" she asked. Her history had told her they were invaders and that King Donald fought to defend his land.

William nodded. "Aye. Many have kin here already as part of the clans. But if they are attacked, these Norse will readily fight back as part of their Viking heritage."

She was quiet for a moment, staring at the knife-nicked wooden tabletop. It wasn't that she didn't have an idea. She did. From her tours with her father, she knew the ins and outs of every part of Dunnottar and the surrounding countryside. That was not the issue.

The issue was how to say it without calling her knowledge into question. How can she tell them of these secrets without revealing her own secret, one that could possibly have her accused of being a witch or touched by the fae, and locked up or killed? William might accept her and defend her, but he was one man in a clan who perhaps did not share his acceptance of her new-found odd nature.

She licked her lips, and with an encouraging nudge from William, she spoke quietly to him.

I know how ye can achieve this. How ye can get into the castle mostly unseen and not take the tunnels?"

"How?" William asked, without questioning how she might know. Those questions would come later, of that she had no doubt.

"Kitchens are odd places. They are the places of women but provide sound access to a tower, a castle, a keep. Most pantries have a small door for access to the kitchens. The Dunnottar castle kitchen has a door in the kitchen storage room to make it easy to bring in barrels and sides of meat."

William nodded his understanding. keeping his chin close to his chest. "Och, lass, what a mind ye have on ye. Our warriors can enter unseen through the kitchens. Now for the more difficult question.

How do we get past the land bridge and palisade wall?" He paused and flicked his gaze to the head table where the men spoke heatedly. Ailith followed his gaze, but her eyes instead met Mairi, who narrowed her eyes at Ailith. She seemed to know of the conversation she was having with William. "There's still the death funnel for the only path that leads to the main gate, as ye've seen. It goes underground in a couple places, is narrow otherwise, with high sides. 'Tis designed solely as a death trap for any invaders."

Ailith turned her head so she spoke directly into William's ear and bit back the inappropriate smile.

"Kitchens were places of women, but the abbey and tower were built by men, warriors like yourself, long ago. What good is a castle if there is no alternate means of escape when it is sacked?"

William lifted his head, his face tight and intense. "There's another entrance."

She wrinkled her nose. "No' quite. There *used* to be. If ye curve around the northern part of the rock, near the shore, there is a rough set of hidden stairs cut into the stone. Some of the stairs are underwater when the waves come in." She held her breath, waiting for him to ask how she knew. Saying that one might see was not exactly the best reasoning for how she knew this.

"So 'tis well hidden," William commented. If he had questions, he was withholding them. She nodded.

"And part of the wall there is a stone-covered door. No' very strong, and 'tis old, like the stairs, and unused, behind the stables, or so I've heard. Over the course of time, it has weakened. A decent shove or a small ram can take it out. Then ye rush your men in, veer right past the stable, and the pantry door will be a wooden door set into the castle wall, right on the ground."

"And this ye also learned from your Vikings? The same who gave ye the knowledge of these lifesaving puddock-stools?"

There it was. Ailith played with the neckline of her kirtle.

"We can say that," she answered, neither confirming nor denying the truth of it.

William shrugged. "It matters little where ye heard of it. As long as 'tis there as ye say." He gripped her chin between his thumb and forefinger and forced her head up to look into his eyes. No longer soft and blue, they were now hard iron. "Is it as ye say? Because, just as with your wee plants, the lives of many depend on this. I care no' how ye know this information. But as my wife, as the woman I love more than my own self, can ye vow to me that what ye speak is the truth?"

His words held a hard edge. He wanted to believe her, but he was no fool. He was a man of violence and defended his land and people at all costs. He would have confirmation of this knowledge before sharing it.

And what was left unsaid was just as loud, that she'd regret it if it was not. This was the first time she'd seen his hardness turned on her, and in an ironic twist, she trusted him more because of it. William was no fool, and he was showing her this.

She lifted her hand to cup his clenched jaw. "I vow to ye on my life, William. What I say is the truth."

With a single nod, he released her chin, drew his finger along her jaw, then leaned forward on the table.

"'Tis a way. A secret way that has been hidden from decades or more," William announced to the chieftains and tanists, and amid the chatter in the hall, the main table and his fell silent.

Once eyes were on him, William explained in shorter detail what Ailith had said to him.

Well, all eyes but Mairi's. She had seen them speaking privately, and Ailith had the sense she knew where William had obtained his information.

"It cannae be that simple," Daniel said. "How has no one attacked before?"

"Who would think both the wall and the stronghold might be breached anywhere other than the sea-facing wall or the main entry?" William rationalized. Ailith gave him credit for the statement. It made sense and kept her out of the conversation. "The keep clings to the outcropping. Who would think to check?"

"Aye," Brian asked. "Who? What did your Gordon lass say to ye? How did she know of this?"

Then his eyes fell on Ailith. So Mairi wasn't the only one watching her.

Feck.

She flicked her gaze helplessly to William. She didn't have a lie, even a bad one, ready for that question. Would she have to answer?

William gave her a subtle nod and moved in front of her, partially blocking her from their view.

"Women would know, as women talk. Ailith spends much time with Leitis and other kitchen maids, as do my own sisters, and they know these things. Mayhap a lass in the village has worked at Dunnottar and has a loose tongue and spoke of it, thinking it harmless. As for the stairs, what sovereign would build a stronghold that might become his prison? I'm more surprised we had no' heard of it before."

Cormag and the other chieftains shared a glance. Bernard raised a curious eyebrow to his son, then gave him a nod. He trusted William even if the tanists did not. That boded well.

"If what ye say is true, then we have a tangible plan," Cormag said. He turned his head to gaze at each man seated with him. "We prepare our warriors, and the MacDougals will have riders near the shores to watch for the dragon prows. The moment we see them, we begin our attack. If God is with us and we have presumed the king's actions correctly, and the Vikings return the attack, and this secret entrance works as ye claim, William, then we have a chance to remove this foul besom of a tyrant once and for all."

Fists slammed onto the table with cheers of *huzzah* that blended in with the general din of the gathering in the hall.

It was settled. They had a plan. And it all rested on Ailith's words. Her chest tightened.

No pressure, Ailith thought, *no pressure at all.*

Once the men gathered together to celebrate their tangible plan, one that would result in victory, William twisted his body and turned his chair so he faced Ailith. With a glance around, he noted Daniel and Ailbert watching him, and this was not a conversation anyone else should hear. Grabbing Ailith's upper arm through the thin material of her sleeve, he leaned in close.

"Walk with me?" he asked. But it wasn't a question, it was a command.

The work with the toadstools was one thing, but Ailith's odd statements and knowledge as of late had been weighing on his mind.

And now her vested interest and knowledge about the Dunnottar? How does she seem to know so much? Something much greater was going on. More than a discussion with Vikings or a passion for plants.

Ailith was still Ailith, but she was something more, something different. And he had vowed he would love her with every breath in his soul until the day he died. But he had to know what was going on with her. Especially since he opened his heart to her in such a raw way. He might not need to hear her words of love right now, but he needed to hear something about *this*.

If she could trust him to love her, then she should trust him to know the truth.

He led her away from the main hall to the darkened hallway. Here, only a few torches illuminated the dark stone corridor, spaced out and forming circles of light amid the dark. Sounds of celebration and pipe music carried in through the wall slits. Dim stone and dull sounds, and that was all.

He stopped at the semi-darkened space between two window slits and looked down at her. In this lighting, her red hair was a deep burgundy black, flowing over her pale face and heaving breasts. Only her eyes were bright, glinting as she assessed him and his motives.

That look was one he was familiar with. It was one that a warrior used to evaluate if one was friend or foe. If a situation was dangerous or not.

He pinched the bridge of his nose and rested his arm on the wall above her head, cornering her against the stones. Mayhap this was a dangerous moment. They would both know very soon.

"Those details about Dunnottar, ye plan military strategy like a soldier." He fell quiet for a long time, trying to figure out exactly what was going on.

Her eyes never left his face.

"I vowed to ye that I will love ye with everything that I am until the moment I leave this mortal coil. And I have told ye that I will accept no' hearing the same words for your mouth, no matter how it pains me. But I need to know, what is it about ye? How can ye know these things that no man, no Highland warrior or Viking can know?" He leaned in so close, his eyes were poised mere finger widths above hers. "I will no' judge ye, I will no' be angered with ye. But this–" William swept his arm toward the main hall. "I must have a something I can tell these men who will risk their lives, their families, their clans, for what ye have shared this night."

She licked her lips, her gaze unwavering. He had to admire her strength, many men had quaked in their boots when William rose above them like this, hard and furious.

"Aye, ye deserve to know everything and more. Ye have been patient with me when others might have set me aside. Ye have accepted my answers when others might have questioned them. And this information, aye, 'tis too large and too dangerous not to know the full measure."

William's mouth thinned as he waited for her answer.

"But here? Now? With clans sitting right on the other side of the wall?" She finally broke their shared gaze and glanced at the opening to the main hall. She was hiding something–it wafted off her like smoke. "I would have a private conference with ye. And I would ask that ye do it after this attack."

His brow furrowed. "After the attack? Why–"

She bowed her head and rested a tentative hand on his blue tunic. "'Tis a fair bit of information, some of it no' quite believable. I would have ye focused and have something that ye must come back to."

His heart shuddered in his chest. Her plea was wrenching, and he understood her motive for it. Would he not ask or do anything with the hopes of bringing her back from a terrible place? Aye, he would.

And he could guess what she might have to say–the words of love he was desperate to hear.

He nodded, but before he could speak, she continued.

"I have one more request. When it happens, let me know so I can stay by the mushrooms. I'll guard them with my life."

"Nay," he stated, his jaw clenched. Was she crazed? To come to the very area where they would be engaged in a treasonous battle with the King of Alba?

She crossed her arms against her deep blue kirtle, shoving her breasts upward distractingly. But he would not be so easily enticed.

"Nay," he said again.

"Ye cannae stop me," she countered. "Even if ye lock me away or try to have someone guard me, ye know I will find my way out. I'll go anyway."

William slammed his hand against the stones. She frustrated him to the brink, and he was ready to grab his sword and take his aggressions out on the nearest drunkard who wanted to fight. How could he come back to her words of love if she was dead because he let her get too close to battle?

"Ye cannae go. 'Tis impossible."

"I'll find a way. I'd rather go with ye knowing, so ye dinna feel I'm lying to ye or disobeying ye."

"Which ye will be doing."

She pursed her lips and tilted her head.

What was wrong with her? Some of the minor changes were easy enough to account for, but this? Going to the scene of battle? To guard paddock–stools? The world seemed upside down, and William was falling off the edge.

He sighed. "Are they that important?" It made no sense.

"So much more than you know. They can save millions, William." She gripped his tunic and moved her face close enough to his to kiss. "Millions."

Millions seemed like an impossible number to him.

He snaked his loose arm around her waist, trapping her. "I hate this situation ye have put me in." His voice was more of a growl. "And I'll say aye under one condition. Ye have your condition, I have mine."

A brief flash of fear crossed her face before she masked it with a tight expression. "What's that?"

"Ye marry me in the next few days. Before the ides of July, whether we have gone to this battle or no'. No excuses, no reasons, no bowing to formalities or decorum. I'll wed ye with a priest or an old druid in the hills if need be. I care naught for information ye feel ye must share. None of that matters. Ye could admit to being the devil for all I care. Within seven days, ye are my wife, in my bed, under my body, by my side. That's my condition for waiting and letting ye guard your plants."

With the last of his words, he shifted his hips to press against her and lowered his face to kiss her surprised lips. Her reticence fell away, and her arm moved up to encircle his neck. That small movement made his body tingle, and if it wasn't for the table of people not thirty paces from where they stood, he would have shoved her skirts over her hips and had her there against the stone wall.

Panting under his ardent kisses, she pulled her lips away.

"But I have a secret," she whispered and averted her gaze. "The reason for all this is so shocking a secret, one I canna speak aloud to ye yet. If we wed, ye must do so knowing that after this battle, I shall have to speak this secret as ye have asked, and ye will have to believe it and accept it. Ye will think me mad or want to walk away, but ye will be trapped with the weight of this secret as I am."

Was she going to tell him something more than words of love?

It was of no concern to him. She had taken the step to move forward with their marriage, and that was as good as words of love. He shrugged before crushing her to him more tightly.

"We all have secrets, Ailith. Aye. I love and accept all of ye, even your secrets, no matter how large or harrowing ye believe them to be."

They returned to the main hall and resumed their seats. Daniel gave Ailith a narrowed glance, and she smiled at him, hoping to reassure him.

Most of the guests had finished their meals, and drinking had taken over for many. The din of chatter grew louder into laughter and boisterous voices, both inside and out.

Seocan remained at the head table with Mairi, and Brian had moved to sit next to him. From the untroubled looks on their faces, the dire talk of treason and removing the mad king had given way to lighter discussion of clan and kin.

Simon had left the head table–Ailith saw his bright red head near one of the lower tables, picking at food with another younger lad of similar age with light brown hair and blue eyes. A handsome lad. One of the MacDougal clan? Maybe with those blue eyes . . .

She returned to her platter and filled it with roasted pork, a bannock, and some preserves and honey. Not quite a honey-glazed ham sandwich, but close enough. Daniel had just refilled her cup when some screamed behind her.

"He's choking! Help! He's choking!"

William and Ailith spun around to see Sine, her face white with panic, standing near the blue-eyed lad, arms open but not touching him as she didn't know what to do. A large man who was not fully drunk and devoid of his sense leapt to her aid and was slamming his hand against the boy's backside to dislodge whatever stuck in his throat.

Ailith stood, not realizing she was in motion as her mind reeled. *Dinna do that,* she screamed in her mind as she pushed past the concerned people gathering around. *Ye'll make it worse!*

The man moved his hand back to slap the boy again, and Ailith used that opportunity to slip behind the boy. The poor thing clutched at his throat, and his body was stiff with his own panic and lack of air. Ailith didn't think, she acted.

She had never had to do the Heimlich before, but it was something she had to learn as part of her tour guide training. That and CPR and basic wound care. As her dad had said, *ye never know who's going to slip and fall on a mossy step or have a heart attack climbing them.*

Now, here she was in the past, wrapping her arms around high around the lad's waist. Making a fist with one hand, she placed it just above where she believed his navel might be. She could hear people shouting, but it was like they were in another room. Her focus was on the boy who was nearly as tall as she was. She grasped her fist with her other hand and gave a quick, upward thrust.

The piece of food that had been blocking the boy's airway was expelled from his mouth and shot across the room. He gasped and coughed, taking in great gulps of air as she held him steady. Those in the room surrounding them fell absolutely silent as they stared at her.

Sine gathered her senses first and rushed to the boy.

"Brian! Are ye well?" she asked, her hands on his chest and head, searching him.

He nodded. "Aye. It's out. She got it out."

The boy, Brian, pointed at Ailith.

Feck.

More attention. Eyes shifted to focus on her, and not all were relieved faces. Some were confused about what exactly she had done. One of those faces was Mairi's

Feck. Feck. Feck.

"I'm glad I was able to help," Ailith replied, relieved that the crisis was over.

William came to her side, his face tight with worry.

"Ailith, what did ye do?"

She sighed wearily. This was just not a good night for keeping things from William.

"I saw a man do that for his lass in the market once. She was choking on an apple, and instead of slapping her back, he somehow shoved it out like that. Like he forced her to breathe out deeply, and it shot the apple out of her mouth." Och, but this lie was a doozy, but what else might she say with all these guests, including Mairi, listening?

She'd apologize for it later. *I promise, William.*

He leveled his gaze at her and leaned in to kiss her cheek. Then he turned his lips to her ear under her hair. "Another secret?" he asked.

She nodded.

Sine stood and hugged her. "Thank ye, Ailith. Wee Brian promises to eat slower next time, aye?"

The lad nodded and from how she placed her hand on the lad's head, Ailith assumed a close relationship. Either a close cousin or a brother. William's close cousin or brother.

The scare sobered many people up. After several of them marveled and thanked her for acting so quickly, including Bernard, William's father, Ailith turned around to sit back down.

Mairi stood in front of her, her arms crossed over the bairn strapped to her chest. For all the commotion, the wee Morgan still slept peacefully against his mother's breast. Mairi, on the other hand, bore a stern look on her face.

"I dinna believe ye saw someone do that. No one can perform such feats like that."

Mairi's voice was hard and accusing, and Ailith was thankful that William's hard body was at her back.

"Mairi, truly, I saw something like that done –"

Her brother's wife stepped closer, poking her finger in Ailith's face.

"'Tis enough, Mairi," William cautioned, and another wave of gratitude washed over Ailith.

"Your brother has had too light a hand with ye. Running about the Highlands, ignoring your chores, speaking about so many odd things. Now this? He may trust ye," she hissed as she shoved her finger toward William. "But he's smitten and thinking with his cock. 'Tis the way of men. I'll no' have it. I dinna know if ye are a changeling or a traitor or the like, but I'll no' have it."

Ailith was at a complete loss for words, and after all, she had been through that evening (*all that? In one night? No wonder I can barely stand!)* she swooned. All her blood drained to her feet.

Then William was there, supporting her weight with an easy grip on her arm and standing between her and Mairi's enraged glare.

"'Tis quite enough, Mairi. 'Tis time for ye to take your leave."

Mairi flicked her glare from Ailith to William and back to Ailith.

"Dinna ride near me on the way home and keep your distance. I'll no' hesitate to say anything to Seocan if ye come near me or my bairn again."

Then she stormed off. Ailith sagged against William, who cuddled her close.

"Lass, I am truly sorry for this eve. Ye have endured much, and though I'd prefer if ye stay, I think 'tis best if ye head back to Glenbervie with your brothers and Daniel. I'll inform Daniel of what has happened with Mairi and tell him ye feel weak after all that happened. He seems to have a care for ye. He'll make sure ye get back to your chambers with no more accusations from Mairi."

He kissed the top of her head, sat her on a nearby bench, and strode across the hall for Daniel. Ailith slumped and held her head in her hands.

Finding her bed could not happen soon enough.

Chapter Eighteen

Leitis was as silent as a mouse when she entered the next morning, but Ailith heard her anyway. She sat up in her bed, her head spinning like she had been steamrolled. In a way, that was exactly what had happened. How had so much happened all in one night? Her father had always said things would look brighter in the morning, but that did not seem to be the case this morn. If anything, things seemed worse.

She wondered if Leitis had heard about all that had occurred the night before because she didn't appear to be her typical boisterous self.

"Thank ye, Leitis," she said, pressing her hand against her head. Not feverish, but achy. The stress was getting to her.

"Ye are welcome, milady," she answered curtly.

Ailith opened her mouth to ask her what was amiss, then snapped her mouth shut. Maybe the striking events from the night were too fresh. Maybe it was better to let that sleeping dog lie, at least for a bit.

Leitis stopped at the door and turned toward "If I might, milady?" she asked in an imploring tone. Ailith lifted up on her elbows toward her.

"Aye, please, Leitis," Ailith answered. Her voice was as croaking and achy as the rest of her.

Though Leitis's bright hazel eyes darkened, her lips parted to show off her crooked teeth in a motherly half-smile, and Ailith found a measure of solace in that smile.

"People will talk. They always do. And they prefer to spread rumors about things and others they dinna like or dinna understand. Let those words wash off ye like water from a graylag's backside, aye? Dinna let the harsh words of others dim your brightness."

So Leitis had heard about the night before.

And regardless of whether or not Leitis believed some of the rumors, which Ailith could readily see her at least considering since Leitis had some of those behaviors firsthand, Leitis was trying not to let those harsh characterizations taint her impression of Ailith.

Even more than that, she was urging Ailith to do the same.

Och, good Leitis. What would I do without ye?

Ailith gave Leitis a weak smile and a nod of her head. Leitis dipped her chin and swept around the door to exit, leaving Ailith to her own chaotic thoughts.

Och. Leitis might advise her to ignore the ruthless words of Mairi or others, but actually doing so was a whole different matter.

A heaviness filled her chest as she dressed, picked at her morning meal, then snuck out of the tower into the gray morning before she might be missed. Ailith didn't know if she was going to see William later that day, what her brother might say about her actions the night before, or what rumors might be making the rounds. As for William, Cormag had mentioned sending out riders to watch for the Norse, and she assumed William was spending the day at the coast, watching the horizon.

Evidently, any rumors about her hadn't reached everyone, as the young girl, Anna, who helped spread feed for the chickens, smiled brightly when Ailith offered assistance. Afterwards, she brought water to the troughs and collected some of the hanging laundry.

She managed to spend the day mostly on her own and avoided Mairi. Instead of taking her evening meal in the hall, she dropped meat and fruit onto her plate and took it to her room. Rain had started to fall that afternoon, and she sat by her open window, the refreshing air on her face, and ate her supper there.

Truly, since the morning she awoke in this new life, this had been the loneliest day she had.

At least she didn't have to suffer another interaction with Mairi. Ailith decided to focus on that as the silver lining to her day. Yet it did not make up for how terrible she felt or the sadness over not seeing William at all. She had grown so accustomed to seeing him daily that she realized how much she cared for him and how much she missed him when he wasn't with her.

She climbed into bed that night, as miserable as she felt when she woke in the morning. A tear slipped from her eye, and she wiped it away. No reason for tears. She had a job to do, and she was doing it. And maybe tomorrow, as her father said, she would feel better in the morning.

Leitis was back fully to her warm and mother hen self the next morn, yet Ailith didn't linger in the tower and was at the sheep pens by mid-morning, patting the nubby black heads of the baby goats who vied for her attention. A few children raced around the pens, chasing each other and teasing the sheep. A young woman was at the well, tugging a bucket off the rope and trying to shyly watch the stable lads brush a pair of horses. Ailith smiled to herself as she observed the dance of glances between the lass and the stable lads.

Several burly men walked toward the barn, carrying peat and haymaking forks. Ailith nodded her and made to return her attention to the sheep when one of the men stopped and squinted into the distance. He grabbed the other man's tunic and the two men rushed toward the tower.

Ailith looked toward where the men had, and she and the lass froze where they were, followed by the wide-eyed stable lads.

Riders. A lot of them, kicking up mud and riding hard for Glenbervie tower.

Who were they? What did they want? *Shouldn't someone close the gate?*

The burly men burst out of the tower with a stern-faced Daniel, Seocan, and several other men behind them. Even wee Simon rushed past the doors, his short sword clutched in his hand.

Daniel saw her at the pens and waved her back toward the tower. Ailith grabbed the lass near the well by her arm and dragged her to the tower.

Ailith kept her eyes on Daniel, letting his body language dictate her reaction. Then he dropped his sword to his side, and she released a clenched breath. Whoever approached was not an enemy.

Men in leather and chain-mail hauberks with shields on their backs and saddles roared past the gates. Dozens more slowed to a stop just beyond the palisade.

One of the men in front pulled his helmet off his light brown hair. It was Cormag MacDougal.

Ailith caught her breath. They were dressed for warfare. They must have seen the Norse boats!

Her heart leapt to her throat. This was it. Tonight was the invasion. Either the clans would succeed with the help of the Vikings, or the king would slay them all and raze all lands west of the land bridge. She suddenly found it difficult to breathe.

Seocan stepped forward. "Are they here?"

Cormag looked down at Seocan and nodded. "Aye. We have come to collect your men and prepare. We will wait in the dense woods southwest of Dunnottar until the Norse land. Brian estimates 'twill be close to sunset. I've sent messengers to the Grants and MacIntoshes to join us."

Seocan dipped his head. "Give us time to prepare our horses, and we shall join ye."

Ailith stood by the tower stairs, shaking under her kirtle. She had to get to the shadowy ridge. How to do that? Closer to sunset and after the men leave the horses to invade the keep made the most sense to her . . .

A rider to Cormag's left dismounted and threw his reins to the rider next to him. He palmed his helmet, and the bright blond head that appeared was William. He shoved his helmet up on the saddle and strode directly to her.

"Come with me," he said in a rough tone, dragging her away from the tower.

"William! Are they here? Is it time?"

She tripped over her own feet as he led her to the barns.

Most of the animals were out in their pens, the musty scent of their hay and fur that lingered in the air assaulting them as they entered. Ailith looked up at William.

"Why are we in the barn? Can ye tell me–"

He whipped her around so his sky-blue eyes blazed at her. "Aye. We saw the prows this morning. And we shall wed as soon as I return."

"What of–"

He pushed her by the bench at the side of the barn. "Bend over," he commanded.

Her eyes flew open wide. "What?"

William exhaled hard and turned her back to him, grabbed her breast over her kirtle and pressed his lips against her ear. His cock throbbed hot and urgent against her backside.

"I need ye, Ailith. We have to be fast, but I must have ye before I ride into battle. If I fall, then at least my last moment with ye was joined with ye, and I'll die with the scent of ye on my cock, and your moans in my ear. And ye will have a memory of my love to take with ye."

Panic flared in her chest. "Ye cannae die, William! I–"

He chuckled as he ran his hand down her kirtle. At her thigh, he grabbed the skirts and hiked them up.

"Will ye tell me that ye know I will no' die? Och, I would love to hear that. But we canna know what the future holds, and I would no' go to my death without the taste of ye on my lips. Please, lass, I dinna have much time."

His lips found her neck where he brushed her red curls to the side, kissing and sucking.

"Please, *mo ruaidh.*" His urgency for her wafted off him in a lustful heat. "Please."

Her hand slid down to his turgid cock, squeezing it through his braies.

She didn't need to say anything more. He shoved her over the bench and flipped her skirt over her rear. Cool air struck her intimate skin, replaced quickly by William's warm thighs. With his hand gripping her hips to hold her in place, his staff dove between thighs and into her welcoming sheath. He groaned as he seated himself to the hilt deep inside her and groaned again as he withdrew and thrust hard inside once more.

"Feck, I need ye. I need your quim. I need ye," he chanted as he thrust over and over, harder each time. No tender words or gentle touches. William was a man with a singular need, and she was the one to give it to him.

His cock brushed over her sensitive skin and that spot in her sheath that made her quake and writhe. She arched upward, supporting herself with her arms, and William shifted over to her. Grabbing at her breast with his left hand, he kept his right hand on her hip, digging to shove her hips back as he thrust forward. They slammed together again and again, rough and fast, until she cried out her pleasure in his rough and needy handling.

Second later, through his gritted teeth, he snarled as he came, pouring himself into her in a hot rush. He stopped moving and pressed his forehead against her shoulder. Then he kissed her neck again and rose upright, adjusting his braies.

Ailith stood up as well and patted her skirts down over her legs, and wiped her hair off her face. Even if no one saw them coupling in the barn, they would be able to tell just looking at her disheveled appearance, she was sure.

She looked up at him to speak, and he grabbed her around the waist and drew her close and kissed her.

"We ride for the wood, lass. I ken ye want to save your plants," he said breathlessly.

"Donald will raze the land if ye dinna succeed," she told him. "He'll burn all the lands the Vikings and their kin touch. If he does that, those plants are gone forever. I'll tear up the rest and race to plant them elsewhere if needed, but I cannae leave those plants. Please, my love. Dinna make me do this against your will."

His face faltered at her plea, and thankfully he didn't ask how she knew what the king would do.

"My love. Och, ye had no' said it in a while, and I feared ye no longer loved me." His grin shifted as his gaze grew more intense. "I love ye lass, and ye are far too invested, but I did make ye a promise. But ye also made me a promise. As soon as I return, I'll bathe, then ye will wed me. Then ye can tell me everything. And I shall make another vow to ye."

He pulled on his arm, raising her up on her toes until she was nose to nose with him.

"I shall return to ye. Never doubt that, *mo ruaidh*. And I am a man who keeps my promises."

William strode back outside with his arm through hers, obviously not caring who saw them or knew what they had been doing in the barn.

Seocan had already mounted, and Ailith saw Mairi standing on the stone steps, her face, normally so hard, was tender and fearful. An epiphany struck Ailith as she gazed at Mairi. Her ire toward Ailith didn't come from a place of hatred, it came from a place of fear. She desperately feared her husband would not return, that she would lose her husband and father of her child, and she saw Ailith doing naught but putting Seocan at risk with her reckless actions.

Poor Mairi. How disheartening to exist in such a frightened state.

Daniel was mounting his steed, and Simon stood next to him, his sword at the ready. From them, Ailith's eyes turned to William.

William marched to Simon and pulled him a few steps away, speaking softy to him. Simon looked at Ailith, then back at William, nodding his head. His young face was as severe and focused as the men on their horses. William clapped the boy on his back and strode back over to Ailith.

"Simon will accompany ye. He's of an age to handle a sword, and while ye might use your feet to kick a man or use his own sword against him, I dinna know what ye will do against an army. At least with Simon, we might balance the fight if 'tis only a few men."

Simon? Wee Simon? Oh no. She couldn't let that young man put himself in danger.

"William, nay. He's too young–"

William shook his head. "He's old enough to ride into battle with his brother, and he makes more sense in a fight than a lass with only a *sgian-dubh.* He's practically a grown man, and I vowed ye could protect your wee plants, but I never said ye'd do alone. I've instructed him where to take the horse, when to leave, and what to do. Ye will arrive at sunset and hide under the ridge. No matter what happens, ye remain there. Dinna approach Dunnottar. And at the first sign of danger, grab all the stools ye can and leave." He ran his hands through his hair, a frantic expression crossing his face. "I still cannae believe I agreed to this."

She stood on her toes to kiss his tight mouth. "I vow I will follow your commands. Thank ye for this, William. I would no' do it if it wasn't so important."

He looked over his shoulder. It was time to leave.

"'Tis also something ye will need to explain when the time comes. I already believe I am a crazed fool to let this happen."

He sighed heavily and lowered his head. "Once more kiss, lass. Then I have to go."

She gave him that kiss, and he cupped the back of her head, crushing her lips to his in a lingering kiss that tasted of desperation and hope.

Then he released her and strode off to his horse and didn't look back.

Chapter Nineteen

He calmly placed his foot into the stirrup, and with a bounce up, William swung his leg over the saddle to mount his horse, then shoved his helmet on. William tugged the reins, spinning Lugh around to face the men who were waiting on him.

William looked around at his clansmen and his future kin, the Gordons. His father Bernard sat on his steed, off to the side and waiting patiently, the only one who seemed calm through this. His uncle Cormag, plus the five men he brought with him, and Brian were steel-faced as they waited for the rest of the Gordons to ready themselves.

Seocan already sat on his mount, looking down at his gloved hands. William knew that look. Seocan was thinking of the blood that would be on those hands before the day was finished. Daniel was mounted, one hand on the hilt of his cherished Celtic sword, while he glanced back over his shoulder at the Gordon warriors accompanying them, making sure all were set to ride. Brian adjusted his shield on his saddle. Brian had brought ten men with him, settlers and kin of his and of Norse blood. At least five of them held axes and shields, with swords and knives on their belts. Those without axes in hand tucked smaller axes into their belts opposite of their swords, and shields hung from their saddles.

The air was thick, tense, as they gathered outside the Glenbervie gate.

Ailbert's horse trotted up to stop next to William's. "When the fighting starts, I'll be on your right," Ailbert said, looking William in the eyes. William just nodded his understanding.

"Everyone ready?" William asked.

No one responded, but all shifted his way and sat up higher and adjusted themselves in the saddle, ready to ride. The tree line where they were to all regroup was a hard hour ride from where they stood, but men would be ready to fight as they rode past Glenbervie. As the rush of battle wore off, they would feel exhausted until the Dunnottar came into sight.

"'Tis your plan, lad. Lead the way," Cormag told him. The faith his chieftain had in William made his chest swell with pride.

But not too much pride. No downfall for him.

The only one with the pride to bring him down was the mad king.

"We'll be riding hard the whole way," William said. "We'll make one quick stop before clearing the woods to meet up with the Grants and MacIntoshes. Then we can go over the plan one last time before the fighting starts. God be with us."

And without a look back, William rode past the gate with the other warriors on his heels.

When they came to the edge of the woods, William pulled up on Lugh, stopping the group. After tying off the horses, they took a short time to regroup and meet up with the Grants and MacIntoshes. James Grant and Lucas MacIntosh each looked ready to battle the devil himself. The king had killed their men and their seconds in command without remorse, and they looked as if they might slay the king on their own.

Vengeance was a dangerous thing.

Their horses pawed at the ground, sensing the tense mood of the Highlanders. The Grant and MacIntosh chieftains each brought a bannerman with him, holding a spear with their colors attached to the end, near the iron tip. Willian didn't see the need for bannermen–the purpose was to sneak in and kill, not announce–but both leaders demanded to have the king know who was deposing him, and William could not fault them for that.

The sun had begun its gentle descent into the horizon. When everyone was gathered, William went over the plan one last time as he looked out at the castle. The stronghold itself was nothing to marvel at, little more than crumbling stones of the old abbey the tower was built upon, but the genius behind the placement of the castle was.

It was more of an island unto itself, rising two hundred feet out of the water. It was not easily connected to the main landmass but by the narrow land bridge that men centuries before had formed into a series of tunnels. His father had been right, three men could hold off an army at that entry gate. It was the castle's greatest strength and the reason for the king's overconfidence and overdeveloped sense of power.

"How many men do ye think the king has with him?" Daniel asked as they surveyed the keep.

"Over a hundred," Grant answered as his horse knickered and pawed at the ground. "Maybe a hundred and twenty."

"There!" Brian shouted, pointing to the darkening ocean.

Three ships with dragon prows broke the tide, heading to shore. It was a difficult angle, and they could barely see where the sea met the land. Church bells from the castle rang in the distance. The king, as predicted, was sending soldiers out to attack the Vikings invaders. William and the rest waited in battle readiness to see what happened next. In the graying light of gloaming, the king's men marched down the road from the castle toward the beach. William guessed them to be about seventy men in total.

William gathered his reins to ride out when Grant spoke up.

"Easy lad," Grant said. "'Tis still not too late for them to turn back. Wait until we lose the shine of their backs and they cross steel with the Norse. Then the soldiers are committed and engaged."

"The king will still have twenty-five or thirty men guarding the castle," Bernard said. "He'll only need three to hold the bridge."

"'Tis the Morays we need to worry about," MacIntosh added. "The king will have scouts out, and ye can wager that as soon as the first clash of steel hits, at least one of the bastards will ride for their help. If we don't own the castle before the Morays arrive, we'll be outnumbered, two of them for every one of us, and 'twill be like the hot metal between the hammer and the anvil."

"Speed is everything," William agreed. "Those of us breaking off for the stairs or the Norse must keep that in mind. If we are all clear in our purpose, let's see it done."

They waited anxiously as the Norsemen came ashore, knee-deep in the crashing waves and pulling their boats onto the stony sand. The welcome was not the one they expected, but one that they were prepared for. The king's men formed up and marched to meet them at the shoreline. The first of the Vikings approached the soldiers, sword drawn but not held as a threat, to see what the soldiers wanted. The soldiers didn't wait for the Norseman to depart the water and stuck out with spears, killing the man.

From that moment of violence, the Norse boatmen changed their disposition, dropped their property, and grabbed axes and shields.

"'Tis time," Grant announced.

They reined in their horses, crossed themselves, and spurred their mounts into a run across the open field. 'Twas a wide clearing, and William wagered the king's men would see them long before they made it across. Or at least, William hoped they did.

They rode hard across darkening grass, but William trailed back slowly, letting Brian and his Vikings pass him, followed by Grant and his men, then Seocan and Bernard. MacIntosh and his warriors slowed with William, as did Daniel, Ailbert, and his uncle Cormag with the MacDougal warriors. MacIntosh pointed to his bannerman to ride with Brian. He wanted his banner there to be seen even if he would not be.

Their horses landed on the dirt road that snaked over the land bridge and led upward to the castle. The road was steep, but the horses barely slowed. When they came upon the first entrance that led to the tunnel bridge, men leapt off their horses and drew their swords.

William, MacIntosh, Daniel, Ailbert, Cormag, and the rest of the men raced down the side of the outcropping that met the land bridge. Since the castle had been built in a way to prevent men on the hill from being able to shoot arrows at men in the castle, so men in the castle couldn't see them run down the hill to the sea. Even if someone by chance saw them running downward, all they would have seen were men running for the water's edge and away from the castle.

Brian and his Vikings would be the first across the bridge to meet the king's men. William just hoped they didn't try taking the bridge, but only cross swords with the soldiers and acted as if taking the bridge was the true purpose of this assault.

Once at the base of the outcropping, William no longer heard the shouting or fighting, only the crashing of the surf against rock. Leaving his helmet behind, he led the men as they scaled the outcrop along the water's edge, then into the water to wade around the island. The water was cold, but his blood was hot and kept him warm.

"Are ye sure 'tis here?" MacIntosh asked over the sound of the crashing surf.

"It better be, or all is for naught," William replied with assurance as he gripped along the rocky edge.

Please, Ailith. I dinna ken what ails ye, but please have spoken the truth.

"William," Daniel called out when they were halfway around the outcropping. "If 'tis no' here, we must call off the attack."

Please, Ailith.

Then, in the shifting gray of late dusk, he caught the rounded corner of a step, followed by another.

Christ's blood, she was right.

Good lass, he thought.

"There," William shouted, pointing up ahead.

The rock had been hammered and chiseled into stairs that emerged from the water and led up to a flat edge. William reached the slick, ancient steps and started climbing. Steel rings, covered in rust, had been hammered into the rock.

"For tying off boats," William suggested, pointing to the rings.

As he climbed, William tried to keep his mind on the attack, but he continued to marvel that Ailith had been right. They had to wade in the water, halfway around the island to find it, but she was right. The only question was how had she known?

Better no' to think on that now, William told himself. *'Tis one of her secrets, most likely.*

What secret? Another part of his mind asked. He shoved the errant thought away.

He reached the top of the steps, but instead of ending at the grass flat bottom, the wooden wall Ailith had referenced prevented their advancement. The sea-weakened wall was a foot from the edge, buttressed with old, warped boards. Using his thick Seox knife to pry two of the boards away, he tossed them into the air and down the side of the cliff into the sea. With a fleeting glance at the more portly MacIntosh chieftain, he decided to pull away a third board so that the man could fit through without embarrassment.

It opened behind a type of shed. Stepping through into the flat, grassy top, he crept to the stone edifice behind the decrepit shed, the rest of the men following. No one was around them, but that was to be expected since they were at the rear of the castle, and all the fighting was at the front.

William ran from the shed, past the stables, and crossed over to the castle wall itself, waiting for the rest to emerge and join him. He risked a quick look over the wall at the other side of the outcropping to the beach and saw that the Norse and king's soldiers were still locked in battle. The king's men had the numbers on their side, but the Norse didn't seem to notice or care about that fact. As Brian had promised, the Norse had gone a Viking the second the king's soldiers attacked.

"The king will be up high where 'tis safest," MacIntosh said with a flick of his chin.

William moved along the shadowy wall, pushing at the stones as he walked. He felt foolish with his clan's eyes on him, but Ailith had been right about the steps, so had no reason to doubt her about the castle entry. He kept pushing as he walked. Then the wall moved under his palm. Not much, not more than a hair, but it was not set in place.

He pushed again harder, and dirt crumbled from rocks as the outline of a door appeared. Rocks had been mortared together to make a five-foot by three-foot door set in place fairly well as dirt and grass had grown over it, hiding it and preventing it from moving.

Ailbert withdrew his knife and bent on a knee, scratching and scraping the ground. He cut away grass and used his blade to dig away two inches of dirt until the wall moved easier.

The wall was like nothing William had seen before. At the top and bottom, he could see that it was built around a vertical iron bar in the middle that allowed it to move without falling. Yet the wall still wouldn't give, even with the dirt removed. William shouldered the right side and as it groaned inward just an inch, the left side slid outward. It appeared to have been locked on the inside. William put his shoulder to the wall again, and with a grunt of effort, the sound of metal snapping broke the air. The wall stayed upright but rotated around.

William ducked inside to find he was in a low storage pantry. Just as Ailith had said.

Good lass, he thought again with a tight smile.

"Ye go get the king," MacIntosh said to Cormag after squeezing through. "My men will go to the bridge."

"Ye'll be facing at least forty men alone," Cormag said. "Forty against ten are no' good odds."

MacIntosh shook his head. "No' if we hit them from the side. If we can open the bridge enough, the rest can flood in. The numbers will be with us."

"Good luck," Cormag said, nodding his understanding.

MacIntosh and his men crouched and ran for the gate. The rest of them moved into an empty kitchen. William drew his Pictish sword and knife as the sound of eight other swords being drawn came from behind him.

They crept from the dimly lit kitchens to the main hall. Two guards stood at the steps that led upward, each with a spear in hand. The two guards dressed in black ran at them, spear points leading their charge.

"Invaders! Traitors! In the castle!" Their shouts announced their presence to others as the guards rushed forward and thrust their spears. "For the king!"

William moved for the one on his left, swinging his sword to knock the spear away as he plunged his knife into the man's side. Ailbert ran up to William's right as promised, slicing down on the second man's spear, slamming the tip to the floor, then slicing upward, taking the man in the belly.

As the two soldiers dropped dead, William spat on the ground next to the bodies. "For Alba."

Cormag and his men ran past William and up the stairs. Daniel, Ailbert, and William followed. At the top of the stairs, the men were making short work of four guards. Daniel ran down the dark hallway, leaving the fight behind him as if he knew where he was going. More guards rushed up the stairs and William turned to stop them.

"We'll hold here!" Cormag shouted to William. "Dinna let the king get away!"

"He's right William," Ailbert called over his shoulder. "We need to help Daniel."

William followed Ailbert down the hallway, the clashing of swords echoing behind him. Daniel stood in front of a doorway fighting three soldiers, and that doorway was the only reason he was still alive. Only one man could swing a sword at him at a time. Without slowing, William threw his knife, taking the first soldier in the throat. As the soldier fell back, blocking the other soldiers from advancing, William ran up and kicked the dying man in the chest, pushing him into his comrades.

Daniel didn't hesitate and stepped in, followed by William and Ailbert. Swords clashed again as Daniel pressed one soldier and Ailbert the other. William moved to help Ailbert when he saw two soldiers run the king through another door in the rear of the room. The king had been dressed for battle in his black leather, and his personal guards of similar warrior build wore matching black leather garb.

"Fools! Ye dare threaten the king! 'Tis treason and if ye dinna lay down your weapons, I'll have ye executed before the sun crests the horizon in the morn!"

William only knew the man who spoke was King Donald by his thin crown and his glinting, dark red ring. Even at this pivotal moment when he should be running for his life, the king had to display his emblems of powers.

Pure lunacy, William thought.

Daniel rushed to William's side, his blade darkened with blood. "Ye must be mad to think ye're in any position to threaten us."

In the dim torchlight, William saw Ailbert smirk as Daniel stated aloud the fact whispered throughout the Highlands.

"Ye have ravaged the clans long enough," William announced. "Ye have robbed us of our land and rights. Your reign as king, mad as ye may be, is at an end. Dinna force our hands to kill ye as well."

This time, it was the king who smirked, a grim smile that made his lips seem too long and too thin. *Aye, the king is more maniacal than we thought!* William reflected as he adjusted his grip on his sword.

The guards in black looked at their king for direction. William inched forward.

"'Tis the last offer. Surrender. Ye have nowhere left to hide."

The mad king's smirk grew uncomfortably wider and William's back stiffened.

"Och, but ye are wrong."

Donald spun with his guards on his heels for the back wall opposite the bed. He pushed on it and it opened to a secret hall. The masked door slammed shut behind then, and William heard a bar slide across the stones.

Without a pause, William leapt over the king's royal bed to give chase. He slipped his Seox knife through the slender gap in the door to shove the bar up. The gap was tight and the bar was heavy, and he struggled until Ailbert reached his side and shoved against his hands, heaving the knife and bar up. The door creaked open and they shoved it wide.

In the next room, they heard the king and his two guards race down another set of hidden steps.

They're heading to the rear of the castle, William guessed as he bolted after them.

Halfway down the steps, one of the guards turned on William. It was a foolish move since William held the high ground. The guard swept his sword for William's legs, but William blocked each swing easily. William returned the gesture by swinging for the man's face, which he didn't block as well, but was forced back each time. The guard knew he couldn't win the fight–he was only buying time for his king to escape.

There was nowhere for the king to go, so the soldier was going to sacrifice his life for nothing. William managed to slice the man across the face. Not a killing strike by any means, but when the man grabbed at his own face, the killing strike came as William drove the tip of his sword into the man's chest.

At the bottom of the steps, William burst through the backdoor, an unstoppable force to be reckoned with. To his right, he saw the bridge, and MacIntosh had opened the way for their forces as he'd promised.

The king's guard, now whittled down to ten men, battled with the MacIntoshes on one side and the Grants on the other.

The Morays had finally arrived and rallied to help the king's soldiers but now faced the same problem William's men had. Brian and two of his Vikings alone held off twenty Morays stuck on the narrow bridge, unable to get past three lone men. William started to turn away when he noticed the burly Lucas MacIntosh lying on the ground, face down, unmoving. William's chest hardened. Another death for that clan. The king had much to answer for, indeed.

William rounded the corner of the castle to see the king and his personal guard slowly shuffle behind the storage shed in front of the ancient steps. So the king had known about the escape steps but had kept them a secret just in case he ever needed them.

William reached the edge of the shed and peered down. The king and his lone guard were moving recklessly fast to get away. From up high in the dark, William couldn't tell the difference between the mad king and his guard. He'd just have to kill both and figure it out later.

Skirting around the shed, William reached the steps. Descending the steps was much more precarious than moving up them. The king was getting away, and William picked up his pace, moving faster. Halfway down, William's foot lost purchase and he slipped. He slid down two of the steps, then off them and was reeling off the cliff face. In a desperate grab, William grasped the edge of a sharp rock, stopping his fall but at the cost of dropping his sword. With an agonizing groan, William pulled himself to the steps and started down again.

William stopped when he heard a scream. Had one of the men fallen? William quickly continued down and found the king's plain crown balanced on one of the steps. When he reached the bottom, he saw one man in black running into the surf and left him to drown in the violent waves. Frantically, William looked around to find the other man face down on the rocks buttressing the churning water.

Jumping into the waves, William grabbed the man and dragged him to the sand. The man's head had been bashed by his fall. Then in a glint of moonlight, William saw it. The king's large signet ring on the man's finger. The Celtic cross was unmistakable, even in the nighttime darkness. In the coward's rush to get away, the king had slipped and fallen to his death. It seemed fitting–he didn't deserve a warrior's death.

Turning the king over, he saw the man's face had been torn off his skull, his lower jaw had been ripped off, and one eye was missing, caused by the same jagged rocks that had almost killed William.

"Serves ye right," William mumbled to the dead king as he tugged the ring off his gloved finger. "Your madness will feed the crabs tonight. Alba and the clans are free."

It was over, but something didn't feel quite right. Mayhap 'twas the fighting still going on above.

William's entire body ached as he slowly made his way back up the precarious steps to the top landing. He was too tired to rush. He made it to the bridge where the king's soldiers and less than a dozen Highlanders lay dead. A dark day for the clans, and it made William feel even more weary.

More than half a dozen of the Morays were dead on the bridge, giving up when they weren't able to press their way through.

William found James Grant on the southern slope of the land bridge, wrapping a bandage around the arm of one of the Vikings.

"How did we fare?" William asked him.

"We lost twelve men in total," Grant answered grimly, his face streaked with dirt and blood. "Lucas MacIntosh and your uncle's man, Brian, among them. MacIntosh opened the bridge for us. We never would have broken through if no' for him."

"And Brian?" William asked. Their tanist and Cormag and his father's dear cousin–their chieftain would be devastated.

"Brian was holding off the Morays with two of his men. They killed several Morays on the bridge before one of them threw a spear. Took Brian in the chest, and he died quickly. It angered his Norse kin, and they went berserk on the bridge. The Morays decided they did no' want to bear as much loyalty to the mad king as they thought. They're still running down the road. Look for yourself."

"And the Norsemen on the beach?" William asked.

Grant shrugged. "Hard to say from this far. I'm told it looks like they won. Lost half their number but slayed all the king's soldiers."

That news did not surprise William. He turned away, and Grant stopped him. "What of the king?" he asked.

"Dead," William answered, handing Grant the signet ring. "Fell from the cliffs."

While Grant palmed the ring, William strode across the bridge. Several Morays were on their horses but weren't galloping back toward their own lands as he expected. They were racing down the hill, heading west into the night. William's eyes followed their direction and in the bright moonlight, saw that they were heading for the depression in the land bridge, the saddle, where Ailith and Simon would be.

William's stomach lurched and stuck in his throat.

Ailith!

The Morays must have seen them and decided to exact a measure of revenge on the woman and boy if they couldn't get it against the men.

With only Simon to guard her. His blood slammed in his head, which burned with fury. He'd known letting her come this close was a horrible idea. He pumped his legs in a panicked run across the bridge toward the horses, searching the ground for a weapon.

Chapter Twenty

At dusk, Ailith and Simon stood on the finger of the hill, at the saddle–the depression where the land cut open to reach the side slope–exactly where she promised William she would be. Ailith leaned against the staff she'd found in the woods. Just a thin branch really, but Simon had been more than happy to quickly cut the smaller branches off for her and smooth any knots.

Though he was alert and attentive as they rode to Dunnottar, Simon kept talking about how he should be with their brother at the castle. At least he hadn't asked why Ailith was there or why they huddled near the grass high on the slope.

"I've a feeling that there will be plenty of fighting still after today, Simon," Ailith told him. An obvious enough statement, but one that held more than an inkling of truth. No matter if the clans defeated the king or not this night, clashes with the Morays and other clans were bound to occur.

Crouched together near the land bridge, they watched as some of the men fought on the bridge trying to cross. In a sudden flurry, they rushed forward and made it across the narrow tunnels. In the dying light, the Morays had arrived as William assumed they would, but they, too, were caught on the narrow land bridge. That fight ended shortly after it began, and from where Ailith stood, it looked like her clan won the day. The Morays scrambled on their horses.

Ailith's chest surged, and she prayed that William was among the survivors. She didn't know if he was on the land bridge or climbing the steps to sneak up the side of the outcropping. She scanned the slope beneath them as she tried to piece together where everyone might be at the moment.

Please let William be alive. Alive and well, she sent up to the heavens

"Look at them run," Simon said, elbowing her. "Cowards."

Ailith stopped to do just that. He wanted to be the protective warrior, but his words belied his nerves. She gave him a weak smile–he was the same height as she was, still growing into manhood–and nodded.

As they watched, several Moray men backtracked down the path while others cut across the field, down the side of the hill. Ailith's blood turned to ice.

They were coming straight for the saddle, right where Ailith and Simon were hiding.

Feck.

Earlier, in their effort not to be spotted, Ailith and Simon had tied their own horses in the tree line. An error in hindsight. A huge error.

"We need to get to the horses," Ailith said as she watched the horror unfold in front of them.

"Why?" Simon asked, then he turned to see what she was looking at. As he stared at the oncoming riders, he realized why.

Simon drew his sword. "Ye run," he said. "I'll hold them off."

She was not about to let her little brother defend her against an onslaught of Morays. Not when they had other options, horrible as those options might be. She hated to leave the plants, but she could do nothing for them if she was killed by the Morays. Better to hide and try to come back if they threatened the plants. Fire she might put out. Fighting a half-dozen men with swords, not so much. *Live to fight another day,* as her father always said.

"Ye'll run with me," Ailith said, and when Simon didn't move, she added, "or I'll tell Seocan and William that ye left me alone to my own fate."

Simon looked at her, child-like hurt written on his face and his mouth in a pout. "Ye would no'," he asked more than stated.

"I certainly would and will," she replied. "Now run!"

Together, they raced towards the trees, she with her branch and her skirts hiked up to her knees and Simon with his sword. The surviving Morays must have noticed they scrambled up the ridge and raced around to cut them off.

Ailith's stomach sank. There were more than a half-dozen of them. All rough-looking men, all looking for payback.

"Do ye recognize any of them?" Ailith whispered to Simon as they neared the Morays.

"Nay," Simon said, stepping up in front of Ailith with his sword clasped tightly in his hand. "Stay behind me."

Brave lad, she thought as she adjusted her own grip on her staff.

The men canted their horses closer, then one of them climbed down and drew his sword. He bore a wicked smile and no mercy as he glared at them.

Simon rushed forward to meet the man and swung his sword, but the man blocked it with no effort, then backhanded Simon to the ground. He'd make a great warrior one day, if these Morays let him live that long.

The grimy, blood-soaked man stepped up to chop his own sword down on the boy's head, but in a flash Ailith leapt forward and knocked the sword out of the man's hand with her staff. They didn't see her as a threat, of course, and that was this man's mistake. The Moray twisted his head her way, but it was too late. The butt end of her staff struck him in the nose, knocking him nearly unconscious onto his back. Her movements were trained and automatic.

The other Morays laughed at her efforts as they all dismounted and drew their blades. Though Ailith shook to her bones, she put on a brave face and let her training take over. Truly, it was all she could do.

Simon had recovered and regained his feet, sword still in hand and a furious glare in his eyes. Seocan would be proud of him, Ailith knew.

The men formed a ring around them to both intimidate and prevent escape. Blood pumped through Ailith's body, fueled with adrenaline, and everything seemed to happen in slow motion.

Simon didn't succumb to any intimidation and rushed the closest man for an attack. This man blocked Simon's swing like the first one had, but Simon was clever–he had learned from his previous mistake–and quickly stepped forward, kicking the man in the balls. As the man grimaced and cupped his injured organ, Simon ran the man through the stomach with his blade.

In that moment, the rest of the Morays decided they were done having their fun and moved forward as one to kill them. Ailith moved to Simon and stood at his back to defend him.

The man in front of Ailith froze where he stood and looked down at his chest, where a spear tip sprang out from his leather hauberk. Ailith lifted her eyes as William, Seocan, Daniel, and Ailbert galloped down the land bridge at full speed. The Morays turned to face the new threat, but it was too late. Seocan rode by without slowing and took out one of the men with a sword slash to the face.

Daniel was not as easygoing and rode his horse right over a man, trampling him into the ground. William and Ailbert were leaping from their horses before they fully halted and ran at the remaining

Moray men, swords in hand, their faces masks of fury. While they approached the Morays, Simon leaped at the lone man near him. Three sets of swords clashed and clanged with such ferocity that Ailith didn't notice the man she'd knocked down getting up until he was on his feet. He bent over and retrieved his sword, then stood upright and, with a vile grin, wiped the blood from his nose and focused on her.

Ailith would have been content to let Seocan or Daniel fight the man – her staff was not a good match for his sharp blade – but the Moray seemed determined to run her through before anyone might intervene.

He jabbed his sword at her stomach, and she smacked it away with the staff. The fact she was able to counter him seemed to anger him all the more. She moved to spin the staff and go for his face again, but he darted at her, closing the distance so she couldn't use the staff. Ailith dropped her staff and grabbed his shirt while allowing herself to be pushed back. She just had to stay out of range of his blade. As she fell backward, she jumped so her feet came up to the Moray's stomach. When she hit the ground, she kicked out as hard as she could, and the man went flying into the air.

From the side of her eyes, she watched as William slashed down, cutting through the man's shirt and skin. He stumbled back but William then slashed across the man's stomach, opening up his gut. The man fell to the ground in a mix of shock and blood, trying to shove his innards back into his stomach.

Ailith spun over onto her stomach and pushed herself up with her hands. The man she threw had lost his sword. He also found his feet and drew his knife from his belt.

Seocan and Daniel reined in on their horses, both men jumping from their saddles to draw swords and stand on either side of her as she panted, human shields against the threat. The Moray froze, knowing the odds had significantly changed.

William looked her way, but seeing Seocan and Daniel with her, he turned back to assist Simon. She watched as William gripped his sword, yet it seemed to Ailith he wasn't going to interfere until he had to. The Moray fighting Simon raised his sword high and stepped in, aiming for Simon's bright red head, but before he could bring the sword down, Simon leaped forward, driving his own blade into the man's chest between his ribs. The sword must have stuck in bone because the sword was pulled from Simon's hand as the man fell.

William's grim expression remained unchanged when turned his attention to Ailith and the man threatening her with a knife. Seocan and Daniel each took a step forward, safeguarding her with swords raised high.

"Hold," William shouted as he walked forward. He waved his hand at them. "Sheath your swords."

Seocan and Daniel looked at him with an odd glance, yet William's tone was not one to be trifled with. This man tried to kill William's wife, and William was most undoubtedly going to kill the Moray himself – it was his right and duty as a husband, and they respected it.

The Moray man realized what was going on and faced William, knife raised high.

"Will ye allow me my sword?" Moray asked with a snarl.

Big talk for a man about to die, Ailith thought.

"Nay," William stated, still walking toward them.

"Is this honor for MacDougals? A sword against a knife?" Moray taunted.

William's expression didn't change. "Nay," he said flatly again, stopping a few feet away. With a flick of his foot, William tossed up Ailith's staff and caught it easily in his hand.

Surprising everyone, William held the staff out to Ailith.

She looked up into his iron blue eyes. They stared at each other for several seconds, and her heart hammered her chest hard enough to bruise her ribs as Ailith realized William's meaning. She *was* different, now at least. He might not know who she really was, but he knew what she could do, and he loved her enough to let her do it.

He accepted her, all of her, even the secret part he didn't comprehend.

She grabbed the staff and spun it expertly in her hand as she stepped forward. The Moray man laughed as he realized what William was doing. Without any warning, he lunged at Ailith, who smoothly side-stepped as she swung out with the staff, breaking the man's already bloody nose. He stumbled back, and Ailith didn't pause. She jabbed his kneecap, trying to push through it like she'd been taught. The crunch of this kneecap as it broke echoed in the field, and the Moray man crumpled to his side, dropping his knife.

William joined Ailith and stood over the man.

"Go back and tell your clan that you were beaten by a woman, you pig," William bit out.

"I'll go back and tell them that she's a witch," the Moray spat out, along with a glob of blood.

"Then dinna go back at all," William said as his sword came down on the man's neck.

Releasing his sword, he turned to Ailith and clasped her in his arms, crushing her to his chest.

Chapter Twenty-One

Leaving the rest of the men behind, William lifted Ailith to his saddle, then mounted behind her and reined the horse around. Not toward Glenbervie but in the direction of the MacDougals. To Drumoak.

"William?" she asked.

He curled his body around her backside as if shielding her from the violence of the world around them. She didn't realize it until he covered her, but she was shaking. The woods were dark, leaves blocking some of the moonlight, and utterly quiet. As they departed the chaos of this terrible night's bloody work, it seemed like only the two of them existed in the world.

"Aye, *mo ruaidh*?" he whispered, his voice raspy in her ear.

"Are ye taking me to Drumoak?"

"Aye," he answered with no hesitation.

"My brother will be worried for me."

"Nay. He knows where ye will be."

Ailith turned profile to him, her eyes lowered under her tresses that were crimson-black waves in the dark woods.

"How does he know?"

"Because he is a man, a warrior. And he knows that after tonight, I'll no' let ye from my side. Ye'll stay with me this night, and we will wed on the morrow."

Her heart froze under her breast. "On the morrow? I dinna have a gown! Naught is prepared!"

He made a noise against her hair. Was he laughing? Aye, he was. That was definitely a low chuckle.

"If we must wait a day or more, I'll agree, but we will be wed before another dawn passes after that. I will no' wait any longer. I cannae wait any longer." The ferocity of his words became more strained as he spoke as if he was trying to hide desperation. His lips pressed past her hair to her ear. "I'd no risk ye again. I'd have no life if I lost ye. Dinna ask me to let ye protect your plants alone again. It took everything inside me no' to ride to the Moray lands and slay them all and let their blood water this plant ye think is so valuable."

Her chin dipped to her chest. She hadn't realized the depth of his care for her, his love for her, and the lengths he would go to protect her. How could she ever return that love?

"Ye dinna want to hear this, but the plant is yet exposed." The thought that it could potentially be destroyed still weighed on her. Would she ever feel as though she had achieved her goal? "I dinna know what to do next." She blinked back hot tears. For the plants and her undertaking, aye, but also for the bloodshed and battle of the day. Shock? Probably.

William released the reins with his left hand and circled her waist. The effect was immediate, calming her.

"'Tis a problem for another day, lass. Too much has transpired this eve. Let us return to Drumoak, wash ourselves of these grim remnants, and find our bed."

"Our bed?" she asked, turning slightly again.

William dug his heels into Lugh's sides, urging the horse into a gallop.

"Aye, our bed."

Muire and Sine and the rest of the keep welcomed them. Ailith didn't miss the side glance she threw at William returning with her, but his sister let any unapproving statement pass.

With the help of several clanswomen, Muire ushered Ailith and William to his chambers, then called for a tub of hot water to be brought to his rooms. She kindled a fire in the narrow hearth at the far end of William's chambers.

"I'd not have ye stain the sheets with the dirt and debris. Wash, and I'll return with cleansing cloths and a léine for ye, Ailith."

With another judgmental glance at William, she exited the chambers.

"She does no' like that I have ye with me before we are wed. We must do that soon so my dear sister does no' suffer any vapors."

Despite all that had happened and the sheer weariness that she felt in her bones, she had to smile. Muire had a sense of propriety, apparently.

"I think ye are using every trick ye have to convince me to wed ye quick."

He placed a warm palm on her cheek. "'Tis the only thing I want to do to ye quick," he said with a sensual grin. How did his eyes manage to dance in the firelight when it took everything she had just to stand upright?

A pair of young women burst through the door with a short, wooden tub between them. A bit of water filled the bottom, and another lass followed them, adding two buckets of hot water. Muire entered after them, leaving a stack of linens and a léine for Ailith, and a wad of grayish-red soap. Ailith sniffed it. Roses and mint ash soap.

Once the door was closed, William whipped his belt off and hung it over a high-backed hair set by a matching table. His tunic followed, and his hair was wild, standing on end as he tossed the tunic over the belt. Wearing only his braies, then turned to her.

Wordlessly, he unfastened her wide leather belt and added it to the pile. In a smooth movement, he crouched and grabbed her skirts, lifting them over her body. She raised her arms so he could lift the entire kirtle over her head. Her léine followed, and she stood before him in her natural body, one untouched by the clothing of man. His eyes blazed, and he unlaced his braies and yanked them and his boots off his legs.

It was the first time she had seen him in his full glory, long-limbed, packed with lean muscle and a fair number of scars, and furred in dark blond body hair. He was enough to turn any lass's head, and he was to be her husband. The fortunes of time had smiled on her, indeed.

He took her hand and helped her step into the small tub. Using a clean linen, he dipped it into the warm water, rubbed soap on the cloth, then with a lingering, gentle touch, rubbed at her skin until he wiped away any reminder of the battle.

Once she was rinsed clean, he handed her a fresh linen, longer this time, and wrapped her in it.

As she dried herself, William grabbed another linen and the soap and stepped into the tub. Dropping her drying cloth on the floor, she grabbed the cloth and soap from his hand.

He stared at her for several heartbeats, then lowered his arms and let her wash him as he had done for her, trailing her fingers over his arms and chest and the sinewy muscles of his back, down over the curve of his buttocks and down his muscled legs. Each sweep of her hand was firm but tender, washing and rinsing his body as he had done for her. When she lathered up a new cloth for his face and applied it to his cheeks, his gaze was riveted to her face, and the heat of the room seemed to come to life, vibrating the very air they breathed into their nude bodies.

She exhaled a shaky breath and rinsed his face, then swept the cloth over his hair to wipe away any clinging dirt or debris. The water in the tub was filthy gray when he stepped out, and she handed him a drying cloth. 'Twas like baptism for them, washing away their sins of the night and greeting each other anew. Washed clean before they became husband and wife in full.

In that deep silence, he tugged her fresh léine over her head, then found a clean set of braies. The fire at the hearth snapped and popped as they crawled into his bed. He threw a plaid blanket over their clean bodies, curled into her back once more with his hand around her waist, cupping her breast, and he kissed the back of her neck.

They fell asleep touching, afraid that if they stopped, they might lose each other.

Dawn broke through William's window slits, casting bright rays of light onto his woven rug. That and the rumbling sounds of the keep woke her. William was still curled against her backside. Had he moved at all during the night? She hadn't–Ailith could not recall sleeping so deeply since she had arrived.

Her stirring must have woken William, who made a groaning noise in her wild hair. Unbound from last night, it wrapped around their shoulders and arms, binding them together.

"Are ye ready to marry me today, lass?" William rasped in a low, sleepy voice.

She didn't respond right away. It was far too early, or at least it seemed too early, for her to answer that question. Because something had to happen before they wed.

"Ailith?" William asked, raising himself over her.

She turned in his arms and stared up at his handsome face. Blond locks fell over his forehead, making him look more like a youthful lad than the hardened warrior she had seen last night.

"Ailith, what silences ye?" His clear brow furrowed, and she brushed those wavy locks back.

"I made ye a promise. I said that after the battle against the king, I'd tell ye how I knew." Her voice shook as she spoke. What would he say or do once he learned who and what she was?

His lips tightened. "And I told ye we all have secrets. Ye can tell me yours in time."

"Nay," she said, averting her gaze. She couldn't say what she had to say and look into those engaging blue eyes as she did. "Ye must know before ye wed me, though I doubt ye will believe me. But ye must believe me, no matter how crazed the words might sound."

"I dinna care what ye must tell me. I love ye, I have loved ye for years. Ye could tell me ye are the devil himself and I'd still want to wed ye."

"Keep that in mind, because ye might no' be far off." She paused and cleared her throat. It was time to tell him, and all she could do was hope for the best.

"Ye have wondered why I seem to be acting so strange as of late. 'Tis because I have been strange as of late. A few weeks ago, I met an old, very old Romani woman –"

"Romani?" he interrupted, his brow furrowing again. Of course, he'd not know that word.

"A traveler of sorts. She needed my help, and I agreed."

"Agreed to help with the yon wee plants? 'Tis she who asked ye to care for them?"

Ailith cleared her throat. "No' quite. Ye see, this Romani, she wasn't from this time, from this year."

He screwed his face up, but he didn't pull away. If anything, his arms tightened around her, holding her as if he might carry some of the weight of what she had to say. "What time? Last year?"

She licked her lips. "Nay. From eleven hundred years in the future. My name is Emilie Gordon, daughter of Jack Gordon, and the last of the Glenbervie Gordons in the twenty-first century. The pud-dock-stools are gone in my time, and only those stools can save most of the world from an illness. The Romani led me back in time, a millennium in time, to prevent the eradication of those stools. I awoke as my own grandmother many generations removed to accomplish this task."

Once she started speaking, the words came out in a rush, having been blocked by the dam of silence for so long.

William didn't move. His face, though tight-lipped and lined with confusion, remained close to hers, his eyes fixed. His arms remained tight. He did not blink or turn away. Ailith released a shuddering breath.

"What ye speak is no' possible, Ailith," he intoned. "'Tis what the priests and abbots oft call witchcraft."

Oh no. Did he not believe her? Of course not! How could he?

"I'm no witch. I know 'tis impossible sounding," she said with an air of desperation, "but every word I speak is true. 'Tis how I knew about Dunnottar Castle. How I knew how to care for the plants. How I know how to fight. These are things I learned in my time, in the future."

William stared at her for several moments, his mind trying to make some sense of what she was claiming.

Believe me, William, she begged with her eyes. *Please believe me . . .*

His mouth worked, and a muscle in his jaw twitched. She waited for him to pull away, eject her from his room, and send her back to her brother and his suspicious wife.

"There are tales," he said slowly. "Tales of changelings. Of fae folk who live with the puddock-stools and walk through the ether. Fae folk for whom time is no' solid and constant, as we know it, but flexible, like a piece of linen that can drain fluid and leave solid pieces behind. And I have seen ye firsthand, what ye know about Dunnottar, how ye fight, these things are also impossible, yet we brought down an evil king with it. Perchance ye are like a changeling, a fae, able to move through that fabric."

Her chest throbbed as he spoke, painful, wrenching throbs as she realized he wasn't turning her away, that he was doing his best to understand her harrowing secret.

"William, do ye mean –?"

He lowered his head so his nose brushed against hers. "I canna begin to understand what ye truly mean, lass. But ye are mine, and ye have always been mine. Ye might be mad, or a witch, or a fae folk changeling, but ye are no' liar, and ye are part of me. If I must love my Ailith who also moves through that fabric of time, then 'tis she who I love. I just ask two things."

Her breath caught in her chest. "What do ye ask?"

"One," he said as he brushed his lips over hers, lighter than a feather. "Ye never tell me what my future is. 'Tis a type of curse, what ye have, and I vow to help ye carry that curse, but I'd no' have that curse turned on me."

Ailith nodded. She understood that curse all too well.

"And two," he said, kissing her again. "That ye tell me ye love me. I'll wed ye whenever ye wish, but my heart needs to know it does no' echo into a void."

Ailith's heart snapped in two as she blinked back burning tears. She lifted her head and pushed her lips to his in a full kiss, a hard kiss, one of need and desire and force.

"Aye," she said as she pulled her lips away. "I love ye, William. I feared I would no' be able to, that 'twasn't fair to wed ye if I could no' return your love. But ye are so full of love, ye loved me enough when I could no' and my heart opened to ye despite all this. I love ye, William, and I will wed ye."

He kissed her again and rolled atop her, releasing his burgeoning cock from his braies.

"But," she said, and he froze over her, cock in hand.

"Och, lass, please, I need ye more than ye know."

"But ye have to give time to make preparations. I dinna even have a gown!"

He grinned knowingly as he slipped his manstaff between her willing thighs and pressed forward, breaching her. Ailith gasped and arched her back at his hot, pulsing entry. He stopped, holding himself inside her.

"We'll find ye a gown and make announcements to your brother," William said in a thick voice. "If no' later today, then on the morrow." He moved, thrusting his hips, and she gasped as he moved in and out. "Tell me, *mo ruaidh*." Another thrust of his hips and his cock deep inside her. "Tell me that ye will wed me at dawn tomorrow."

As his cock slid in and out, driving her to the brink, she dug her fingernails into his bare shoulders and arched into his movements.

"Aye! Dawn tomorrow, William."

He dropped his head to hers and kissed her as his hips increased pace. "I love ye, Ailith. No matter who ye are or where ye are from." His thrusting increased, as did his breathing. "I will love ye until my last day until my last breath is ripped from my body."

Then he was riding her, and she was losing herself in the movements of William's cock claiming her.

As her body approached climax with him, her mind spun. She didn't know if she managed to protect the plant. She didn't know if replanting the mushrooms would work. She didn't know if everything she had done would work to protect everyone she loved in the future, and she certainly didn't know if she would ever be able to go back to her own time.

But that was all in the past.

What she did know was that her future here, with William, was certain.

The End

Content
Warnings

- **Sexual Content**
  - Medium Kick - May contain explicit sexual content, or have mild sexual content throughout.

- **Sexual Abuse**
  - *Sexual Assault: No.*
  - *Dubious Consent: Yes. Main Character takes over the body of her ancestor without her sexual partner knowing.*
  - *Sexual Activity Involving Teens: No.*
  - *Sexual Activity Involving Minors: No.*

- **Substance Use**
  - *Alcohol: Yes.*
  - *Drugs: No.*

- **Violence**
  - *Violence to Animals: Horses involved in warfare.*
  - *Domestic Abuse: No.*
  - *Hate Crimes: No.*
  - *Extreme Gore: No.*
  - *Torture: No.*
  - *War: Yes. Depictions of medieval warfare.*

- **Character Deaths**
  - *Main Characters: No.*
  - *The Kid: No.*
  - *The Baby: No.*

- **Self Harm & Suicide**
  - *Self Harm: No.*
  - *Suicide: No.*
  - *Suicidal Ideation: No.*

Michelle Deerwester-Dalrymple is an award-winning author of historical romance -- Scottish, Highlanders, and Ancient! To Dance in the Glen was recently a bestseller! She also writes contemporary romance as M.D. Dalrymple -- police and campus romances, and as Strawberry Chase, paranormal romance author.

Winner of the Top Ten Author Academy Award for 2018, Best Indie Book 2019, and N.N Night's 2021 Winner for Scottish Romance.

For upcoming events, please review her social media.

Michelle is also a wife, mother, and college writing professor. She has worked with students of all age levels – from elementary to graduate school – through her college teaching, tutoring, and charter school courses.

Her favorite historical romance genres include: Scottish (love those Highlanders!), medieval, renaissance, ancient, and Viking, but she will read just about anything!

If you are interested in learning more and receiving some free downloadable books, want to follow her social media, or just learn more, start here: https://linktr.ee/mddalrympleauthor

Also by

Swept into the Highland Past:

Highlander's Dawn – Book 1

Highlander's Awakening – Book 2 (coming soon)

Highlander's Morning – Book 3 (coming soon)

Glen Highland Romance

The Courtship of the Glen – Prequel Short Novella

To Dance in the Glen – Book 1

The Lady of the Glen – Book 2

The Exile of the Glen – Book 3

The Jewel of the Glen – Book 4

The Seduction of the Glen – Book 5

The Warrior of the Glen – Book 6

An Echo in the Glen – Book 7

The Blackguard of the Glen – Book 8

Christmas in the Glen

The Celtic Highland Maidens

The Maiden of the Storm

The Maiden of the Grove

The Maiden of the Celts

The Roman of the North

The Maiden of the Stones

The Maiden of the Woods

The Maiden of the Loch – (coming soon)

The Before Series

Before the Glass Slipper

Before the Magic Mirror

Before the Cursed Beast

Before the Mermaid's Tale

Before the Emerald Crown – (coming soon)

Glen Coe Highlanders

Highland Burn – Book 1

Highland Breath – Book 2

Highland Beauty – Book 3

Historical Fevered Series – short and steamy romance

The Highlander's Scarred Heart

The Highlander's Legacy

The Highlander's Return

Her Knight's Second Chance

The Highlander's Vow

Her Knight's Christmas Gift

Her Outlaw Highlander

Outlaw Highlander Found

Outlaw Highlander Home

Contemporary romance, as M. D. Dalrymple:

Tactical Protector Series

Night Shift – Book 1

Day Shift - Book 2

Overtime - Book 3

Holiday Pay - Book 4

School Resource Officer - Book 5

Undercover - Book 6

Holdover - Book 7

Tactical Protector Series: Marines

Her Desirable Defender

Her Irresistible Guardian

Campus Heat Series

Charming - Book 1

Tempting - Book 2

Infatuated - Book 3

Craving - Book 4

Alluring - Book 5

Made in the USA
Columbia, SC
28 June 2024

37734584R00163